T0285115

THE
BLUEPRINT

THE BLUEPRINT

| A NOVEL |

RAE GIANA RASHAD

HARPER

An Imprint of HarperCollins*Publishers*

THE BLUEPRINT. Copyright © 2024 by Rae Giana Rashad. All rights reserved. Printed in the United States of America. No part of this book may be used or reproduced in any manner whatsoever without written permission except in the case of brief quotations embodied in critical articles and reviews. For information, address HarperCollins Publishers, 195 Broadway, New York, NY 10007.

HarperCollins books may be purchased for educational, business, or sales promotional use. For information, please email the Special Markets Department at SPsales@harpercollins.com.

Excerpt from *How it Feels to Be Colored Me* Copyright © 1928 by Zora Neale Hurston.

FIRST EDITION

Designed by Elina Cohen
Ship art courtesy of Shutterstock / Morphart Creation

Library of Congress Cataloging-in-Publication Data
Names: Rashad, Rae Giana, author.
Title: The blueprint: a novel / Rae Giana Rashad.
Description: First US edition. | New York, NY : Harper, 2024.
Identifiers: LCCN 2023023633 | ISBN 9780063330092 (hardcover) |
    ISBN 9780063330122 (ebook)
Subjects: LCGFT: Dystopian fiction. | Novels.
Classification: LCC PS3618.A756 B59 2024 | DDC 813/.6—
    dc23/eng/20230929
LC record available at https://lccn.loc.gov/2023023633

ISBN 978-0-06-333009-2

23 24 25 26 27 LBC 5 4 3 2 1

| FOR MY MAMA. FOR HER LIFE. FOR HER MEMORY. |

THERE ARE NO BONDS SO STRONG AS THOSE WHICH ARE FORMED BY SUFFERING TOGETHER.

Harriet Jacobs, *Incidents in the Life of a Slave Girl*

| PART ONE |

FOR *HAMMADI*

MY HENRIETTE

THE MEN CALLED HER HENRIETTE, BUT IT WASN'T HER NAME. SHE PROMISED HER-self she would never think it, never say it, never answer to it. It wouldn't be her name.

Henriette was named by Henri Rousseau, whose belly she warmed on the voyage across the Atlantic from Senegambia. The captain of *L'Aliénor* had the first pick of the wenches. This he coveted. He chose from the comely—the tawny, copper, or yellow, as described in his slave manifests. He created one little Henriette for each trip through the Middle Passage, and when he was done, he ushered her from his bed to the auction block.

Dazed Henriette, fiery Henriette, timid Henriette. His Henriette who held a clasp knife to his throat while he slept and later leaped from the bow of the ship, leaving only tattered nightgown cotton in his hand.

I imagine there were dozens.

Henriettes, scattered and windblown through the port of New Orleans like ashes.

Henriette, confused by the strange tongue of these pale men with sun-reddened arms and hair like savanna grass, understood enough to know although she didn't desire him, Rousseau was a small refuge. The men could've forced her to dance before passing her down through the ranks, from dirt to filth, from bed to pallet, until there was nothing left except to return to the lower deck's darkness that nearly suffocated her. There, she couldn't see the lives next to her, but she smelled them. Heard them. The ship's stretching groan couldn't mask the sobs of terror and agony.

Rousseau understood things, too. When he found a bowl of beans behind his dressing table, he understood Henriette was saving it for her brother, one of 309 men shackled behind the nine-foot wall forged with spikes and swivel guns. Which one, he didn't know. The men were identical to him. Names and ages of the inventory in his slave manifests were rarely accurate, but Henriette's marks in the fine layer of dust on his desk meant her brother had seen only twelve years to her fifteen. She didn't want him held like the men, shackled to another body and vomiting in the lower deck that smelled of shit and decay and anger.

Under a blanket of dark, she did what pleased him. She placed his hand over her heart, and though it stumbled off her tongue, she said the only word he taught her. This name, Henriette. It lay in repose between them.

The following day, Rousseau brought his Henriette below deck to find her brother among the broken bodies. Some dead. All longed to be. He made the boy a pallet in the corner of his cabin.

Clutching an amulet the Fulani people believed offered protection, Henriette—sweet Henriette—finally slept. She wandered through dreams where Rousseau kept them safe and together in America.

The predawn haze settled over the cabin, and outside the ship, the cages on the shore of New Orleans. Rousseau considered Henriette's arm entwined with her brother's and studied the message she traced in dust. Three linked circles. One large, two small. He didn't miss the hope in his Henriette's eyes.

He let her cling to it.

When he lay next to new Henriette, her body thin and shivering, he thought of *sweet* Henriette.

The year is 2030. I am Henriette's descendant.

CHAPTER 1

NOW

I LAY AWAKE UNDER HIS ARM, IMAGINING HIM DREAMING IN COLOR ABOUT TASTE-fully decorated cages on the shore and umbilical cords turned into tethers. Children anchor you to the home and to the man the algorithm assigned you to. The more babies, the less likely you are to run. Fifteen studies compiled from quantitative and qualitative data have confirmed this.

I breathed too deeply, head shifting against the concave between his neck and shoulder. In answer, his trigger finger twitched against my hip as if to access data from the chip embedded in my thumb.

"Stay with me, Solenne," Bastien said, starting the ritual with this.

"Always."

A kiss on my neck, shoulder, and instep. Then he was up, sweeping his firearm off the nightstand, stretching his neck, rolling his shoulders. Feet whispered against heated tile in the bathroom. The only sound was the bathroom's sensor on the automatic doors, clicking them shut. A soldier is silent. He leaves no record of where he's been.

I rolled over and rested my head against the pillow that held the shape of him. His gaze was on me, always. I could ignore it for only so long. Thomas Jefferson stared at me from the antique French frame above the dresser—powdered wig and skin, wispy ribbon knotted around his throat as if it were the only thing keeping his head attached. A story lived behind this portrait. I stared back at him sometimes and wondered what she saw in him, or whether she saw anything in him at all.

If he could speak, he would warn Bastien I planned to leave him. He would remind him he could never trust a Black woman. Hypersexual, manipulative, destructive. In polite company, the men called it sassy. Distrust lips that no longer mention home, he would say. Don't be fooled by no longer finding train schedules in her search history. She memorized them.

"You're ready," Bastien said. Not a question, a command. He was wrapped in his black uniform, damp hair darkened from sandy to brown.

I sat up and stuffed a pillow behind my back. "Unless we can skip today."

His eyes gave me nothing. He held Source six inches from my face, the thin glass-like device dwarfed in his hand. I didn't speak until its lights changed from blue to green, ready to scan my retinas and voice patterns for untruths.

"Solenne Bonet, twenty and five months. Locale, Government District. Austin, Texas."

"Continue."

"I'm not conspiring against Bastien Martin or the Order. I have no plans, current or future, to leave my locale without permission." My eyes shifted from the lights to Bastien's face and gave him my other truth, what had kept me chained to him for five years. "I love you."

He gave me one of his long looks, robotic blue eyes analyzing every movement. Palm against the headboard, he leaned to kiss me. "Don't go past your pier today." His footsteps faded into stillness.

I sipped from the lukewarm glass of water he always left for me on the nightstand and waited for him.

The front door's locks would click as he approached. Out on the porch, he would wait for the lock's electronic whir before walking down white concrete steps. He would open the MV's driver's-side door, and fix a boot on the running rail, but he wouldn't climb in. He would lift his chin to the clot of thunderclouds, read the gray as warning to manually check the house's eight exterior doors even though Source reported no irregularities. He would come back to our bedroom, shoulders filling the doorway, boots filthy, eyes seeing something I hadn't done.

I would look up from the tangle of white sheets. "What are you checking, darling? We live behind a ten-foot fence guarded by agents you handpicked."

If he had a sense of humor, he would say, "UFOs."

But patriots don't laugh.

"You'll stay with me, Solenne."

"You're all I know."

Even without Source, we would know it to be my truth.

Later in his office at the Order's Capitol Building in downtown Austin, the other ten councilmen would narrow blue eyes at platinum timepieces that reported their interim councilman was eight minutes late. Bastien's father would say, "Official, that girl is driving you insane."

Julian Garnier, his chief strategist and master negotiator, would remind him I have layered security—cameras, shadows, and Source's monitoring software embedded in the chip in my left thumb. In everyone's left thumb. The software Bastien wrote himself.

Bastien's trigger finger would twitch. He would steeple his fingers to hide it, but not before Dr. Bouchard noticed. He would park his interlaced fingers on his swine belly and remind Bastien of the leading cause of death in white men in the Order. Eyeing the collection of firearms suspended on hooks behind Bastien's desk, he would say, "Stress is the real silent killer."

THE PIER YARDS FROM OUR BACK porch was named for me, but by law, it could never be mine. The treated pine became property once assembled into a raised structure. Its deed was filed in the Office of Property Assessments, the same office that held my certificate of birth.

I passed the tilted palm trees, our empty hammock a strange nest between. I saw us there under an orange sunrise muted by matted clouds, a gentle sway, fingers skimming rebellious grass climbing through sand beneath us.

Damp wood underfoot, I stared out over the lake. I imagined wading ten feet away, limestone sandpapering the soles of my feet. I'd done it before Bastien. That's how I measured my life now. Instead of days, hours, and minutes, time was broken into two—when I belonged to Bastien and when I didn't. I was fifteen when he decided he had to have me. Sixteen when he became obsessed with running his fingertips over discontinuities in my body—between my lips and fingers and toes—like these natural separations were cracks he needed to fill with himself. *I'm not wrong,* he said once with the world outside of us, the distant sound of boots patterning past a locked office door, lamplight dimming us to unnatural shadows. *Not when this is the world we were given,* he said, reasoned that I wouldn't have been better off in any other time, with any other man whispering promises that only the wounded make. I would never leave. Never lie. I promised my love. I promise, my love.

The wind sent scrawls through the water's surface below the pier. I could just make out the Fulani girl's reflection before the waves stole it. I saw her there, distorted and alone, forever fifteen.

Bastien thought she was gone, but I kept her with me. He didn't understand she had nowhere else to go.

CHAPTER 2

THEN

I WAS FIFTEEN MY LAST SUMMER IN DALLAS, COLLECTING AND LAYING AWAY memories of home like old photographs—the cicadas' hum in the twisted arms of the live oak trees, the sun-eaten liriope leaves, the papery wasp nests cloistered above the patio beams.

The night before the Monroe Gala, I sat on the living room floor between Mama's legs flinching against the heated brush. She liked to stretch my curls into smooth sheets before braiding. Length meant I was beautiful, she said. Length meant she was a good mama, she didn't say.

A childhood habit, my fingertips slipped down the curve of her calves and over the tawny birthmark, her one-winged butterfly. If I kept my head straight while the brush made straight paths out of curls at my nape, she didn't mind. These were moments for my journal. Turn the page, and I could read Mama's memory of my birth. I was her miracle, a startle of limbs and feathery black hair from my hairline to my eyebrows. She thought she was happy in the gap between my birth and my daddy losing his mind when I was seven, but she learned happiness was found in stillness, the quiet of mind. I never asked what that meant. Instead, I dissected her moods and curled against her anytime she was motionless.

In those moments, the world was no bigger than us. We didn't think about the algorithm or the assignment system. We ignored that as female descendants of slavery, our lives lay in the hands of the Order's men—our father, the patriot who paid to hold our contract, and finally, a husband. A set of three, like the hands on a clock moving us through the cages of time.

The sage burned in smudge bowls. White tendrils of earthen smoke twisted against one another in three corners. Daddy paced the living room, palms facing upward. "My wife, my daughter, my world. Please, God, walk with them."

He murmured different versions of his soldier's prayer until Mama finished my braid and it was his turn to sit in front of her with his dark eyes closed. Mama dipped her fingers in a jar of oil and rubbed the calm into his scalp and temples. He sagged against her legs and said, "My love," like punctuation to a long, lyrical sentence.

One day, I would have that. I would blend shea and blood orange in an amber glass jar and press my oily fingertips to my husband's scalp. Together, we could watch the depression evaporate like sage smoke. When he called me love, I would gather that sound with the sight of a pink skyline over the late-blooming pomegranate shrubs. My tertiary muses. I would write.

THE DESCRIPTION OF THE MONROE GALA on my Source's calendar: *An annual event honoring esteemed soldiers of the Code.* The real purpose was for high-ranking Black soldiers to browse women in the assignment pool. Officers didn't accept wives assigned by the algorithm like poor men or low-ranking soldiers.

Black bodies gathered on the dance floor, swinging satin dresses and box braids, blotting sweat from hairlines with cloth napkins from dinner tables.

I sat between my parents messaging my friends and waiting for their amused eyes to find me through a hollow of champagne glasses.

SOLENNE: I want champagne.

DALENA: Me too.

NATALYA: They won't give it to y'all. We can't drink until 21.

SOLENNE: We graduate this month. One glass to celebrate is OK.

A group of officers passed, fresh from deployments spreading the Order's view of democracy in Europe. We lowered our devices at the same time, the white glow of Source's lights no longer obscuring our faces. None of the men looked in our direction. They ignored the clusters of girls—sibling sets of three and four with their shea-buttered knees and updos—at these galas until they were in the assignment pool.

DALENA: I'll get an officer to get me a glass.

SOLENNE: The lower ranks are easier. Try a general.

DALENA: Nope. Watch me.

Dalena, with her rust-colored coils and a scatter of freckles on brown skin, never let us forget she knew more because she was two years older than us. One at a time, she circled men with military emblems crowding stiff black sleeves. The men laughed and "run along, darling'd" her. Dalena pretended to toss her fork at one when he turned. We laughed behind cloth napkins. Pretended to cough. Our mamas said never laugh in mixed company. *Laugh in front of a Black man, and you'll slip and laugh in front of a white man. He'll think you're mocking him.*

When Daddy took Mama to the dance floor for a slow dance that embarrassed me, I tugged on the sleeve of a passing general. He agreed to get me a glass of champagne.

I was smiling across the room at a stunned Dalena when Officer Charles Decuir sent Lower Rank in the opposite direction and settled into Daddy's chair. Unsolicited, a server had a glass of champagne in front of him in seconds.

The room didn't breathe. This man with acorn-colored eyes and locs gathered at his nape breathed. Red and green emblems mingled under yellow lights until I had to squint at his sleeve to separate the threads.

Mama's juniper satin dress swirled around Daddy. She tapped a finger against her bare shoulder, and like a string puppet, I corrected my posture—arching my back, lifting my breasts, and pushing my hips against the chair.

Never make him speak first, Mama would say.

"Thank you for your service, Officer Decuir."

"For the Order."

His locs were waist length and neat like cane rows. Daddy's rarely grew to his shoulders before he cut them to the new growth and had me retwist the tufts of hair.

"How do you have so much hair? It's beautiful."

A trumpet's blare eased into the jangly piano melody. Decuir let his silence play. His gaze journeyed over my almond-oil-slicked ponytail and down the length of my braid that hung over the shoulder of my white satin dress. He lifted his eyes back to this mask on my face—the mix of admiration and innocence, the squinting eyes unencumbered by glasses even though Dr. Clairmont told Mama I needed them at ten. *I'll be damned*, Mama said under her breath in his office because my face was hers and our faces were too pretty to be hidden behind lenses, frames, and screws. So I squinted and pursed my lips because Mama said that's how pretty women smiled.

"I'm too blunt to be a poet. You already know you're beautiful, don't you?"

I had been aware of myself from the first time a man said, "I bet you have all the boys fighting over you," and "Girl, you look just like your mama." I was fifteen—a woman now. It didn't matter that I still felt like a girl when nobody could see a difference between my body and Mama's. Breasts too big for my frame. Hips that swung when I walked. I hadn't asked for either to rise from the straight lines that used to be me. Maybe the swing was natural, or maybe I unconsciously mimicked Mama and other women who weakened men just by being. Mama said in the Order, the only things lower than Black girls are roaches and ugly Black girls. We didn't choose to be pushed to the bottom of the hierarchy, but we use what's given, like our ancestors who made meals out of pig intestines and softened kinks and coils with kerosene.

Decuir tilted his head toward mine, reclaiming my attention. "Do you believe in destiny?"

"Nothing is real unless it's written," I said, eliciting a quick smile to check off as an accomplishment to report to my mama.

Forbidden bubbles quickened in the sweating glass of champagne Decuir pushed into my hand. I looked over his shoulder at Daddy staring down at Mama gathered in his arms like his world started and ended there. A small sip became a long one. I passed the empty glass back and dried my hand on the diamond-patterned chair fabric underneath me.

Decuir smiled a second time, let it fade, and touched my chin. "Destiny."

Then he was gone, ballroom lights tunneling the dark, the hush of champagne on my tongue.

THE PATH WE WALKED TO BECOME Black women wasn't straight; it was a loop. Starting from nowhere, it brought you back to nowhere. A man at one end, a man at the other, humming the same song, "It's just a body. Nothing special." If that were true, why did they want it? Why couldn't it belong to me? Mama called it child's want, something you grow out of. But the moment I recognized this loop existed, I poked holes at it to find an exit. There were times light shone through the pinpricks, but inevitably, reality was patchwork, sealing and stealing until there was only me and the dark. Like the beginning. End. Beginning . . .

From six years old to fifteen, Mrs. Guidry trained you to survive men. After fifteen, school was no longer necessary for Black girls, Descendants of Slavery, DoS.

Guidry hustled down our school's hallways, worn-leather boots slouching around her ankles. *Bridle that tongue. Hips and lips, keep all of that still. Sit down somewhere, fast-tail heffa.* After graduation, she watched you board trains to places where the white men waited for you as it was done since Civil War II.

I never could remember which of the eleven founders of the Order started the system where a DoS was assigned to a white man temporarily, but I remember it started as a system to punish girls who rebelled after Civil War II. A patriot corrected her behavior then sent her home to marry a Black man. We were expected to have three children by twenty-two, four if at least two weren't boys. The endless supply of soldiers for the borders.

Things evolved subtly after those first assignments like a slow drip behind a wall staining it black with mold. Within six years, millions applied to become contract holders. They created a rating system for behavior and appearance. Facial symmetry, waist-to-hip ratio, skin tone, curl pattern, blemishes . . .

In those early days of the algorithm, the men who opted into the system paid a flat fee and prayed for the best. We prayed, too. Who we were assigned to determined how they'd use our bodies and for how long. Some wanted you in their office, fingertips and backs numb from cleaning, typing, or researching. Some wanted you by their side in bed. Most wanted you for both. When you were spent, wrung out, and dry, they replaced you.

The teachers held their breath when you came home and the algorithm switched your occupation to wife. They found you in the grocery store and called you a failure if the algorithm assigned you to a Black man so tight with his money, he slept in his boots and jewelry. *Uh-huh, I told you. Didn't I tell you?* they said, holding their Source displaying your husband's name, rank, and salary. *This happened because you don't like to listen.* We didn't miss their smiles of approval when hearing about a DoS who maneuvered her way into emancipation and moving to Louisiana, the only state where she could be free. In their smiles, we remembered the lessons that were as much a part of us as breathing. A Black man can sign his name on documents so you feel free for a moment, and they did sometimes, like my daddy who signed for my mama to move her hair and skin cream business out of our shed to a small shop on Bishop Avenue. A white man's signature on a certificate of emancipation can free you from all men. Never take him at his word. Get him to write it or it's not real. Never ask for that signature. Asking could make things go wrong. A smart girl made men believe everything good was his idea.

If that failed, catch the interest of the officers. Collect enough bodies, and the white men turned a blind eye to the officers who built wealth and chose their own wives. My daddy worked for years to increase his rank to officer so he could circumvent the algorithm and marry my mama.

Officers' wives didn't whisper to wounded reflections in public restroom mirrors about running away from this motherfucker and disappearing where he would never find her. Officers' wives looked like closeted American history—redbones and yellowbones. They looked like my mama with hazel eyes and our dance instructor with breasts so perfect, when the drum solo flowed into the studio as she danced the Erzulie, I hoped one would shimmy from her wrap shirt. I needed to know they were real. When I was home alone, I was her—dancing in front of mirrored walls, palms to the sky, to the floor, toes spinning against polished wood until I was breathless. I left my fingerprints on everything. My music was an echoing internal chant. *I am the goddess Erzulie. I am Erzulie. Officers' wives look like me.*

We became what they called us. Who wouldn't want to be set apart, deemed beautiful by men with houses in gated subdivisions with clusters of lilacs and polished floors that gleamed in sunlight? A Black girl gives and gives, why is she wrong when she takes? If you had to have a cage, it was better to have a beautiful one. Wasn't it?

THE WEEK AFTER THE MONROE GALA, Guidry gave us an end-of-the-year aptitude test. We sat at our desks in ordered rows while Guidry whisked by. She stopped next to me and frowned at my black screen. I clicked random answers on my Source and finished the 109-question exam in eighty-three seconds.

"Chile, you may as well settle in because you missing lunch to retake this."

"No ma'am, I'm not. Why find out what we can achieve if nothing will come from it? If you want a score, you—"

Guidry connected her yardstick to my forearm. My mama brought me to school the next day, her skinny bat in one fist and my bruised arm in the other. Mama couldn't stand the thought of my being hurt. Until I was four, she bit my fingernails instead of clipping them. She was afraid to cut me.

Guidry looked at Mama's ponytail and her flats instead of heels and pursed her lips hard enough for grooves to sprout on her face. "Loren, if you think Solenne's too precious to be hit, do better about fixing her sassy mouth. I warned you when she was in first grade. Mister Jesus. *Lord*, your baby don't listen. She do whatever she want. You encourage it."

Mama said something about her child making mistakes and learning from them, but Guidry talked over her while she ushered us into her office, musty with old books and whatever food she had wrapped in foil on her desk. "You know as well as I do making mistakes don't apply to us. They expect her to know better by now. If we don't fix her mouth, that algorithm will assign her to men who will. She can run her mouth for only so long before she turn ugly, and they'll knock ugly's head off her shoulders with no hesitation."

Guidry spoke to Mama's biggest fear. Her daddy knew how to fix a sassy mouth when he was alive. He called the black leather belt hanging around his neck Black Magic.

Loren! Make this girl sit down some damn where before I put Black Magic on her ass. She got in my tackle box and ate up all my peanut brittle and broke my damn flashlight.

Guidry sat behind a beaten desk with too many manila file folders stacked on top. "And I told you that girl needed eyeglasses. What you plan to do about it?"

"Nothing," Mama said. "Twenty/forty. Dr. Clairmont said she was fine."

"Hmm," Guidry said.

"Hmmm." Mama said her final word.

Guidry opened a file folder and told Mama the aptitude test I took at the beginning of the year identified me as a gifted writer. I squinted out the window behind Guidry. That wasn't a Black girl's life. We served the patriots we were assigned to until they sent us home to become soldiers' wives. That part was almost certain. Using aptitude tests, the Order assigned 90 percent of Black men to the Code, the Order's military.

Three women from three generations, we understood this.

Guidry closed the folder and dropped it onto a pile of others. "Bridle that tongue and when you come home, you'll be an *officer's* wife."

The shriveled smile was for herself, not me. In the teacher's lounge, she could brag about marriages to high-ranking men, not aptitude scores. *One of my girls married an officer,* she would say, lips perched on her chipped yellow mug, thinking of the men who cherry-picked the beautiful, planted them in the sun with lilacs, laced their boots, then left them behind.

CHAPTER 3

THEN

I SLEPT ON THE COUCH THAT NIGHT, SOMETHING I DID BEFORE MY DADDY LEFT FOR deployments. The sycamore in our front yard cast a maze of shadows on our living room floor. Daddy found his way to me and rested his large hand against my face. It was warm there, that undiluted light. Neither of us needed long goodbyes. I didn't tell him I loved him, pulling him against me like Mama would, an open wound, bleeding when they separated. Wouldn't that feel like the end of a story?

The front door closed softly behind him.

The engines were alive outside, the headlights, the May winds.

Upstairs, Mama stood at the picture window watching the convoy of MVs until darkness won. I knew that. It was what she had done since she was seventeen.

I couldn't sleep either. In the kitchen, I pulled rotting cherry tomatoes from Daddy's plants on the windowsill, the flesh broken and black.

I ARRIVED AT SCHOOL THE NEXT morning, still yawning and listless. I found my class, sitting in the empty courtyard that used to be a basketball court when our school was coed, discussing graduation. I nudged Natalya until she scooted over in the circle. I wanted to sit next to Dalena.

"I'm getting my signature in a year and moving to Louisiana.

Watch me," Dalena said. "I'm not coming back here to play baby factory for one of these bird-chested idiots I don't even like to make more soldiers for the Code."

She read her handwritten plan for the man she expected to be assigned to. We'd seen him in the front row at our dance performances or loitering around our school. Soft and doughy, soot-and-ash-colored hair everywhere except his head. He called out through our school's chain-link fence using her full name like she already belonged to him—

Dalena Batiste! What size shoe do you wear now, darling?

—until Guidry saw them together at the gate and hollered, *Take your ass away from my girls. Wait for the algorithm like a decent man.* Even white men listened to Guidry. Head down, he shoved empty hands in his pockets, climbed in the driver's seat of his MV, and drove away with his three brats in the backseat. Then Guidry swatted Dalena on her behind even though she was too old for that. Said Dalena was too hot in the ass and constantly pulling her from fences or closets would be the death of her. Said Dalena would end up like Charlesetta if she didn't stay away from that fence howler.

FIVE YEARS AGO, CHARLESETTA, AN OLDER girl with a broad forehead hidden under ear-to-ear bangs and the patience to herd us younger girls from the bathrooms to class on time, disappeared. Source couldn't pull location data from the chip embedded in her thumb. USER DOES NOT EXIST, Source said. Her parents reported her missing, and the men and bloodhounds searched for days. Nothing, until thirteen days later when she appeared in front of the school, silent and empty, holding a plastic bag with a three-pack of those assorted, rolled and taped panties, a nightgown, and a half-used box of sanitary napkins. I'd seen the man with bright hair and shifty eyes drop her off. Hooked my fingers through the chain-link fence and, like a moving picture framed by steel wire, watched him roll down Davis and stop at the Corner Store, where he bought stuff he couldn't buy in Austin: boudin and crackers and those long ropes of beef jerky I hated. Maybe he needed it to keep him sharp for the 180-mile drive home.

Charlesetta wouldn't name him even when her daddy said he would take a switch to her legs, and he didn't care that she was too big for that. So I told Guidry I saw an executioner's truck. One function of the Office of Strategic Services was to handle reports of DoS abuse, sexual or physical. Charlesetta's daddy reported the incident. *Abuse of the system*, he said in the OSS office. *Strip him of rank*, he told the Council. Source tracked the man within seconds. Only one man used an executioner's vehicle for a round trip to Dallas within two weeks. One man from Austin visited the Corner Store. Twenty-six-year-old David DuPont II, agent and executioner, employed by OSS. They investigated internally, found David had done nothing wrong, and dismissed the case. Three months later, the algorithm assigned Charlesetta as housekeeper to David DuPont I. When Guidry read her assignment aloud, Charlesetta shrieked like someone stabbed her right there in the middle of the cafetorium, where lips were supposed to stay still. The older girls cried with her. On the stage, the teachers fanned themselves with folded papers, saying, *Lord have mercy on this child. God is not pleased.* The little girls watched it unfold where we sat in bone-white uniforms, cross-legged, in rows facing the stage, until Guidry ushered us outside. We stood under a spindled limb live oak tree competing to see which of us could scream like Charlesetta. God, we didn't understand. Now I know exactly what that scream meant. Shock. Despair. Anger because the system found new ways to remind us who we were. Never open your mouth. *Never* tell. A way out was never given to us. We had to make our own.

Two weeks after Charlesetta arrived on Big DuPont's porch, Little DuPont completed his forty-fifth public execution, and OSS promoted him from general to official. His daddy was so proud his son did in eight years what took him twenty that he gifted him a crystal decanter of cognac and Charlesetta. When Charlesetta came home five years later, she wasn't quite right in the head. Maybe it was David. Maybe it was the toddler with the coily blond afro hanging

THE BLUEPRINT | 21 |

from her hip. Our mamas called those types of babies hip babies or lap babies. Always needing arms around him. He shrieked like his mama did five years earlier anytime she sat him on his own behind.

Guidry said Charlesetta was home only because Big DuPont finally put his foot down about giving him grandchildren. Reluctantly, Little DuPont opened his fist and sent Charlesetta home with a two-year-old son, three bags, and a five-hundred-dollar-a-month stipend until the algorithm assigned Charlesetta to a Black man who would become daddy.

When the teachers saw her around town, they spoke softly and slowly, coaxing a jumper off a ledge. *You stronger than that, child. You got to get past this.* Voice barely there, Charlesetta said she was tired. *Why won't anyone let us break?* As she walked away, the teachers said, *Oh, child, oh.*

And I watched, nails biting my palms, letting the words echo as they had since I was ten. It would have been better if I had stayed silent.

"... SCORE LOW ON THE GRADUATION APTITUDE test so they believe I have no skills." Dalena looked around the circle to make sure we were listening. "That increases the chances the algorithm will assign me to a soft man. The Order hates soft men. They assign them the scraps."

"You're gambling," Natalya said, loud enough for us to actually hear this time. She was all glossy black skin and hair, pinned from her face with her auntie's rhinestone clips that had more puckered glue than rhinestones. "If your plan works, cool. If not, you just told the Order you're a dumbass, so guess what's waiting for you back home? Marrying a broke, dumbass man."

You could get Dalena to stop and think in only one of two ways. One was to threaten her with being assigned to a man who was broke like her daddy. The men hated him. Said he was henpecked and a man could take only so many ass-whoopings before he became a woman himself. Three to be exact. The only job he earned in the Code was as a glorified housekeeper.

The other way was to mention her twin brother. Dalena had started liking men only two years ago after Guidry found her and another girl in the art room's water heater closet and told her she better get those strange thoughts out of her mind. *You know better. If you think for one second the Order will allow two of us to be together like that, you're dumber than Twin.* At seventeen, Twin was still laughing at odd things and saying the names of shapes when someone asked him to solve a simple math problem. Every morning, he sat in his navy velvet chair, waiting for Dalena's kiss between his eyebrows, waiting for Dalena to say God kept him a child so he would love her right. But they both couldn't be children. Those early mornings crammed next to that water heater that hissed and hummed enough to hide all that was inside was something she would forget. *Y'all love bringing up old stuff*, she said when anyone asked, then louder, *That was kid stuff.* She preferred doughy men she could press and manipulate in her hands like the fence howler.

"Not worried because I won't lose," Dalena said. "Just because y'all's mamas didn't show you dodo birds how to win doesn't mean mine didn't."

I didn't like when she talked to me like I was no different from the other girls, a shard from everything she hated about the Order.

"If your mama knows so much, how come she's not free?" I asked.

Dalena gathered her coils into a ponytail with too much malice. "Let's not talk about mamas when your mama is a fraud, selling hair products that don't work."

To dig into her, I called Twin stupid, but then she called my daddy crazy. We were two screaming octopuses on the faded concrete until Guidry pulled her off me, calling us heathens. Dalena smiled when she saw my curls snagged in her broken fingernails. The Black girl's proof of victory.

....

CHAPTER 4

THEN

SINCE THE DAY WE MET, I COULDN'T STAY AWAY FROM DALENA. SHE WALKED INTO our classroom when the bluebonnet petals colored the hills a tempo-rary blue, thirteen when we were eleven, round where we were flat. She missed two years of school because she had almost died from meningitis, she told a group of us at a table in the cafetorium, but as soon as she caught up, she was going to eighth grade. I was obsessed with this Black girl with freckles and rust-colored coils. I was swept up into her impermanence, the threat that if I blinked, I wouldn't witness her do what no one else had done—disrupt the system and flutter to the high school in a separate wing of our school in a mat-ter of weeks. I'd always been better at writing than speaking, so I slipped notes into her desk asking her to be my best friend. She ig-nored them each morning, hand over her heart, reciting the Texas Pledge. "Honor the Texas flag; I pledge allegiance to thee, Texas, one state under God, one and indivisible." After school, I found her by the back perimeter fence, upsetting ant piles with the scuffed toe of her leather school shoes. "No," she said when I offered her my soul. "You ain't tired of being somebody's something? Assigned to this man you don't know. Assigned to marry another one. Being mama to a houseful of kids you don't want. Look, we hang out if it's fun. When it's not, we don't. Cool?" No, it wasn't cool, but neither was it cool to tell her it wasn't. She was the bluebonnets, fading from blue to brown too quickly, dry, like the grass on roadsides.

That summer, we shared lime slushies in paper cups and waved away the desperate honeybees. We made music by slapping our hands on the sandstone tables under the magnolias in Reverchon Park. Then she disappeared for days without warning. I stared at a digital image of her in a black leotard and paint-smudged jeans. Her coils were in two ponytails, two thin gold necklaces hung between her breasts, and she held two fingers next to pursed lips. When I pulled my hair into two ponytails and made guns with my fingers, a little girl stared back at me in the mirror, not a painter who didn't need anyone, not even a best friend. Because of her hair color, I typed *water bug* over her image then erased it the day she rang my doorbell. All she needed to do was hook her finger at me, and I followed, racking my brain for a discernible pattern to her arrivals or departures. Never did figure it out.

Once, she stayed away for three weeks. Mama knew I was hurting. She came to my room holding thick pages with perforated edges loosely bound with a black ribbon. Dot-matrix paper, Mama called it, and it held the story of Henriette, our first American ancestor. My grandma typed Henriette's original letters and handed down that printed copy to Mama.

I couldn't think of Grandma Shawna without seeing her as she was framed in Mama's dresser drawer. She was perched on the edge of a wooden church pew. A praise tambourine lay abandoned on her skirt pleats, like it had been placed there by an unwanted hand. Her desolate eyes. My mama sat beside her, a tiny afterthought with plaited hair and folded hands, frilly white socks and shiny black shoes.

Then the evening came that, on the surface, looked like any other evening with Grandma Shawna tying my mama's hair down with a satin scarf before bed. But she lingered. She ran her fingertips over my mama's face as though she were transferring a memory to a place time couldn't touch. My mama had the answer to the question she'd had for too long. When would her mama fly away and leave her behind?

At the bedroom door, the blues of her mama's Praise Tabernacle canvas bag were vivid in the semi-dark.

"Can I go with you to choir practice? Please, Mama. Just this one time."

She thought if her mama gazed out at her from the choir loft instead of those old double doors that kept her trapped in this life, she wouldn't leave.

"Not tonight, baby. One day," her mama said. "One day, you'll go." She stepped out into an evening weary from dry heat and flew away. A year later, my mama found Henriette's story tucked in her church purse she no longer had use for. The pages still smelled of pink peppercorn and coffee, of her mama who was dead or alive but gone all the same.

"Henriette was fifteen when she made it through the Middle Passage," my mama told me. "Read her story so you learn early what too many of us learn late. First, never hang on to anything too tight. Second, nothing in this world, not even the Order, is enough to kill you."

I stayed up all night, reading. When sunlight filled my room, I understood Mama, Guidry, and all the other Black women who put lessons in my ear and parts in my hair. I would never know how it felt to walk boldly because this world wasn't mine. My tears would never be a weapon. There was no patience for my softness, my wounds, my unraveling. There was no protection for me, a Black girl, no tender touch, no consideration for a delicate exterior. No space to scream.

Somehow, Dalena was born knowing this. But I wasn't Dalena or Henriette, who had formed calluses on the inside. I still wanted.

AFTER OUR FIGHT AT SCHOOL, DALENA stayed away for six days.

"You wanna go to the Corner Store?" she asked from my driveway.

"My mama said she doesn't want me talking to you anymore."

"My mama said I have to apologize for calling your daddy crazy."

"Well?"

"Well, what?"

"Say you're sorry."

"Heffa, I just did. Do you wanna go or not?"

Mama was behind me. Dalena shrank like most women did when in Mama's presence. "Mrs. Bonet, can Solenne walk with me to the store?"

Mama roped her thick braid around her hand, a habit I'd picked up from her. *No* was in her eyes, but she'd said earlier I was worrying a hole in her head, following her around the house complaining about being lonely. "I guess," she finally said, "but you better keep your hands off my child. Be back on this porch by eight."

"Yes ma'am."

"And tell your mama to call me. I have some boxes of things for her." Hand-me-downs. An officer's wife's reminder to those who hadn't married a high-ranking man of her status. Mama said she felt bad for Dalena's mama, marrying a man who had nothing but yellow skin and good hair. Even that was worthless because he hadn't passed on those genes. She would slide a heated brush through my hair, breathe her relief, and say the twins had a bad grade of hair. She didn't blame Dalena's mama for spending her electric bill money on keeping Dalena's hair done. How else would she attract a man who could afford to circumvent the algorithm?

Dalena walked too fast, her stride doubled by legs longer than mine. I wouldn't hang on to the back of her shirt to get her to slow down like I used to. I could keep up in that field of Dallis grass and sweet gum trees that separated the gated subdivisions like ours from everything else. Homes hugging shared driveways and shrubbery, the postage stamp backyards, the random potholes drivers intuitively swerved to avoid.

Dalena knotted her shirt so her belly showed. "You like my waist beads?"

I raised my eyebrows at the amber-colored jewelry hanging below her navel. "They're all right."

We insulted each other's shoes and hair until there was nothing new to say and the novelty wore off.

At the Corner Store, young men leaned against the dingy brick storefront. Harlem and Kingston, named after countries, cities, or neighborhoods, like half of the boys from Dallas. A natural consequence of being born to women who were restricted from leaving their locale. We didn't go to school with them, but we saw them often. They worked cashier or stocking positions until they were old enough to have their quick smiles erased by deployments. Dalena went back and forth with the boys, soaking in mindless chatter. Before we were assigned and they were deployed, we were equals, entwining ourselves in banter. In a few years, we wouldn't dream of saying much more than, "Thank you for your service." Guidry said God gave women a tongue as her weapon, and she could shred a man faster than bullets could. We needed to be mindful of our words. The world was hard enough for Black men.

Harlem grinned at me. Same short locs with faded sides as Kingston. Same black tee skimming the thigh of his jeans as Kingston. The difference was Harlem was cute, and he knew it. "What's up, Sol? You can't speak?"

Harlem let me read old magazines the store owner kept hidden behind a movable ceiling panel above the drink coolers. Back pressed against those clammy cooler doors, I read and imagined myself living in the time when Black people published Black stories through Black publications. But the last time I was here, he said my new dress made my butt and tits look nice, then laughed and ducked the rolls of duplex cookies I threw at him.

"Not to you, I can't."

"That's why I don't talk to her," Kingston said. "She got a smartass mouth. My ti-ti told me what you did to the cafeteria deliveryman."

"Ask me if I care."

Guidry was his auntie. She said I was disrespectful to the man delivering breakfast stuff when all I was trying to do was verify his ID through Source. He told me to shut up and hold the school's door open. I lifted my eyebrows at the tape on his boot and the dirty sock peeking out despite his efforts, looked into his eyes, and smiled. But I never said anything.

"Are y'all going to ring us up or stand out here looking stupid?"
Dalena said.

They leaned to watch her walk into the store, her hips swaying
and twisting.

Inside the small store, Dalena sloped over the glass counter, peer-
ing at packaged snacks in boxes lined on the linoleum. "Give me
some salt and vinegar chips."

"You got some money?" Harlem asked. They loved making jokes
about us never being able to earn a salary. The government issued us
a $325 stipend after we were assigned. Nothing before then. Noth-
ing after we married.

She smiled, a tulip blooming beneath her perfect nose. "No, but
you do."

He laughed and rummaged through three boxes until he found
her a bag of those reeky chips.

Kingston watched Harlem scan his Source to pay and slide the
bag across the counter to Dalena. He shook his head, tongue darting
out against the skin of a cigar to open it.

The three disappeared inside a room in the back of the store to
smoke. I was alone with the steady buzz from the walk-in drink
coolers and the boot-scuffed linoleum. I opened the drink cooler and
stepped on the middle shelf that boosted me high enough to reach
the movable ceiling tile. The delicate pages of a magazine were in my
hand. *Jet* magazine, April 1952.

DO CAREER WOMEN MAKE GOOD WIVES?
WHO DO NEGROES WANT FOR PRESIDENT?

Hazel Scott's face floated disembodied next to the words, sleepy-
eyed and coiffed curls. Guidry told us she was outspoken about Jim
Crow laws and discrimination. Only two short years after this picture, the second civil war began.

Source vibrated in the pocket of my shorts at the same time the
old Source screens lit blue behind the counter and above the drink
coolers.

ALERT: RUNAWAY—20,000 REWARD

Shea Boyd. Locale: Gov District, Austin
23 y.o., 5'6", 135 lbs., dark complexion
Reported by contract holder 58 minutes ago
Fugitive believed to be headed to Louisiana by vehicle

The chip we couldn't see or feel embedded in our left thumb twenty-four hours after birth was part of us, but it wasn't perfect. Move under unsuspecting skies, escape to the free state of Louisiana, go off grid. That was how the bold did it.

"Dalena?" She didn't answer the next six times I shouted her name down the dark hallway. Outside the store, the mile-long field home was dark and abuzz with the katydids screeching their name.

"What took you so damn long?" I asked Dalena when she emerged from the store a half hour later with an open bag of chips. "Your Source is working fine. I know you saw the alert."

"And? I'm tired of jumping for things that have nothing to do with me."

I jogged to catch up with her down the sidewalk. "So I was supposed to walk home by myself?"

She pushed a foul-smelling chip in her mouth. "Yep, why not? It's just a mile."

Because the field scared me. She knew that. I should've told her she didn't have to take her frustration out on me because our lives were built around alarms that reminded her of who she was. Instead, I slapped the chip bag from her hand. She looked up from the chips littering the sidewalk and shook her head like I was something to be pitied.

"You're gonna have to grow up." Her voice rose over military deployment helicopters sweeping overhead. "What will you do when you're assigned? You think the man they send you to will babysit you? Solenne, are you listening?"

CHAPTER 5

NOW

M Y SHADOWS TRAILED ME. SHADOWS WHOSE QUALIFICATIONS INCLUDED shared DNA with well-known slave catchers from nineteenth-century Virginia, the smudges in my periphery who bragged about owning the handcuffs their great-great-grandfather slapped on 350 souls before returning them to their rightful owners. Shadows who clenched their teeth, made a *tssst* sound, and ejected streams of spit.

"The official requested you return to the house before the Council meets. That's before seven," a shadow said at my elbow. "Solenne, are you listening?"

If God was listening, none of them would climb through the ranks. They'd never become one of the eleven men preparing to convene in our library tonight.

In front of me was Lake Travis. Wind-driven waves rushed the shore, grated against pebbles, stole the worthy ones.

Behind me, our house breathed as Bastien's extension. Window walls separated rooms from the shore and an iron perimeter fence. Cameras rooted to corners whirred to find movements and droned for secrets. *He sees everything before you do it*, they hissed. *You've loved him since you were fifteen*—their answer why I had to love a man who wrote laws that buried us, a man who strayed from the promise to write my emancipation papers at seventeen.

I remembered his whispers on nights we lay tangled like insects in a cocoon, slick and blind-reaching for each other in the dark. Then I remembered my mama's advice the night of her last visit, to file away that promise as pillow talk and to never rub him raw with my words. Over idling wind, I heard her disquieted murmur as we fell asleep, fingers intertwined, braids mixing on the pillow.

At least he doesn't hit you.

FOR YEARS, I DREAMED IN BLACK. Black armor-plated military vehicles leading trails of exhaust, black aircraft slicing through dusky skies.

That evening, the councilmen swarmed past my writing room into our library like black-winged wasps. Their security detail and teams followed in order of rank: officials, generals, then the marshals with sallow skin from long work hours and whiskey instead of water.

They bragged about their accomplishments in private, boasted about the difference between them and their brother. But skin quality and quantity of sleeve emblems aside, from neck to ankle, the men were identical. Descendants from Europe. Ramrod straight backs from the hubris of rank. Standing collar, black brass buttons lined on the right, black tactical pants the younger men wore stuffed into boots and the older men wore hemmed to boot collars. The black ski masks were for when they wanted to remember. Black uniforms and rifles, eating the space until there was none.

Councilmen were the Order's most decorated men. The talented, skilled, brilliant. Engineers, physicians, cryptographers, developers. But fundamentally, they were soldiers. Killers. Eleven gun-wielding psychopaths who signed opinion into law.

In speeches and articles, the councilmen became the adoring grandpa, the gentle husband, the everyman who maintained order and kept our borders safe.

They identified as either Traditionalists or Modernists. The main difference between them was their philosophy on DoS. Traditionalists believed in strictly adhering to the Founders' original framework where rights were almost nonexistent. Modernists flirted with the idea that DoS deserved some autonomy, mainly based on reports of abuse and letters written by lobbyists, white women like mama's friend Margaret Ann.

The moving wall of rifles opened enough for a councilman, Dr. Bouchard, to notice me. His eyes lingered. Our presence offended them unless we were in awe of theirs, silent, or beautiful. "*The* official's beautiful Sol," he would say if he were close enough, even though we hated each other.

The official. Forgetting to emphasize *the* before his title was disrespect Bastien would not tolerate. Many officials earned the title through oil, military, banking, medicine, or technology, but only he wrote the software that updated Source from a simple communication device to one that tracked our entire existence through a chip in our thumb. "Many want what I've accomplished, but they're unwilling to sacrifice the blood and sweat I've sacrificed. They deserve nothing," Bastien said when worknights merged into a slow dawn. "I was given no advantages. No head starts."

The Council adored Bastien since he was seven. Brilliant and reckless, he loitered outside the Legislature Chamber, listening in on meetings. He studied languages, cryptography, and the philosophy of leaders from across the globe. The Council didn't expect anything less from Abraham's son, the president's son. They fed him the nuances of bipartisanship and groomed him into becoming the prototype for all men. The Council remarked on his ambition and strength through the loss of his mother at ten. While his father grieved privately under the supervision of medical doctors for six months, Bastien stood in for him, sitting in his father's oversize chairs while the Council convened at their house or the Capitol. *Remarkable*, they said. *A man already.*

There weren't bonfires at the lake or shared flasks of whiskey with girls on dusty blankets. There was the Santa Monica Mountains and Edwards Plateau at eight, a rifle and a ripstop nylon sleeping bag, and alone in the dark, the snapping twigs and screaming mountain lions. There were the slaughterhouses at fifteen—conveyer belts of animals wailing in terror, shuddering cows suspended on chains, the blood and cow fat on his rubber boots. At seventeen, there were bombs in Yemen, Afghanistan, and Novosibirsk, bleeding children with doe eyes, blue or brown. He scrubbed his nails with a brush five times a day and rolled camphor under his nose when the phantom smells wouldn't fade. I was everything pure and beautiful in his life, he said on nights he couldn't sleep. I knew that to be true.

The Council never worried about their golden boy's future until I became an aberration that never resolved itself. They lectured him on approval ratings and garnering enough votes to make his interim position on the Council permanent. He needed to focus on winning over the fickle administrator of Georgia. No councilmen in the Order's history had won his seat without the support of Georgia. They admonished him, using the story of former US vice president Richard Mentor Johnson. The electors in 1837 Virginia refused to vote for him because he publicly treated a woman he enslaved as his wife.

I was the storm. That's what Abraham said when I was sixteen. Now I was the uprooted tree the storm sent careening through windows. I would wreck everything.

WHILE THE COUNCIL MET IN OUR library, I sat staring at myself in the wall mirror above my desk. Dark eyes, full lower lip, long black hair captured in a single braid. In Africa, I would be a Fulani girl. Before the second civil war, I would be a Creole in Louisiana. In the Order, I was a descendant of slavery.

Henriette, I wrote in my journal, blue ink forming silken letters. *Solenne is Henriette—*

A door opened somewhere in our house. My fingers locked on the pen. I ripped the sheet into halves, fourths, smithereens. Breathed. The words didn't exist anymore. They were confetti, sprinkled and buried in my potted orchid that never left me, never died. I stood and left them behind.

Two soldiers flanked the heavy library doors, underneath the Order and Texas flags, reassuring themselves the world was still theirs with a brush of a thumb against rifles tethered to their chests. One stepped forward and waved Source from my head to toe.

"Is this really necessary, General?" I asked. "I *do* live here."

He avoided my eyes. "Our president's protection protocol super-sedes *the* official's clearance."

Invasions by other countries were always a threat, but since the second civil war, the most immediate threat came from the Order's citizens. There were insurgents found huddled in basements, restaurants, and bank vaults, planning assassinations that would result in the reinstatement of the US Constitution. Abraham had already had three near misses on his life.

When the guard was satisfied I wouldn't murder Abraham, the doors slid open. The sting of whiskey was so thick, it burned my eyes. I paused, allowing the mask of warmth and admiration to tug and snap against my profile. A useful skill, really, and you either had it or you didn't.

The hypocrites shoved their chairs away from tables, gently up-setting stacks of papers. Knees bent, half of the councilmen crouched over their chairs like frogs. They hated this disruption, being torn between ignoring me because of my skin color or honoring me be-cause the official treated me as his wife. I liked the disruption. At least here I existed. Outside our fence, I was no one.

The soldiers lining the room twitched, waiting for Abraham's command to see me out. The president sat behind Bastien's over-size desk. Mononymous, he was called Abraham with no preceding titles or surname. No one else would be called Abraham in print, digital, or verbal form in the Order. I hated his ridiculous name. I hated that down to the hawkish nose, meticulously groomed beard and mustache, and deep furrows between his eyebrows, I saw the sixty-five-year-old version of Bastien. I couldn't see through the il-lusion when I was younger, but they weren't handsome men. They were attractive how the highest-ranking men usually were—wealth shaping their bodies, mannerisms, and voices. Their uniforms fit as if they were born wearing them.

My own uniform clung to me. Three-inch heels Bastien buck-led daily, giant fingers nimble on silver clasps. Knee-length dress in ivory, oat, nude, or clay. The colors that do you justice, Bastien said when he pulled a dress from our closet. Sapphire clips wrapped around my braid made him pause in appreciation. Today was ivory, the color Abraham was partial to.

Abraham acknowledged it or me with a curt nod. The men settled into their chairs.

Bastien.

He was God, enormous in the high-back leather chair at a table in the center of the room. He twisted the obsidian ring on his right ring finger once, a muted expression I interpreted as a smile. He was all solid edges, like canyon rock. When I was younger, I made a game of searching for soft spots—the lines of his palms, wisps below his knuckles, the beige scar between his pointer and middle fingers from a hot rifle cartridge. Another on the pinky finger he broke ten years ago that curved slightly inward. To become an official, you must complete one twenty-four-month tour of duty overseas. The rumored body count is fifty. Ten percent at close range. Rumored, because that number isn't printed anywhere. It's understood. He couldn't have ever been anything other than this when even his flaws were created by the Order.

Dr. Bouchard's sharp expression forced me into a chair by the door. I averted my gaze to the mural of the eleven Founders of the Order hanging behind him. Eleven sets of painted eyes judged me. Light, navy, cornflower, milky, sky, but always blue.

"We move forward with Proposition Forty-four. A yes vote amends the Order's abortion policy to include an exception for rape, incest, or to save the life of a pregnant woman," Abraham said.

The votes followed without a single man voting in favor. It was smoke and mirrors introduced by lobbyists, they agreed. It was a ploy to weaken a man's right to the highest honor—contributing his progeny to the Order. Provide women the verbiage to end a pregnancy, and that's the verbiage they would use to end every pregnancy. It was sinful, criminal, and unconscionable to not protect the Order's most vulnerable citizens. I bit down on my lower lip until it burned.

The number 1058 flashed on a digital screen above one of the fireplaces. Propositions labeled with high numbers dealt with issues surrounding Louisiana, the Order's only nonrestricted state. The Council voted on issues surrounding Louisiana constantly.

"Proposition 1058. A yes vote gives citizens in the nonrestricted state of Louisiana the ability to vote in national elections, as represented by a certificate of voter eligibility," Abraham said. "Denied."

The other four Traditionalist councilmen denied, and the five Modernists confirmed. The men glanced expectantly at Bastien. He says he makes decisions within seconds, but it's important to periodically test your power by forcing "the wait." Much is learned during periods of silence.

He swirled whiskey in his glass. Sipped. "Denied."

Voice raw with power, the word hung in the air like he'd spoken it twice.

The proposition appeared before the Council yearly, but Bastien said it would never pass during his lifetime. New Orleans and its bars and parties and the wards of nonrestricted women bothered him. I would never become like DoS in Louisiana, Bastien said. They weren't taken care of the way he took care of me. They were dressed and jeweled and used by men for their bodies until they were confused, empty, broken.

"EARLIER THIS EVENING, THE OFFICIAL INTRODUCED Proposition 1077. We amend the Constitution tonight with a majority Council vote." Abraham glared at the pinky nail resting against my lower lip. Hidden behind the hill of my crossed knees was a better place for my hands. One-half-inch nails, pink rounded tips like smiles. Bastien couldn't tolerate anything more or less. "Proposition 1077 is on the matter of Louisiana's asylum policy for descendants of slavery, DoS."

"Need I remind every man here, this issue has been debated since my confirmation to Council thirty years ago," Vice President Newman said, tired lips and neck leathery under the lights. "The name of the proposition changes; the issue remains the same."

"The number of DoS leaving their locale, applying for asylum, and becoming Louisiana Nationals increased forty-two percent in the last four years," Bastien said. "The state's infrastructure cannot withstand these sudden population increases. It's overrun with—"

"Louisiana's asylum policy is necessary," Councilman Russell said. "No man, Black or white, should have the power to interfere with asylum. It was part of the Treaty of 1960 after Civil War II." He blinked at Bastien's left hand curling into a loose fist. "For the Order. For Texas."

"I have the floor, Councilman," Bastien said.

"You've had the floor all evening, Councilman. Must we sit through another sales speech before we put this to a vote?"

Vice President Newman talked the men down as usual by rapping his knuckles against his leather-bound copy of the Councilman's Declarations, reminding the two that although the Order was a two-party system and they fell on opposite ends as a Traditionalist and Modernist, they were still brothers.

Abraham held up his empty glass tumbler. He didn't meet my eyes, but I was the only woman in the room and the only one he would expect to serve him.

The order came from Bastien. He nodded once at me, then watched me cross the room and take the bastard's glass. The decanter of whiskey sat on the end of the desk.

"Yes abolishes the Order's recognition of certificates of emancipation issued by Louisiana, thereby enabling her contract holder, service or marital, the right to pursue the fugitive without restriction and return her to her locale. Confirmed," Abraham said.

The decanter swayed in my hand. If it passed this time, Bastien would be in a good mood.

"Confirmed," Vice President Newman said.

"Denied," Russell said as I took my seat. "My stance on the right to seek asylum has always been clear."

The men continued confirming and denying. Pushing and pulling. Bastien's eyes were on me, his impetus to block the path leading to a Black woman's freedom. He steepled his fingers. "Confirmed."

• • •

TIME TICKED AFTER THE COUNCILMEN AND their men left our house. We sat without words in his office, my anger fading to something I could bottle and bury.

"You shouldn't sit in these meetings. It only upsets you," Bastien reminded me from behind his desk. He used his gentle tone, the tone he used only with me. "You have nothing in common with those women, so you don't need to worry. I've always taken care of you, haven't I?"

Bastien's chief strategist slipped in with a stack of papers and settled at a table near the window. A stealthy, blue-eyed man as large and well-groomed as Bastien—the only hint of Julian Garnier's Black grandfather who fled the Klan in 1950s, small-town Mississippi with his white wife was his dense black waves and smile that either meant "I've been sent to put a bullet in your head," or "I'm happy to see you." He was the antithesis of Bastien. When I molded a smile on Bastien's lips, it was Julian's smile I mimicked. Vital records had no information other than he was a former highly decorated drone pilot. I guessed he was thirty-five, two years older than Bastien.

"Notes from Abraham about the meeting?" Bastien asked, tense.

Julian read Abraham's notes about his performance tonight, mostly favorable. Abraham wasn't always so generous.

"Plans to reintroduce Proposition 1077?" Julian asked.

"It's dead. Six to five, split between Modernists and Traditionalists. Modernists cannot comprehend how dangerous this policy is. I don't foresee that changing."

"This is your platform, Official. I recommend reintroducing it before Newman retires and is replaced. He favors your legislation."

The men moved to smooth the corner of their mustaches with a thumb, an imperceptible difference in timing.

"Replaced by a Traditionalist. If a Modernist is confirmed, that will shape policy for another fifty years."

"An effective Traditionalist, not another Bouchard. Are you

aware he went on record admonishing you for introducing Proposition 1077?"

Bastien froze. "A proposition he voted in favor of? I'll hear his notes."

Julian scrolled Source. His facial expressions shifted from amusement to disgust. "He says, and I quote, 'Interim councilman Bastien Martin is not the future of the Order. He caucuses with Traditionalists, then retires each evening with an insolent woman he's had in his possession for the past five years. One only has to catch a glimpse of her to see her conspiring to flee the district.'" Julian glanced at me, the storm. "'Bastien Martin, Traditionalist in legal rooms, Modernist in his bedroom, and never the twain shall meet . . . until a weak moment in his tenure as councilman, and it does.'" He checked Bastien's face. "Christ. Okay, I'll make some calls."

Julian left the office, shoving his earpiece in place.

Bastien looked across the office at me as if I had a plan for my life that didn't include him. He was always on alert, running a thumb along seams, searching for gaps in the certainty. I was still here, but he saw me in an alternate universe, squinting at the sun that bronzed and burned. He imagined me five hundred miles away watching the parade of nonrestricted women in Louisiana, red-jeweled skirts swirling to the rhythm of the drums. He saw me in another life, standing on the deck of a steamboat, watching the silver waves push me north to freedom. He hated it.

In my dreams, I had seen myself there, too, unsure of what lay in front of me and wondering where I got the strength to leave Bastien behind.

CHAPTER 6

··

THEN

THIS TIME IN MY LIFE WOULD ALWAYS BE MARKED BY THE HEAT. THAT SUMMER, IT was relentless in its taking, destroying lake levels and cracking foundations on homes. The dry winds pushed the grass fires from the hills off the highways to the subdivisions behind, leaving blackened perimeter fences and dead shrubs. I was restless, wondering what it would consume next.

Then the night came, the one we hoped to avoid by burning sage and kneeling next to our beds in prayer. Prayer hadn't protected me from my bedroom door opening, my blankets being pulled away, or my mama's face indistinct over mine, her hair in long, wild ropes. Headlights pierced through my window blinds. Men murmured in our living room downstairs. Mama's lips moved, but I couldn't hear. She squeezed my hand until my fingers ached.

"He's gone, Solenne. Your daddy is dead."

I REMEMBERED LIGHT SPRINKLING AND FADING, those trembles of yellow in a field of blue-eyed grass. My daddy held me. His summer-damp temple rested against mine. *Lightning bugs putting on a show just for you.*

Once, the world was small and simple, the wind a whisper that this would always be mine.

I remembered.

• • •

IN THOSE DARK DAYS, WE BECAME marbles rattling around an empty box. We filled the house with pretty things that meant nothing. We ate too much. Too little. We slept in each other's arms. Cried until dry. I loved my parents equally. I told myself that lie. But I watched my mama lace Daddy's boots before deployments, strained fingers and desperate sounds, and learned he was our world. Without him, life was cemetery quiet. Nothing changed that silence except anger. I spent days, pissed at myself, slipping into memories of him cracking the windows in the MV, letting the air conditioner run to cool the steering wheel before he got in, and me on the porch, *Daddy, can I go?* He smiled and pretended he had no choice. *Get your shoes on, girl.*

Why hadn't I learned that one day, I would ask that question and there would be silence?

GRADUATION WASN'T A CEREMONY. IT WAS emptying your locker, hugging the teachers you liked, and giving a solemn nod to the younger girls who watched you file out of the school's metal doors for the last time.

That night at the kitchen table, Mama scrolled Source for saved images I drew when I was little, two brown stick figures with black scribbles for hair, half circles for smiles, the larger figure under a yellow sun or blue moon waving goodbye.

"Say something," I finally said.

She gazed across the table, not at me but at the canned soup in my bowl. Her hazel eyes were more brown than green under dim lights. "Nothing to say."

I didn't know until he was gone how much losing my daddy would change my mama. My mama was fierce, always had a plan, always ended her stories where she achieved the impossible with, "I descend from Henriette." Now she couldn't figure out how to work a can opener.

"Say you're scared about where the algorithm will send me because of my mouth. Say you're scared Daddy's not here to get me a better assignment. Say, 'But we'll work it out because we have Henriette's blood in our veins.'"

She left the table. The whiny sixth stair carried her to her bedroom, urging me to follow. Mama looked younger than her thirty-three years standing at the picture window in her white shift dress, arms wrapped around her waist like she was clinging to Daddy, melting until her skin was his. Love, quiet as breaths but thrashing against what waited for him somewhere at some border—what stilled Black men's lives too soon. *I'll die if you go*, she said. Then his promise to her, *I'll be right back. I always come back to you.* Waiting for the convoy of MVs to return spiraled into waiting for the moment the bereavement officers turned down our driveway to deliver a folded green flag, so she could fling open the front door and scream at them not to bring their asses on her porch. They could keep that fucking flag. She wouldn't be a good officer's wife who bowed her head and accepted fabric instead of the man she loved. But she was someone's mother. Mothers couldn't retreat inside themselves and leave their children behind. She told me that. What was I supposed to do here alone besides see her with new eyes? I decided then to never love a man, not when his absence singed edges of you, creating different versions that not even your mirror double recognized.

Later, we sat on the back porch in front of the potted lilacs, knees touching, sipping from the same mug of jasmine tea with creamed honey—warm, but we would never be whole again. White light from the moon fragmented the dark. The trains rushed past Oak Cliff into Downtown Dallas while we imagined we were anywhere but here.

THE CHASTE TREES THAT BLOOMED IN the summer began a slow death that fall. Leaves and purple petals littered the driveway and backyard. But the days were still warm with relief found only hours after sunset.

"We have to get out," Mama said, pulling the curtains back on a day that was mostly gone. "This bed will still be here tonight. We can lie in it and hate God later."

Walking through a world of people smiling, ordering brisket plates, setting hair appointments, and breathing as if I hadn't lost everything would only piss me off more than I already was.

"For what?"

She sat on the bed and held my face in her hands. "Because I see you in this bed, and I see you sinking. Neither of us can climb if the other one is buried, and I don't plan on burying my only child."

So we did what brought her joy—walked through neighborhoods carrying her mango butter hair cream in black wicker baskets. She had straightened my hair and tied the edges down with a silk scarf so the humidity didn't curl it until after the last jar was sold. It had rained that morning, but in our tomb of a bedroom, we didn't know it. *We needed the rain*, people sitting in the shade of their porches used as pleasantries. *It's too hot.* But that never cooled anything off except the grass, then made the rest of the day muggy and unbearable like Houston.

Mama talked to women who answered their doors and reminded them her shop was reopening in two months. Then she used me as a model, telling the same lie. My hair had grown five and a quarter inches in the last year from using the mango butter. They knew she was lying, but they looked at my beautiful mama, and she became their map to all they desired. One woman asked to barter by exchanging plates of smothered turkey legs, yams, and greens seasoned with neck bones. She was tall with thick hair and long legs under a short housedress. Four little girls already in their pajamas of tank tops and shorts took turns peeking through their mama's legs at me.

The woman unscrewed the lid and sniffed the cream. "It was easy for you to charge these crazy prices when you had your man propping you up, whispering you were better than everybody else since we were in school. You don't have a high horse to sit upon now. I'm only looking to trade."

Mama glazed a smile, and I almost felt sorry for the woman.

"You gave him four babies, and now you can't even get him to take care of y'all's hair? If your man is tight with his money, or you haven't learned how to keep the boot off your neck, say that."

A standoff followed. She could buy a jar she couldn't afford or close the door and wonder if mama was somewhere gloating about her having a husband who wouldn't give her hair money. She sent her daughter to grab her Source off the kitchen counter to pay.

Mama's old walk, her sleek walk, came back, and for a moment, I thought we'd be all right. Then her thoughts swam to the surface of her face, pushing me back to hopelessness. When Daddy was alive, she saved the money she made. With a widow's conservator, where would the money go? We wouldn't speak the name of the bitter-faced man the Order appointed to hold the deed to our house and distribute funds Daddy left us. He was our god until Mama remarried, which she wouldn't do, or until she had a son-in-law. When the algorithm assigned me, it was his signature that finalized the assignment or marriage. Daddy said the Order worked it that way to make Black men feel they had some power over the process. It worked. That bit of power deepened the conservator's onion-smelling laugh. Mama returned teary-eyed from a visit to his office, and I knew then we ended up with a dishonest conservator who wanted sex in exchange for our own money. I asked why *he* couldn't die, then I closed my eyes and saw the lumps and sags under his shirt. *Fat bastard*, I said. Mama was so mad, she didn't notice I cursed. All she said was, *Don't wish for it. The devil you know is better than the one you don't.*

Behind the rows of houses, the sun settled into the thinnest yellow line in a graying sky. The men in the neighborhood emerged from garages cranking lawn mowers to take advantage of the lower temperature.

Mama stopped at the curb in front of Dalena's house, a sepia ranch style with too many red lava rocks in the landscaping. "Carleen had her baby. Josephine put something together for her."

"I'm not going in there."

I hadn't talked to Dalena or anyone else in months. I didn't want to listen to a bunch of hens oohing and aahing over Natalya's new sibling as if my daddy hadn't died.

"Bring your *ass*," she hissed at me just as Dalena's mama, Josephine, opened the door.

The women hugged, nodded against each other's shoulders, and murmured in the other's ear.

Inside was the smell of sausage and vanilla and Mama nodding through more hugs and murmurs of "The Lord don't make no mistakes. He called your husband home for a reason."

We sat on a suede love seat. Someone handed us plastic cups of punch frothing with sherbet.

Carleen sat across from us, thick glasses on a puffy face, a newborn curled like a shrimp between her swollen breasts. Gray knit hat and blue socks. This one was a boy.

The women hovered over them singing blessings. Stroking the baby's thigh, tan and mottled red, his true skin color just under the surface begging entry. "He ain't gone be too dark." Stroking his hair, still bone straight and plastered to his forehead and neck. "His hair gone stay just like this, too."

They said this about every baby, even though Carleen, her husband, and the other six children all had glossy black skin, vibrant and unblemished.

Carleen smiled, too much gums showing. One end of the burp cloth stretched between the baby and her chest was for the spittle escaping puckered lips. The other end was for the fog on the thick lenses of her glasses. This baby was destined for greatness, she told the women. His birth was the easiest of the seven. Easy, as if almost delivering squatting in a shower was nothing at all.

Carleen found my eyes. "We'll be getting together like this for you in a few years."

"No, we won't," I said. "Ovaries, uterus, tubes—I hope mine are shriveled and black like raisins."

I knew I didn't want kids when Guidry forced the pretty baby doll into my arms to practice on. Why have a girl the world would treat like nothing or a son who'd die in the Code? My mama had me at eighteen. No way I could do it. I couldn't teach her what too much eye contact meant to men, or watch her learn choice doesn't exist.

"I used to say the same thing," Carleen said, "but you grow out of that. You have your baby, and you love them as soon as you see them."

Mama sipped her punch. "That's a myth. It's not the same for all of us." She continued through disagreeable silence. "You get married. The Order clears you for a family. Then you're pregnant. Your body is beaten for almost a year. You have that baby, and you feel like an animal. Nothing works on you but the parts that ooze. First, all you care about is making sure you and that child are all right. Survival. Responsibility. First, you're human. Love comes later."

But that wasn't the story she told me for my journal. She said she loved me the moment she witnessed my first breath. I was something precious my daddy gave her. Proof that she did something right in her life.

"Can we go now?" I whispered to Mama.

"No." Mama looked around the room of women. "They can tell me which part is a lie."

The women looked away from the grieving widow who was going on about nonsense. They picked at sausage rolls and sipped punch.

"Loren is saying what don't nobody else want to say," Josephine said, lips still pressed to her cup. "We don't talk about it enough. We listen to women who loved their baby as soon as they felt it moving about in their stomachs, and then we're ashamed because our moment happened weeks later during a middle-of-the-night feeding." She wrapped her arms around her chest as if she were cradling a baby. "Doesn't matter that it doesn't happen in seconds. We're still mama."

INSIDE DALENA'S ROOM WAS ART. CRUMPLED tubes of paint, brushes soaking in jars, small canvas panels in various stages of becoming a finished piece. Gold cloth pinned to a mannequin torso on a tripod stand. Styrofoam wig heads on her dresser. Candice Jr., the wig cut into a bob with wispy bangs, sat in the middle. Dalena's mama claimed the original Candice as her church wig.

I sat on the carpet and sorted through the canvases propped against the wall. Most were of the French Quarter. Dalena could paint anything after seeing an image once. Her mama said that was useless. She needed to learn how to do something reasonable like make clothes or do hair. Bartering worked only if you could exchange something useful.

The last canvas in the stack was larger than the others. It was a portrait of a woman, of me, gazing into the distance from underneath a 1950s pompadour. I outlined the sad eyes with a finger and imagined Dalena mixing paint until she had the perfect shades of brown to create me on this canvas for the first time. A yellowish-brown for my skin, beige for my lips and earlobes, near black for my eyes. It must have taken her days.

I pulled my hair up in a ponytail with Dalena's hair tie and snapped on her amber waist beads I found twisted between the wig heads. Lying in her bed, I burrowed into her pillow. The smoky scent of castor oil and something else I couldn't identify was buried in the threads. A secret. Like Dalena. I thought of New Orleans at night and Dalena in all white wandering through nightclubs and restaurants. Drinks in one, a main course in another, dessert on a white plate decorated with sauce and chocolate shavings in a place where a man in a suit said, "Reservations only." That her life had such a clear path to freedom when I couldn't see my own bothered me. What was so different about us? Born and raised to be owned, and yet, I knew in my bones that wasn't how it would end for her. *Why?* I wished my daddy was still here, the safety of his footsteps and words. No longer could I assure myself as long as he was somewhere staring up at the same pale moon, we'd always be together. So childish that I had ever thought that.

The bedroom door opened. Dalena stood in her doorway zipped in her red satin jacket with *Oak Cliff* stitched on the chest. She'd been with that idiot who wore a leather jacket in the summer, rode a motorcycle, and threw lies at her feet.

"What are you doing in my room?"

I sat up. I didn't feel like arguing with her. "Your mama sent me to lie down in here."

"And you're going through my stuff? I swear you're like a toddler constantly rambling through things."

She stared at me fumbling with the clasp of her waist beads before sighing and telling me to keep them.

"I'll wait in the living room."

"You'll be waiting forever. Your mama is only halfway done lying about her hair creams." She sat next to me, shrugged off her jacket, and kicked off her sandy shoes. "I was at the lake with a friend. He dropped jewels in my ear. Gave me a few names to use when I make it to New Orleans, so I'll have places to stay."

I hated the excitement in her voice and how casually she talked about leaving like the possibility of never seeing each other again never kept her awake at night. She should've felt guilty about having plans for freedom that didn't include me, but she never did. I sorted through words to find the hurtful ones.

"I'll probably end up assigned to an idiot like Charlesetta did while you're living it up in New Orleans."

"No, you won't—"

"It's true, and you know it. But I don't care where they send me anymore."

We listened to the *slip-thump* of the ceiling fan. One of the women in the living room clapped and laughed. A front or a back door opened and closed.

"We're not kids, Solenne," Dalena said softly.

"I know that."

"Then what do you want from me?"

I wanted her to look at me instead of the magenta polish on her nails. I wanted her to remember me.

"Nothing."

"You have to want something. Your daddy being killed is not the worst thing that can happen to a Black girl."

In her words, I found fear instead of comfort. With my daddy gone, the world had opened wide enough to swallow me. Its darkness reminded me Mama was the only person left on earth who loved me.

"Then what is? Losing my mama?"

She wrapped her arm around my waist and accepted my head against her shoulder. She smelled earthy, like grass and dry wind. "Never being free. Find your way. Wherever they send you, get him to write your papers. Get on a train. Nobody owns you unless you believe they do."

CHAPTER 7

NOW

I LAY IN BED MESMERIZED BY THE RAIN AND WIND FORCING THE MAPLE TREES INTO a sultry dance. Bastien stood at the window wall as if his presence would force the rain to continue bleeding into his precious lake. He rarely took his boat out now. He couldn't stand the uncertainty of change. Waves didn't lick as high on the limestone cliffs. Drought sucked at the water levels until Sometimes Islands resurfaced in Lake Travis, becoming a peninsula of salt cedar bushes and juniper stumps jutting from the earth.

"What are you doing?" I asked, knowing he was annoyed by Dr. Bouchard's notes about the meeting. Knowing he was analyzing his performance for anything that could be perceived as a misstep by his father.

"Thinking."

"What are you thinking about?"

"Confidential."

I traced my name against his silhouette with my finger like I did when I was younger, when I wanted him to stay. "What are you thinking about, darling?"

"Drafting a response to Dr. Bouchard's notes about my vote tonight. The fucking idiot."

He slid into bed next to me, skin still dewy from the shower.

"Would you still do anything for me?" I asked.

"Anything."

One of the first lessons I learned from Mama. Never ask for what you want upfront. Men are programmed to deny the first ask.

"Send Julian back to the box drone piloting the border."

"Explain why Julian is an issue."

By now, he was sifting through my Julian interactions for any signs Julian had failed him. He wouldn't come up with anything. The serpent. The wolf. The man who talked himself out of the brain-shredding position as a drone pilot and into a position in the highest office in the Order. To the men, Julian was a genius.

"He's around too much. Isn't that enough?"

"Let's talk about it in five days." He kissed the top of my head, then settled against the pillow. "You failed your truth assessment this morning."

"Maybe you need to recalibrate."

"I don't need to recalibrate, baby. You passed all sections except where you stated you had no plans current or future to leave your locale without permission."

He was rigid beside me, unforgiving of things that were thoughts, weightless, without the chance to become fully formed.

"I thought about visiting my mother back home—"

"You are home."

"I've been thinking of my daddy and our old house. Source probably picks that up, but that doesn't mean I want to leave you."

He didn't blink. "I need something outside your assurances."

"Why don't you ever believe me?"

He ignored the question. "Last month, the Council discussed my health file."

His creeping blood pressure, increased resting heart rate, and headaches—all my fault.

"I'm not the issue. I'm not stressing you out."

He ran his thumb over my stomach, still hollow and not serving the Order. The conversation would flip to my health data that used to be available to me but became a grayed-out box on my Source's screen three years ago.

With one quick motion of limbs, I was pinned under him. "Vice President Newman recommends a child. Two within thirty months."

Bastien reviewed eighty years of data, and the conclusion was clear. Children anchor DoS. Give her a child, and she'll never leave. A child would reduce his stress by ensuring I would never disappear like the rain. In his head was the crisp image of a child with his coloring, eyes, and beliefs—his DNA diluting any part of me. I never wanted children. It was the quicksand that grabbed at us, filled our eyes with grit, and pulled us into nothing more than *mama*.

His eyes met mine when he guided himself inside. He held them there so we could watch the storm.

We lay there afterward, sweating and undone, his arm tight around my waist as if I would wander and lose my way while he slept.

"Bastien?"

"Yes." The post-sex haze clouded his voice, but still, he answered too quickly for where I was going.

"When your financial planner came last week, neither of you mentioned me. What happens to me when you die?"

I continued without stopping for a breath.

"Children of DoS follow the condition of the mother. Without you here, your sons would be assigned to the Code. They'd die at the borders. What if we had a daughter? I would have no control over who the algorithm chooses for her. Who would provide for them financially? That little stipend from the Order until I'm married? Abraham? You know he hates me. Yes, he does. He wouldn't give us anything because he'd have to acknowledge them as his grandchildren. You know he'd rather die. We'd struggle. You wouldn't like that, would you?"

"Of course not."

"Then sign a certificate of emancipation. I could earn a salary. I wouldn't need anyone to take care of me or our children. Plus, you promised you'd give me emancipation at seventeen."

"Never."

"You did. You told me—"

"You will lower your voice and correct your tone."

Eyes closed, I wrestled with myself to hold on to the things I couldn't say.

"You swore to me—"

"Nonsense."

"So I'm fucking insane?"

"A *filthy* mouth. I won't tolerate it." He separated his body from mine, prompting the auto lights to spotlight over our bed. "Look at me."

It was his soulless gaze—nothing or no one behind it.

"Stop it. This is about security. At the very least, you could file the document for me and your daughters . . . for when you die."

Behind him, Jefferson sent his reminders. Hold her as a child, hold her as an adult. Hold her in death, Official.

Bastien finally spoke, but I wished he hadn't. "You will never convince me to give you a document that puts distance between us." He tapped my temple with two fingers. "Your life. My love, all that you are or will be—every cell in your body—belongs to me. Without end. Without fail."

Outside, the storm quieted into windless rain, fine and gray like smoke.

THERE WERE LEFTOVERS FROM THE STORM. Pieces of our conversation about emancipation were scattered like debris throughout our house. Bastien tried to put things back in order with shiny boxes with shinier things inside. I flipped open lids and swallowed the confirmation he never intended for me to be free until it overflowed.

I found him in his office. He and Julian stood at the weapon's cabinet preparing for the two-and-a-half-hour drive to Houston for his Address to the Order. Rifles, handguns, machetes, knives. Rehearsed until second nature, they moved in sync without a word. Weapons were shoved in holsters, strapped here, attached there. The Dance of the Arming of the Officials.

I used the one weapon I owned. "Dr. Bouchard isn't right often, but he was right about you."

Julian's hand paused on his rifle. One of the jobs he inherited was to make sure I didn't stress Bastien out. "Solenne—"

Bastien held up a hand.

"You're one speech away from the idiots who come to listen to you speak figuring out you're just like them."

"This serves no purpose. No matter what game you play, I won't send you back to Dallas."

My body was on fire. The calm I collected to go toe to toe with him wasn't mine anymore. "You can't stop me. The Order guarantees me time home."

His eyes met mine in the cabinet's interior mirror. "I am the Order."

A light smile twitched on Julian's lips.

Like doubles, the men saluted the mural of the Founders behind Bastien's desk who, seventy years ago, had given Bastien more power over another human than should ever be possible.

In the doorway, he kissed me. "Your train to Houston leaves in ninety minutes. I'll see you at my address."

I couldn't ride with him. My proximity to him in public had to be carefully curated by Julian, but Bastien never had to see me to know I was standing backstage to the left of a swath of curtain. Always absolutes and certainties for him. Never any for me. I was a guest, walking on the periphery of spaces designed for him.

I would write before I took the train to Houston. Insert metaphors for that place where anger is indiscriminate from pain. That place where my ancestors whispered in my ear, telling me I was done.

CHAPTER 8

THEN

Sitting at the kitchen table that September morning, we couldn't have imagined the snare lying in my path, the cinch of a wire noose for girls like me.

Mama nodded at the Assignment Notification on my Source. "What does it say, dear heart?"

"Frank Pettit. He's a narrative writer in Austin. I move into a dorm with the other . . ." The Order used words like servants, servers, in-service. We didn't know what to call it. "With other girls next week." I closed out my Assignment tab and shut Source off. Assignments in Austin were known to be easier. Those placements were coveted.

We laughed, and the sound belonged. We didn't think about Mama alone with the mocking sounds of Daddy returning. An MV turning down the wrong driveway. The storm door rattling. The neighbors' dogs in mournful conversation about the dry wind.

But a Frank Pettit placement wasn't meant to be. Three days before I would arrive in his office, he had a stroke on the train home and died at fifty-two. We made okra creole the night Source notified us of the death and auto-reassignment. While the name of my new contract holder rolled in my brain, Mama chopped sausage and tomatoes in quarters. Without looking at me, she scattered handfuls into the onion and bell pepper I had simmering in tomato sauce. She skipped adding hamburger meat to the pot the way Daddy liked it.

Same pot, same spices, same galley kitchen too warm from eight windows facing the sun, but everything had changed.

"This never happens. The assignment is always the assignment."

"Then why did it have to happen to me?" I asked, angry because one step forward was always two steps back. Why couldn't anything ever work out for me?

OUTSIDE MY BEDROOM WINDOW, THE EXECUTIONER'S high beams swept over lilacs languishing in pots next to our mailbox, the hopscotch squares, and the jump rope with missing handles abandoned during his earlier sweep. The neighbor girls were trained to listen for jouncy tires. They screeched an alarm to anyone unaware. *The Boogeyman. The Rougarou.*

They learned early that we were parts, unformed and unsafe, until the algorithm placed a man's name in the ASSIGNED TO box in Source. UNASSIGNED meant the parts belonged to anyone who reached out with greedy hands at the end of the hunt. *Be sweet. Be quiet.* It hurts worse if they take. I knew that. So two years ago, when an electrician saw me dragging a bag to the school's dumpster and told me to get in his truck, I did. *Don't make me take it*, he said, Adam's apple floating underneath keloid scars, bubbled snakes on brown skin. *Don't waste my time taking your skirt off. Just lift it up.* I couldn't lift my skirt, couldn't recline on filthy tan seats, couldn't let him insert himself into my memories. "No sir," I said, and again when he had me by the throat, again when Guidry opened his scalp with the brick I used to prop open the back door, and again when he screamed for the rag gray with motor oil wedged under my feet. He didn't get me. He almost did, but he didn't. My daddy watched him hang.

Not finding girls out past curfew, the executioner rolled through the stop sign to the next bank of darkened houses with green flags hung in a second-story window for a father or son lost in the Code. Those with flagless windows listened to the embittered sound of ticking clocks. When I was still, I could hear them waiting.

• • •

OUR COHORT WAS THE LAST OF DoS in our area to board trains that took us to our new assignments. Brown girls huddled on the platform in front of trains streaking into the station.

I saw Dalena with the man she was assigned to, but they only saw each other as they drifted in front of me. Arms brushed, heads slanted in conversation. A boy of about twelve wearing his rifle on a chest sling walked next to the man. A chubby baby hung from Dalena's hip.

I followed.

When we neared the L42 platform, she saw me pleading with my eyes but pretended she didn't. She said something in the man's ear that worked. He switched his rifle from his chest to his back and plucked the baby from Dalena's arms.

"Mama." He twisted in his father's arms, reaching. *Mama.* The babies didn't belong to us, but they had no other word for what we were. Mama.

Stone-faced, the man stood near a concrete pillar and watched Dalena avoid a group of Black men in mechanic uniforms and sidle next to me on the platform. If she drifted too far, he would monitor her through Source. That's how they did it. The tether we couldn't see but felt like the early churn of thunder.

"He only gave me two minutes," she said.

"I wanted to tell you I think I'll be all right. I'm assigned to James Gibson. Narrative writer. Frank Pettit's former assistant."

Her pretty features fluttered, the clue she was impressed or relieved I was going to Austin where the councilmen lived and violence didn't happen in front of schools.

"Guess it didn't work out for the fence howler. I'm assigned to Lucas Magnan. Litigator."

"He doesn't look like a litigator."

"That's what he is. I looked him up. Supposedly has a genius IQ like the councilmen. He's running for administrator of Georgia."

"You're going all the way to Georgia?" I sifted through memories for a time a girl had been sent so far away.

"It's far, but he said I can talk to Twin whenever I want."

She raked her nails through her bangs, and I was eleven again, following her around the neighborhood. I didn't know how scared I was of the answer until after I asked if she would call me, too.

"Yeah," she said, but I couldn't analyze her voice.

She gave Lucas Magnan the phony smile that got her whatever she wanted, chipping into his stoicism and sending his gaze to a group of passersby. Eyes on me, she snorted. "He named that baby Bear. *Bear?*" Hand pressed to her chest like the 1950s actresses from the magazines, she slipped into the fake voice we used when we had what we called company. "The name fits him so well. You should have lots of children so you can give them beautiful names."

I pretended to cough to mask a laugh.

"Anyway," she said in her normal tone, "Lucas said the older boy is his nephew, so I'll only have to help with the baby. It'll be easy."

Lucas. Not my contract holder or Mr. Magnan.

"Is he married?"

"Two years, but when has that ever mattered to them? He said I'll love Atlanta in the spring." A train gusted past, lifting coily bangs from her forehead. "Can't be too much of a genius if he thinks I'll still be there in six months."

CHAPTER 9

NOW

IN THE BACK SEAT OF THE MV, I THOUGHT OF MY PLACE BEYOND BLACK STAGE curtains separating me from Bastien, the podium, and the thousands gathered in a Houston stadium to hear his speech.

By the time my shadow parked at the train station, the rain was coming down in slanted sheets. Outside the MV, it tore at his umbrella and glued my dress to my arms.

We were a sight—the shadow shuffling behind me holding the rogue umbrella over my head, and both of us trying to keep enough distance between us that would satisfy Bastien.

Down the concrete stairs, we passed lines of DoS new to Austin. They exited trains, goddess braids or twists pulled into neat buns. I counted the beautiful ones and wondered how many would find themselves in lifetime contracts.

Thunder vibrated off the walls. The Arrival-Departure screens flickered then cut the digital voices on the intercoms off midsentence. An outage.

A hush fell over the station. The DoS assembled into obedient clusters against walls, waiting for instruction from Source. Something my cohort never did. We took advantage when the chips glitched during an outage and couldn't track our location.

My shadow moved closer to me, scanning the crowd like this brief interruption in electricity was some ominous threat. He checked Source and warned me of a fifteen-minute train delay.

I was looking for an empty bench when I saw Daddy, locs pulled away from his face. He coughed and became the only Black man in a line of six chained at the ankles. Mournful faces and sour smelling, they shuffled past led by two agents through the station where a flatbed truck waited for them. They wouldn't see another sunrise.

What happened next was in blocks of time. The man at the end of the line shoved the man in front of him. The chain of men fell to the ground like downed dominoes. I saw it before the agents did. The man at the end was unchained. He rolled to his feet and bolted through the station, pushing two women between him and the agents' guns.

My shadow's eyes darted between me and the commotion. He brushed his thumb across the pistol holstered at his waist. If Bastien reviewed the footage from the station's cameras, he would say it was a weapon's check. I knew it meant "You better stay right here, or else." Then he was gone, doing what a shadow does, involving himself in something that didn't involve him. The crowd swept him into the confusion.

The agents circled the remaining prisoners, cursing and checking chains.

The Black man lifted his head from the concrete. Red trickled from his hairline to the bulging eye forced shut. The near-dead animal in the trap looked at me with his one good eye.

Me. Like I could do something when I was wearing my own chains. I found one of my scarves in my bag and brushed past the agents.

"What do you . . ." the agent stopped short when Source buzzed against his hip. The tautness eased in his shoulders. He'd learned I wasn't just any Black girl. My ID said I had government clearance and belonged to someone at the Capitol, maid or staffer, and that was a significant difference.

I crouched next to the insurgent and pressed the scarf against his hairline. I wished I had words that would comfort. He should never doubt his decision to stand up for what he believed was right.

"Thank you." His voice was a rough thing, scouring itself into my memory.

"Ma'am, I need you to step back now."

But I wasn't listening to the agent. Behind us, the bullet train to Louisiana sang its arrival. It was the sound of escape, a hymn, the hopeful notes of my ancestors' map songs.

I STOOD, THOUGHTS WAVERING BETWEEN BASTIEN and the high-speed bullet train.

Knotting myself inside of him standing next to a fountain in a courtyard.

The train's hum.

My disquiet the first time Bastien kissed me on the sofa in his office, holding me so tight he said he could feel my nerves.

The train *humming*.

The first time Bastien told me I would be free. The night he denied ever speaking those words.

The train's doors sliding open.

The tingling in my body was a surge of adrenaline. I hung back against the current of bodies sweeping me toward the glass doors gaped open like everything—this day, the storm, and what I was considering doing—was normal.

I looked over my shoulder and found my shadow's back. He had the escaped insurgent on the ground. I couldn't let him see me standing near the bullet train, vacant-eyed, clutching my bag. He would know *everything*, and that would go into his daily report. Bastien would find the mental box I packed and unpacked for years when he told me he needed me and I needed him. Had anyone ever beat Bastien? Had anyone ever stood between him and something of his, including a fifteen-year-old Black girl?

He's not here. Get on the train.

What if I did? If I tried this and failed, he would close his fist so tight, I wouldn't be able to use the bathroom without an escort.

Henriette did it.

But things were different then. Overseers and pattyrollers eventually ran out of time, money, desire. How do you leave a man whose software runs through your body? A man with unlimited resources who never tires. You don't.

This is what you want. If you don't leave now, you'll never leave. One pregnancy after another. You'll never leave his sight. Once you have his child, he—

"I'll never let you go."

I whirled around, looking up where I would find his eyes. But Bastien wasn't there. No agents. No shadow. Just me.

This was stupid, and it would never work. Louisiana was freedom, but it was also the unknown. Where would I sleep? I had no money. I didn't know anyone.

But being unknown is why this works.

Wasn't that how enslaved people disappeared before the first Civil War? They relied on anonymity and the kindness of strangers.

Bastien would be livid if I got on this train. Black women would feel how livid for the next three generations. But should I have to shoulder the burden for everyone who looked like me for my entire life? I was a twenty-year-old nobody. Any woman would do the same thing if they were standing next to a train that could get them out of here.

This was how it worked. No planning, no money, no safety, just going. If you were neat about leaving, you'd convince yourself to remain in chains.

Eyes frozen on the train's doors, I moved. One foot in front of the other, and my God, when did the platform become so long and narrow? I was *pulled* toward the glass doors, the leather seats, Louisiana, and the idea of putting distance between us. There wouldn't be a warning from the station's speakers, but would the train start? There must be an internal mechanism that prevented the train from shuttling me off to an unapproved area even if the power outages caused my chip to glitch. Bastien said it once, casually. *It's as simple as one line of code, love.*

I would get on the train, and nothing would happen, like my dreams of being on an elevator that wouldn't move because I couldn't

THE BLUEPRINT | 63 |

get my finger to align with the buttons. *Oh, you stupid little girl. You didn't think this would be that easy, did you?*

Sometimes, it is. Isn't that why he had me shadowed? Technology, even technology created by Bastien, failed sometimes.

I conjured the image of Bastien looking out over the crowd of adoring faces, his men behind him, assuming I was in my place behind the curtain. During the speech, Source would alert him I wasn't. It would alert him of surging adrenaline and an elevated heart rate. I would be a warning in an earpiece, a crimson dot on a screen, moving far, far away from him. He would break.

It's his turn to break. He'll never give you emancipation.

Could I hurt him that way? Since I was sixteen, he said I would. Said I was cruel and selfish and no matter what he did for me, I always wanted more. Said I was a product of my upbringing, brutal and self-centered, like my mother and grandmothers.

Maybe he was right.

There was a part of me I didn't understand, the part of me that loved him, but there was a larger part that was tired, so tired. With time and distance the divider between us, I could undo the mistakes I made. For the first time in my life, I could be alone. Free.

I clutched my bag to my chest and let the tide take me within inches of the doors. No alarms. No accusatory stares. Only people minding their own business. On the train, I donned a mask of confidence because I remembered who I was. I am Henriette's descendant.

| PART TWO |

FOR AUGUSTIN

MY HENRIETTE

THE STORM DIDN'T PITY ANYTHING. IT ROLLED IN GREAT SHEETS, BREAKING THE doors apart on the carriage house and washing out the grave path to the cabins on the slave row.

Drenched to the bone, Henriette traveled that dirt path for the first time thinking of the hundredth. Henriette, property of Antoni Dubois. Henriette, inked on the page after the names and ages of his mules:

Gus, 5 years.
Sainte, 9 years . . .

In a cabin she would share with the old midwife, Delphine, Henriette wept with the sky.

TIME DIDN'T PAUSE. IT MOVED ON, endless, like the black ocean Henriette once stared into searching for souls who chose freedom there. With patient hands, Delphine taught her how to feed the chickens. She scattered a handful of grain into the coop.

—Here now, c'est bon. Here, c'est bon.

While they worked, Delphine sang Henriette the rhythms of

Creole—that blend of French, Spanish, English, and African dialects. When the nightmares came, Delphine held her close on the pallet they shared.

—You stronger than that, child. Thinking while you sleep won't help you none.

Henriette couldn't guard her thoughts while she slept, so she rose before sunrise each morning. She scrubbed dust from the grooves in the cabin's floors, shifting it under the cliffs of her fingernails, transferring it to the elbows of her frock. If she was moving, she didn't think. If she didn't think, she didn't hurt. She paused only to listen to the enslaved marching past their cabin to the fields. Hundreds of them. Mournful songs rose rhythmically over the cadence of their steps on sodden ground.

—Master ain't buy you to pick no cotton, Delphine said from her pallet.

FIVE MONTHS LATER, THE DRESS ARRIVED. Delphine accepted it from her master's driver and asked no questions. She bathed Henriette, buttoned her in the new dress, and fixed her hair in two long braids, using a bit of kerosene from her rations.

That night, she walked Henriette to the big house. Darkness blurred the raw-fingered field hands bent over cotton bolls in the distance.

—This is good, child. This where you stay now.

Uncle, a man who worked in the house, led them down a dim hallway. Alabaster oil lamps colored their shadows along the walls and up the staircase.

Antoni Dubois opened his bedroom door before Delphine knocked.

—Master, Delphine said, her face and voice worn not by the fields but by doing Master's bidding. She picked no cotton; she picked enslaved people off the auction block. In the rows, she sang no sorrow; she sang rumors of uprisings in Master's ear. Her latest task had been to guide Henriette into understanding that like Master's horse and rifle, she was his possession. He liked all three pretty. She pulled him and two of his brothers from their mother's womb; it surprised no one that Delphine was one of six enslaved people Antoni brought to New Orleans when he fled the Saint-Domingue slave revolts and yellow fever. Together, they'd seen too much.

Henriette averted her eyes and curtsied. Delphine's lessons. *Don't you look in his eyes unless he tell you. Don't you talk unless he ask you something.*

Antoni nodded once to dismiss Delphine.

Beside the bolted bedroom door, Henriette memorized Delphine's footsteps fading down the stairs. Delphine wasn't coming back for her. Baths and dresses meant it was time for another piece of her to be clipped off. Her gaze fell upon the four-poster bed with the blankets turned down.

—Mercy, Master, she whispered. The words she heard an enslaved man scream to an overseer before being bound and dragged naked from the slave quarters, accused of ruining fifty pounds of pork by letting the fire go out in the smokehouse.

But mercy didn't come for her. No, it never did for Black girls.

THE BABY CAME ON A RAINY spring night a year later. Henriette knew the day it would come. She knew it would be a boy. She knew she wouldn't love him.

She was afraid to see, so she didn't look at the whimpering flesh Delphine pulled from her body and placed on her belly.

Delphine dried the baby and did what she usually did. She checked his cuticles and ear cartilage for the color that would emerge in the following months. White as the skin on his daddy's thighs.

—Won't see too much color, but he beautiful, child.

Delphine wiped her eyes with the end of her apron. The mother could be twelve or forty, and the pain for her was the same. She was first to see the women search for signs of themselves—the full lips, a rounded nose, something that said God intended for this child to belong to her. She found nothing but distance in Henriette's eyes and her trembling hands looped around the sweaty blanket instead of the baby.

—Don't matter who his papa be. This your child. After no more breath is left in your body, you'll still have somebody who love you.

In that splintery cabin with one window, Delphine helped her put the new baby to breast. The tugging from the pink mouth inspired no thoughts of love. It inspired thoughts of Black bodies at dusk carrying pinewood torches and small coffins to the burial grounds. Even when they were wanted, half the Black babies died before they weaned. How soon did the unwanted die?

Within days, Antoni decided Henriette had enough of Delphine's help and demanded that she move back into the big house.

—Do you presume to tell me how to manage my property? Mothering is instinctual, he shouted down to Delphine from his horse. He'd seen it firsthand. Mules, cattle, slaves.

That evening, Henriette was restless. She carried that baby to the big house, the weight of him against her arm like a smooth, swaddled stone. Her room across the hall from Antoni's, the room she never slept in because Antoni called for her every night, had changed. The rectangles of diaper linen stacked on a table were for that baby. The pine rocker shrouded by fine mosquito netting was for that baby. But he didn't have the one thing he should. A mother who loved him. Henriette couldn't love anything on that plantation.

So she left Antoni's son in his rocker when she fled under the secrecy of night, still bleeding and leaking milk through the bodice of her dress. She didn't know she was miles from where *L'Aliénor* arrived, where her brother was sold, or that no American or French custom allowed her to trade one boy for another. Her only thoughts were of the boy with skin like hers who understood her words. While the world swayed beneath them on *L'Aliénor*, she promised he would never be alone.

CHAPTER 10

THEN

CLIMBED THE STAIRS LEADING FROM THE TRAIN STATION AND STOOD UNDER THE sun on Government Avenue. Circling, I took everything in—the State Archives and Library building, monuments, and the medical research building. Everything was paved in stone. Source flashed from storefront windows, on benches, above stoplights, reporting time, temperature, and updates on fifty-two insurgents tried and executed for conspiring against the Order. At the heart of Government Avenue was the domed Capitol building with the Goddess of Liberty statue perched on top holding a star high in one hand. I was colored glass, a drop of rain in an ocean, nothing for men and women with black umbrellas resting against their shoulders to notice. My pulse drummed in my ears.

The dorm I would live in until James Gibson either sent me home or wrote my emancipation papers was on Guadalupe Street, a few miles from the Capitol. The cream two-story Victorian house looked more like a bed-and-breakfast than a dorm. In an outdated kitchen and a large living room with blackout curtains to protect wood floors that were already sun-faded, I counted sixteen girls. We were together but separate, stealing glances like it was the first day of school. Head straight, hips swaying, I was Dalena in those hallways, scanning doors for the one that was mine. I didn't need anything or anyone, especially not any friends.

This room with its empty corkboard, chain-suspended fluorescent light, and twin beds opened its mouth to swallow me. I unpacked my journals and clothes with stiff fingers and tried not to think of this as home.

NOTHING COULD'VE PREPARED ME FOR JAMES GIBSON. James didn't look at me as if I owed him myself the morning I stumbled into his basement office at the Capitol. He brought his hands to his face and closed his eyes. "Dear God, what am I going to do with a fifteen-year-old girl? Do you know how many times I've asked myself that? Okay. Okay. We'll figure it out." He hadn't asked for me. He didn't believe in the assignment system, but I was a gift from the Order after he lost Pettit, his mentor and manager. He showed me an image of his family—a gigantic pet rabbit named Baby and his husband, something I never thought possible before meeting James. This was his second marriage. His first marriage to a woman in Fort Worth ended when he met Robert, and he and his wife grew tired of pretending. They really *could* do anything they wanted. What would it be like to have that choice?

James had thin fingers that swept over translucent letters on his keyboard like a piano and charcoal-framed glasses that enlarged his blue eyes into innocence. His position as a political speech-writer made him the manager of fiction and nonfiction relics from before Civil War II. *Fahrenheit 451*, *Their Eyes Were Watching God*, *Annie Allen*, *1984*, *For Whom the Bell Tolls*. James had read them all, and watching the love in his eyes as he discussed prose and plot, I had all I needed. He introduced me to his hidden copy of "How It Feels to Be Colored Me" by Zora Neale Hurston. Highlighted were the lines "Sometimes, I feel discriminated against, but it does not make me angry. It merely astonishes me. How can any deny themselves the pleasure of my company? It's beyond me."

He listened when I talked about Henriette. The questions came next. How much of the story did I remember? When I laughed and told him I read the letters a hundred times and could rewrite her words line by line, he said he would help me turn her letters into a biography. I could use Louisiana history and geog-raphy books from his library and write without fear of refractions for writing unapproved American history. *Writers write*, he said, *and no one can take that away from us. Henriette's biography will be your raison d'être, your reason for existing. Two voices. You could hand the biography to your own daughter one day.* That day, the cramped basement space of the Capitol, where James fit a navy sofa, a coffee bar, and a desk for me, held the glamor of the councilmen's offices overlooking the city four floors above us.

Nothing had ever belonged to me, not even my own body, but now I would own part of a world.

THE NEXT MORNING, JAMES GAVE ME a brown leather journal. "Now, you're officially a biographer." He hooked his arm around my waist, pressed his lips against my cheek, and puffed his own as Source captured our image that marked our beginning. I laughed in front of a white man, and Source caught that, too.

Source recorded him saying, "I already adore you."

Cautioned before we could walk, every Black girl knew better than to feel this free with a white man, and yet, I soaked in this strange comfort and said, "I adore you."

And I did.

I FOLLOWED JAMES AROUND THE SMALL basement, matching my footsteps with his so I wouldn't miss a word. We weaved through rows of floor-to-ceiling bookshelves, reshelving relics that councilmen and their assistants borrowed.

He talked about the yearly writing convention in Oregon. Narrative writers from all over the country met in Brookings and shared oceanfront cottages for eleven weeks out of the year.

"I'm allowed a plus-one. You'll come with me this year."

"I can do that?" I asked, dizzy at the thought of leaving Texas and traveling like a nonrestricted woman.

"As long as it's not Louisiana, we can travel wherever we want without written permission from the Council. You'll love it. At night, we meet in the larger cottages to unwind. We drink too much wine, smoke too much, and criticize writers we will never be. The night ends with poetry recitations. It's godly."

I closed my eyes and put myself in front of a fireplace on a fluffy white rug. A poet in all black stood in the middle of the room holding a crisp sheet of paper. When she read, there was a melody of peace, no pain. Writers write what's inside, and she had nothing but beauty to share with the world. When she finished, she looked at me to pass on her gift.

The overhead light fell over James's face, now flushed red from the excitement of planning. "You could share pages from *My Henriette*. I already see you have a spectacular writing voice. Maybe one day, one of the writers will share your pages with the UN to convince them to intervene in the Order."

That was enough to make me curl up on the couch long into the afternoon writing. James walked to an offsite deli and came back carrying a plastic white bag, fragrant with a spice I didn't recognize. We unpacked the bag on his desk, sorting through lidded bowls of soup and hummus and pita bread wrapped in foil.

"We'll start eating in the café soon. It's onsite, but it would still get you out of this basement."

I nodded, but I wouldn't go. I didn't need more than him and the basement. Eating in front of men with stone faces and emblems sewn on everything wasn't appealing.

"Do the councilmen eat there?"

"God, no. Councilmen have their own chefs. I haven't seen a councilman all year." James frowned at the soup in my bowl. "You don't like hummus or pita bread."

I didn't, but I took both, shoveling hummus on a plastic plate like he did. I picked at it while I alternated between writing in my journal and searching databases on James's computer for articles on enslaved girls on the slave ships and plantations. Zero returns. If the Order erased these stories, where in history would I exist?

There were only articles about councilmen detailing their education and contributions to the Order. The fifth article I read was about Official Bastien Martin, *the* official. The president's son and the interim councilman as of a year ago. It was about his first tour of duty, arriving in Yemen at seventeen years old with thirty-seven undisciplined men. He returned. They didn't. That taught him the importance of discipline. "The idea of privilege is a false paradigm," he was quoted as saying. "Discipline is available to every person on this earth. Work ethic doesn't cost a penny. Discipline and work ethic determine success, and sometimes they are the difference between life and death."

Simple words that rubbed salt in wounds. Was my daddy and all the other young men who became RIP tattoos on forearms or murals under bridges or on abandoned train cars simply undisciplined?

"It's almost eight . . ." James said until he saw my face. He shifted uncomfortably, like he didn't know what to do with his limbs. "Oh no. Don't cry. I'm terrible at this. If you cry, I won't know what to do."

If he was magic like I thought, he would hold me and say he would make sure I never lost anything else and that I wasn't wrong for feeling overwhelmed at the thought that life could never be more than this.

He ran his hands over my arms until I was standing. I pressed my forehead to the buttons on his shirt. After a moment, he wrapped his arms around me. It felt familiar.

"I know it's hard." His voice rumbled in his chest. "I've had my share of heartache, but I still walk through this world as a white man. I can't pretend to know how hard it is for you."

Long into the night when I should've been in my dorm and he should've been home with his husband, we sat on the couch in the basement. I pulled at the cushion pilling while he spoke gently about the 1950s Beat poets in smoky jazz clubs, the women in jeans, pencil skirts, and sweaters, all black, because they had something to say to the world. I drifted. My head against his sleeve, I breathed hints of amber and cedar from his cologne and garlic from the hummus and fell into something close to sleep, a mind quieted by the breath of cool air from the vents. I was back home with my daddy.

"Are you asleep?" James whispered.

I pretended I was so I didn't have to hear him tell me it was time for him to leave.

WE AWOKE HOURS LATER TO STIFF backs and thirty missed calls from James's husband.

James jumped up from the couch, eyes already on the elevator doors. "Shit. It's two a.m. Robert is probably beside himself."

"You have to go."

He looked down at me apologetically. "We all have something that keeps us from becoming birds, flying away free. Robert is mine."

"I hope I didn't mess things up for you." I meant it.

"We should get home and get some sleep. We'll clock back in this afternoon." He grabbed his thin jacket off the coat rack near the elevator, stopped. "You know how I feel about the assignment system."

I ran my tongue over my teeth. My throat was too dry. "I know."

"The way I found you earlier . . . I never want to see that again. I'll write your emancipation papers this afternoon."

Stunned by my refusal, James let the elevator doors close.

This pull toward freedom was surrendering all you knew. Non-restricted women couldn't stay in Texas. They had to relocate to Louisiana within seven days of emancipation unless they petitioned the Council, which never worked. Robert was his something that kept his wings pinned to his side. Mama didn't know it, but she was mine. We'd already lost Daddy. At that moment, knowing I could have my papers anytime was enough. To be in control, to have choice—that was what it meant to be free.

CHAPTER 11

NOW

OUTSIDE MY WINDOW, CALCASIEU PARISH, LOUISIANA, BLURRED PAST. TEXAS
was behind me. I traded the chafe of Lake Travis's lake bed for the
drone of a train's engine under my feet. I crossed both arms over my
purse and let the weight remind me that sometimes, things align.
Like standing alone in front of a high-speed bullet train that could
get me to New Orleans before dinner. Align, like a Fulani girl mixing red wine, saffron, cinnamon, and laudanum and convincing her
master to drink a full glass so he'd sleep through her escape.

Source buzzed continuously in my purse. It was Bastien, barely
containing his anger, and Julian with a fresh story to coax me into
seeing things differently. He would play on my fears. Someone
would hurt me like the electrician tried to. I knew no one. I had no
money. But they forgot I had my account with the last of my stipend
from four years ago. It wasn't much, but I could pay for food and a
room after I paid for my train ticket. I had jewelry. I grew up bartering. I reached into my bag and silenced Source without looking
at it. Access denied. Both of them could go to hell.

An hour outside of New Orleans, I thought of my mama.

CHAPTER 12

THEN

BACK THEN, ALL I WANTED WAS TO BE WITH JAMES. WHEN HE CLOSED THE DOOR to his small office to take a call, I was restless, searching the air for escaped murmurs. I wondered if I was worrying a hole in his head like Mama used to say when I followed her around, but he came out of his office with a sheepish, dancing smile. "My dear girl, my Piglet, why do you always look so worried? Let's have lunch."

I exhaled, smiled, because James wasn't too good to be true.

"THERE'S NO REASON TO BE INTIMIDATED," James said, guiding me inside the Capitol's first-floor dining room. "Officials like believing they're a glass of whiskey away from becoming Abraham, but really, they're just arrogant little boys."

His words were magic. The men became normal people. A young man blotted water from a tablecloth. Another dropped his fork on the floor, then, satisfied no one noticed, he speared a cube of chicken from his salad.

Men served themselves from silver warming trays lining the room. A young woman with box braids greeted each man by name before handing him a set of silverware. Her black flowing skirt masked curvy hips.

James kissed her knuckles and introduced her as Annette.

"You don't sleep," he said as we walked away, "but you'll eat while you're here."

At the salad bar, a man with a round face turned as if expecting us. He spoke to James but kept watery blue eyes on mine. "They said you were hiding your beautiful girl in the basement."

"She's not mine—"

"Not on a writer's salary, she isn't." He winked at me and introduced himself as Dr. Bouchard, councilman. "I could use some help in my office. Temporary, of course."

James shifted completely in front of me. "I keep her busy—"

"My assistant will be in contact."

"I can't stand him," James said when we were alone. "He walks around citing a sixty-year-old, non-peer-reviewed study that concluded descendants of American slavery sexually mature earlier. Pseudoscience. In another space and time, he'd be in a cage. But this is the Order, so it won him an appointment on the Council. God, I'm sorry." James was always apologizing for the behavior of men he didn't know personally. His apologies didn't make me feel any better, but maybe they helped him in some way.

A young man with pale blond hair passed. James gazed after him, forgetting about me until I pulled on his sleeve. "Do you know him?"

"That man with shaving nicks and pants a half-size too small is Albert Goldman, assistant to Vice President Newman."

"Are we going back to the office?"

"If you don't mind, I'd like to eat here."

I did mind. I wanted to sit across from James at his desk and watch him tear off pieces of roll to dab in his soup while he discussed why Ginsberg dedicated his poem *Howl* to Carl Solomon, not watch him stare across the room at Albert.

A hush fell over the room. Silverware clattered to plates, chairs screeched, and every man stood. The entrance doors opened. *The* official.

His size reached me first, as a ship's does when standing on a pier watching it dock.

He moved down the middle of the path the men created for him. They saluted, measured themselves against him, straightened their backs and lifted their shoulders, searching for an extra quarter inch in height.

I averted my eyes to my hands as Guidry trained me to do in a classroom of other six-year-old girls. My God, he stopped in front of us. My hand found James's almost by instinct. Breathed.

"Thank you for your service, Official. Novosibirsk is better because of your service there," James said in a voice that wasn't his. "Congratulations on your appointment to Council."

Only silence where there should've been acknowledgment.

No emblem on his wrist identified him as Modernist or Traditionalist. Black brass buttons on his shirt, the newest emblem on his sleeve detailing how and where he proved his loyalty to the Order, then his face. He studied my hand in James's like he needed to make sense of it.

Our eyes met.

His face was too still, like the portraits Dalena painted with haunted eyes that followed.

Everything inside me stuttered. I shifted behind James. I was afraid. I didn't like that I was.

THE HOURS PASSED, THEN WEEKS OF quiet. I pretended the impending doom stirring in my gut like silt didn't exist. I could stay in this basement with James. I could close my eyes, hold on tight, and stay rooted. *Stay with me*, I wanted to say anytime James left me alone. Everything would be fine if he knew how to block everything out and stay in one place.

JAMES LOOKED UP FROM HIS NOVEL. "Do you know I'd make more cleaning bathrooms in this building than writing for and about the most influential people of our time? Our Treasury is a joke."

It was easy to forget how different we were until this discussion came up. This happened almost daily. James sprawled on the couch complaining about the lack of money in the profession, me hiding my annoyance. He didn't mean anything by it, but he forgot Black women weren't paid a salary at all. Black men in Dallas were paid half of what citizens in Austin were paid for the same job. The Council claimed the cost of living was lower in Dallas, so salaries were set accordingly.

"Why are you worried about money? You're rich."

"*Robert* is rich. I lost everything in my divorce. The Order says I'm free to do as I want, except what they perceive as making a fool out of the daughter of Fort Worth's district attorney."

The blue light flashed from his earpiece. Incoming call. It was probably Albert, the man from the café, planning their daily meeting in the server room—their thrill of arguing behind metal racks, voices muted by equipment fans, the scant scent of burning plastic. I would never like Albert, with his tight pants and white hair and his insistence on ruining James's perfect family picture of matching robes and ridiculous pet rabbits. Albert's existence also meant I spent hours in the basement alone, watching the elevator doors, waiting for James to come back and remember his promise to read to me. He never remembered. He'd press his hand to his chest and say he was in love for the first time in his life, that Albert reminded him so much of himself when he was younger, and that it was absolute poetry falling in love with your younger self. Then he'd spend the next hour messaging Albert like he hadn't just seen him.

"Solenne Bonet?" James's voice deepened. He climbed to his feet. "With all due respect, she's assigned to *me* . . ." Eyes closed, he sighed. "I'll send her tomorrow at ten." He snatched the device from his ear, checked to make sure it was disconnected, then tossed it on the table. "Asshole."

"What happened?"

He flopped on the couch and pushed his nose into his novel. "The official wants to see you in his office tomorrow."

The official. The stillness of his face when our eyes met in the café.

I fumbled with my braid.

James's fingers shook when he turned the page.

• • •

THERE WAS AN ORDER IN THE official's office that shouted I should be on the other side of the door. The cushion underneath me that wouldn't yield to my weight. The firearms on the black panel wall behind his desk. The locks on everything. White walls with paintings of dead men who built societies by taking. Impersonal because it wasn't cozy, but it had all been designed specifically for him. What would he think if he walked into my dorm with twin beds, five towels, and the water-stained desk I moved under the window to focus the scattered light?

He was too young to have this office, that many emblems on his sleeve, or sit behind this desk, yet he did. There was something odd about his eyes. They burrowed into me like they were unearthing answers to dark questions he already knew but wanted to cross-check. He moved slowly like Daddy. When someone was afraid of him, he kept his hands in plain sight and his voice low.

An hour of sitting in his office, and he still hadn't spoken to me. He walked around taking calls in a foreign language. German, maybe. Russian? The air conditioner kicked on and the cool air from two overhead vents dried the slickness where my palms rested on the chair's leather.

An eternity later, he walked to the office door. "Ten a.m. tomorrow."

My eyes met his. Three seconds of eye contact was the general rule when an official addressed you directly. Enough to show respect, not so much that he thinks you're challenging him.

I WALKED BACK TO THE BASEMENT, but James's small office space was darkened. A copy of *The Pursuit of Love* lay cast aside like a forgotten plan. I sat in his leather chair, tilted back and forth, listening to it groan in discomfort. I drank from his stainless-steel mug of coffee and regretted it. It was black, not a hint of sweet, and still warm like he left in a hurry. Albert probably called. Mama would tell me not to trust James if I told her about Albert. She would say he wasn't a good person. To cheat on your partner, you have to lie, and we could never trust a liar. But then I thought about how my birth story differed from the one she told at Josephine's house. I thought about her hair butters and how quickly her voice changed when she told customers her products worked the same on each person regardless of curl pattern. Was there a difference between her and James? Maybe we all tell different stories depending on who was listening.

Besides, if we had to place blame, this was Albert's fault. What kind of person wanted someone who wasn't free?

THURSDAY MORNING, I WAS BACK IN the official's office, ignored in the same seat. For two hours I practiced answers to questions I expected he would ask. I would be careful to never slip into DoS dialect like I did with James occasionally. The Order said it was disrespectful.

Friday, he took an in-person meeting with two councilmen. Devin Russell, from Unmanned Technologies, and Dr. Bouchard, who I figured out worked in Medical Genetics. Russell updated the men on his software that improved the accuracy of self-propelled vehicle routes based on user history while I fantasized about the cherry chewies in my bag next to me. Although he was the youngest, newest to Council, and spoke the least, the official led the meeting. He slanted back in his chair, his long fingers splayed on the desk like bars on a cage. His black uniform was vibrant, like he'd never worn it before and would never wear it again, even though it fit like it was made for his chest, his arms, his wrists alone.

Bouchard spoke about his current genetic testing project that hadn't gotten the support from the Council he thought it deserved. Russell nodded each time Bouchard raised his voice for emphasis. The official sighed and looked at the pig in a way James was too afraid to.

"Safety, liberty, and freedom from tyranny for all citizens," the official said, cutting into Bouchard's speech. "Principles the Order was founded upon."

Bouchard's face pinkened. "I'm aware of that, Official. Say what you intend to say."

"Did you consider the research is the problem, rather than your brothers denying support without cause?" the official asked. "No one owes anyone anything. The Founders structured the Order into a meritocracy to ensure each citizen has equal opportunity to succeed . . . or fail. The quality of your research is abysmal, at best."

I hid a smile by touching my fingers to my nose, though it didn't matter when I was invisible. They wouldn't see me free two chewies from the plastic or sneak the candy into my mouth. Russell. His amused expression said he'd seen everything. I swallowed, crossed my legs, and smiled. The official frowned at us and stood, cutting Bouchard off midsentence. "We'll pick up in three hours." Then to me, "Ten a.m. Monday."

Silent, we followed him to the door.

I slipped past the three pairs of boots, the arms crossed over chests.

"A masterpiece," I heard Bouchard say when I neared the elevators. "Facial symmetry 2.6, .67 waist-to-hip ratio . . . at fifteen years old. Amazing how much faster DoS mature."

CHAPTER 13

THEN

Like a bird with a broken wing, I stayed close to my dorm when I wasn't with James on Saturday or Sunday.

Two girls with metal smiles and box braids poked their heads into my room. They could've been sisters, but they weren't. The Order wouldn't send two girls from the same school to the same work dorms, let alone family members. "Deedee from floor one said the chips aren't working. Everybody's going out."

Two years ago, the official's software updated it to restrict us from entering certain buildings by setting off door alarms. *God don't like ugly,* I heard Guidry say to another teacher. *Every software bug this side of the Mississippi gone take up legs and walk right into his code. That update gone give him more grief than it gives us.*

The train took me to restricted places. In doorways of glass-like buildings, sensors didn't shout that I didn't belong. I ate popcorn from white paper bags spotted translucent by butter and licked salt from my fingers when nobody watched. Coffee was richer in the café where potted plants framed the stairs. I sat in a chair that looked like the inside of Mama's red jewelry box. Granite tile and cathedral ceilings in museums and art galleries memorized my echo. In a shop that sold silk dresses I couldn't afford, I smiled at the prune-y saleslady. Lies came easily. *Yes, my contract holder sent me here.* In the dressing room's orbit of mirrors, I admired the blue silk tailored to my reflection. I. I. I. *Me.* Make yourself small and soft. Disappear inside. In this space for young white women, I thought of Joy.

. . .

MAMA AND I WOULD TAKE THE train to her friend Margaret Ann's house in the Bouldin Creek neighborhood of Austin when her husband was away. Her daughter Joy and I ate shortbread cookies stolen from her daddy's office. She read me princess stories from a blue-covered anthology and made up scenes when she stumbled upon missing pages. We performed plays for our mamas, pretending a stadium of hundreds watched. *You're my beautiful princess*, Joy said. *I'll be the prince since my hair is short.* She tied her auburn hair back into a twiggy ponytail, and her sword was a wire hanger shoved into the towel she tied around her waist like a sheath.

Then Joy had to turn sixteen, and I had to turn into glass.

We visited and Joy looked through me that time and the next. That pain. It made my eyes and chest burn.

I sat in the living room, laughter from Joy's bedroom stabbing me. I prayed like the day Guidry told us to. *Pray for the seventeen men indicted by the Council.* That was a big word for a twelve-year-old. Indicted. I closed my eyes and prayed like the other girls. After class, I asked Guidry if the prayers worked, and if the men who left my neighborhood in the executioner's truck would return. She said, *Chile, just keep praying.* So I did, and I prayed everything would be the same with Joy. I was so stupid that when her friend poked her blond head into the living room and curled a finger in invitation, I clawed at the chance. My mama's smile said, *See, I told you she'd come around.*

A trapdoor opened, and I descended into another world. Joy's pink and purple bedroom was now shades of blue and gray, except for the cherished white blanket her auntie made her. I brushed blond and auburn hair and painted bitten nails red while they talked about sex and boys. *As long as he doesn't put it inside you, it doesn't count as sex*, the friend said. But Guidry said the spirit is willing but the flesh is weak, and even kissing was sex because you think about sex when you're doing it.

They didn't use the art galleries and museums to study. They used them to meet what they called potentials, the good patriots eager to serve the Order. *It's never too early to think about marriage*, Joy said, but I remembered when she once said she wouldn't marry a man in the Order. While our mamas smiled, she said since I couldn't do it myself, she would move overseas and get the United Nations to intervene in the Order.

When I passed the nail polish to the friend so she could paint mine, she laughed and asked if she looked like a slave girl. I don't remember her name, but I'll never forget how she smiled and flipped her arm over to show the palest part, the seediness of her eyes. *No, I didn't think I turned Black.* Then I understood what I should've when Joy first left me.

I threw the open bottle of nail polish, and the white blanket caught it. A child's violence, the need to take to cope with the confirmation that Joy could be more like a girl she'd just met than the little girl who'd nicknamed her Joy from Joyce. *I hate you more now*, Joy shrieked. *Get the hell out of my room.* The friend said, *They ruin everything.* Joy said, *Destructive.*

On the train home, Mama told me I couldn't behave that way. It didn't matter that I'd seen Joy get upset and throw things. We couldn't be angry and draw attention to our messy thoughts. Ever. She wiped my tears and said she knows it hurts, but Joy would come around. She was raised by Margaret Ann, a kind woman, a lobbyist who dedicated her life to improving conditions for DoS.

I didn't want to wait for Joy to come around. I wanted her to say I was her beautiful princess, wave her sword to the sky, and save me from towers while everyone watched. I wanted her to love me like she used to. Like I had never done anything wrong.

MONDAY MORNING, I WAS BACK IN the official's office watching him take calls. He found me watching him. He looked away, then looked again, stretching out the seconds until we looked away at the same time.

After hours of listening to his side of arguments wrapped in legal jargon, I patched together things I never cared to be clear on—how the Council worked. The official was in his first year as an interim councilman. At the end of the sixth, he needed 65 percent of the citizen vote to gain a lifetime appointment. He spoke as if this would be easy for him. Meetings, speeches, and appearances were for the sole purpose of earning the vote of Traditional white men in six years. Black men didn't have large enough numbers to influence the vote. White women did, but that was of no concern to him. Over manicures and brunch, they would pretend to be outraged by his voting record, then they would leave and vote however their husbands voted. They followed the flow of power. History supported this.

Still in conversation, he turned his omniscient eyes on me. "We'll continue this discussion in the next meeting," he said into his device.

I tracked his hands—plucking his communicator from his ear, setting it in a cradle next to a silver mug, pulling a topographic map of the Order from a desk drawer and spreading it over the length of his desk like a tablecloth. "Tell me about yourself," he said without warning.

My tongue was stuck. I shrugged and twisted a curl around my fingers.

"I don't converse through gestures."

Glancing between him and the wall, I fumbled through a narrative about Dallas, my parents, and James. Meandering, I told a story with a nice beginning, but the middle was a jumble of unrelated details that got messier the longer I talked.

His face never changed. What did he see when he looked at me? Curls pulled back into a high ponytail, humidity-damp and bushy. Squinting eyes with a hint of mascara. My blue dress worn into comfort.

I heard myself say, "I'm marrying Officer Charles Decuir. I'll be an officer's wife."

It wasn't my voice, not quite. It was a blend of my mama, Margaret Ann, and how I guessed Joy would sound now.

Was the tick in his eyebrows surprise? "Do you see him often?"

I said yes, though I'd only seen him in person at the Monroe Gala, then again at my daddy's funeral.

"Why am I here every day?" I asked, surprising myself.

His timepiece clicked. The white tails of the curtains drawn over the bank of windows fluttered against air from floor vents.

"Thomas Jefferson once said that slavery is a moral depravity, a hideous blot, and a threat to the United States. I agree with that, yet, here we are working through a similar system created by the Order's Founders. The system enables DoS to contribute to the Order through work and family, but it also creates men without integrity, men who exploit the assignment system instead of using it for its intended purposes." He took a breath, apologetically. "You're here because the alternative is the bathroom in Dr. Bouchard's office or the backseat of his MV."

We held each other's gaze far too long, understanding passing between us. His eyes were soft enough to send me back to our living room, Daddy consoling me after what happened in the electrician's truck. *Let me worry about this. Let me keep you safe.*

The official nodded to the brown leather journal on my lap, asked why I carried it around every day, and watched my hands curl around my secret.

"It's just drawings and words I hear that I like."

"What do you draw?"

"Sunsets," I said, thinking of Dalena's last painting. My answer was quick enough to sound authentic.

He eased into a story about the sunset on the shore in Indonesia and the deep golden pearls he'd seen. I couldn't re-create his image in my mind. I'd never seen anything outside of Texas.

CHAPTER 14

NOW

FACE TO THE SKY, I EXCHANGED BREATHS WITH THE WIND, THE PALM FRONDS reaching to the sun, and buildings with so many windows, they looked like they were paved with glass. I memorized the traffic sounds of the Pontchartrain Expressway behind me. I closed my eyes so I would never forget this moment.

"I made it," I told Henriette, who surely felt the same as she stumbled along the Mississippi River during her escape that night in 1802. The stars were impossibly similar to the ones at home ninety-three days away, and the dark shaded the trees into muddled lines that arched and folded around her. She heard whispers under the scurry of leaves and followed the faint scent of cedar and ash. Eight faces of rebellion lustered by campfire flames welcomed her. The men escaped a sugar plantation where the cane stalk grinder chewed away limbs and the overseer's whip never rested. *Where your chil'ren?* they asked suspiciously. Women didn't run like the men. Navigating swamps and forests with children crying out for food, comfort, and all they knew as home was too difficult. It was also common for the master or mistress of a plantation to keep an enslaved woman's children locked in the big house if they saw rebellion in her eyes. She would never run and leave her children behind. The man sitting next to her offered his name, Royger, and a chunk of salt pork skewered by his knife. He leaned so close that the firelight illuminated eyes green like Antoni's. *Go home to your chil'ren.* Henriette accepted the meat still warm from the flames and said she had no children.

She laid hands on the men and wished she were a healer like her grandmother. Her fingertips found scars where an ear once curved below a hairline and traced the fleur-de-lis branded into a brown or yellow shoulder. Penalties for the first escape attempt. Next time, their master would brand them again. Next time, instead of their ears, they'd have their hamstrings cut. There with the mosquitoes and water moccasins and the earth that oozed black water, they swore there would be no next time.

"Sugar, if you wanna sightsee, take an SPV. Set it to scenic." I looked at the man hovering over my shoulder. Bald, dark skin, gold hoops lining one ear. "Better for your feet. And . . ."

"And?" I stepped back, checking for weapons. None visible.

"You won't be blocking the path for the rest of us that have things to do other than spending some top brass's money." He winked and moved past me.

My hands fluttered to my ears, neck, and wrists to remove anything that shined. I stuffed them in my dress pocket and twisted my promise ring, so his mother's diamond hid against my palm.

Shops on both sides of the street lit in red, blue, and green lights advertised everything imaginable on digital screens above awnings.

Silks Here!

Sweet Oranges/Two For Ten. NO Credit. Don't Ask.
Have You Upgraded Your Firearm? Do it now for free.
Home Goods. We Have It All. No Money, No Sale.

I moved with the crowd. Other than nonrestricted women with makeup as bright as their shop lights on their eyelids, cheeks, and lips darting out to lure me into buying their dresses or sampling their glazed-covered chicken speared by toothpicks, no one acknowledged me.

I ignored Source chirping in my bag. I was programmed to respond, so it was a numbers game for Bastien. He knew eventually, I would crack. I always had.

A man sat in front of a bar using an overturned orange bucket as a drum. He wailed over the beat, singing about a man in a war that took place across the ocean. A place he'd never seen, but one he visualized through his ancestors' eyes.

At the end of the block, I found two cafés detached from the endless rows of buildings. Instead of an advertisement about their imported coffee beans, creams, or syrups, the digital screen under one awning read:

THE FALLACY OF MERITOCRACY. THE ORDER IS A DICTATORSHIP.
JOIN US THURSDAY AT 10 A.M. FOR COFFEE AND A LIVE PANEL DISCUSSION.

An overhead bell chimed when I pulled the door open. Other than the middle-aged barista grinding coffee beans and two men sitting at the counter sipping from mugs, eyes frozen on a horse race on a screen in front of them, the café was empty. I welcomed the gentle sound of normal, the bitter smell of coffee, the scent of sweet. My stomach awoke.

I wasn't sure if I would be shown to a seat or if I could choose my own, so I waited, scanning the place. White walls, silver tables, bright red booths, and bucket chairs with peeling faux leather. A place Bastien would never allow me to enter.

A man I hadn't noticed before sat in the far corner. The darkest brown skin, gray beanie over shoulder-length locs, shoulders hunched over an empty glass. He wasn't dressed like the men in Louisiana. He wore a lightweight green jacket, a white T-shirt Bastien would call rags, and a leather necklace with a gold piece hanging from it.

The grinding paused. "Get you anything else, Memphis?" the barista called in the man's direction.

Memphis. In his name, I saw and heard his lineage. His mama hadn't been born free.

Still staring into his glass, Memphis lifted a hand to decline.

The barista tilted his head to an empty seat at the counter, but I chose a booth in the corner where my back wouldn't be to the door.

The barista shuffled to my booth. "Name's Ed. What can I get you?"

The hair on Ed's cheeks was cut into a pattern that reminded me of lace fringe. I tried not to stare. "I'll need a moment."

Ed stared at me without moving, so I said, "A few minutes, please."

Back in his place behind the counter, he told the customers he was closing up early today for Mardi Gras. His granddaughter was dancing in a parade, and he'd be damned if he missed it. Mardi Gras. Bastien said New Orleans was chaotic because it never slept, but I'd just walked in on the busiest time of year.

Outside the coffee shop window, the crowds moved. There were more people here than I could've ever imagined. Enough so that, barring Source's location capabilities, I could disappear for years without being found. Would I hurt Bastien that way? Slip into the thick of the crowds and pretend—

"You gone sit there and look cute? Take up space?"

I looked into Ed's impatient eyes. "I'm waiting for someone."

"I keep my seats open for ordering customers."

I looked around the near-empty shop. "A glass of water, then."

"Three."

"Three what?"

"Three gators. What you think I mean? Three dollars."

"Give me a moment." I pretended to access the digital menu through Source as he lumbered away. My query function was disabled, no doubt to make it difficult for me to find my way around or to locate Immigration. On my currency panel, the option to enter my usual account, Bastien's account, was grayed out. My old one with the last of my final stipend was still accessible. Only thirty dollars. I clicked on the activity report. Bastien transferred 203 to his account an hour ago. Judging from a quick view of the shop's digital menu, he left me enough so I wouldn't starve. It was nearing lunchtime, and he would want me to eat. He would want to know *what* I ate. He tracked macro and micronutrients to make sure I was getting my daily allowances for nearly a year.

At the counter, I ordered a glass of water, a mozzarella, tomato, and basil sandwich, and a muffin. Ed tugged a payment reader from his apron's pocket.

"Thirty-five."

I mentally calculated the prices on the menu again. "You mean twenty-nine. Three for the water, nineteen for the sandwich, seven for the muffin."

"Plus tax."

"What?"

"Tax to the District." He widened his eyes at me, the idiot who didn't understand. "Tax to Austin on each sale. Are you really gone argue about six dollars? Top Brass got you on an allowance?"

A man at the counter snorted a laugh without looking at us.

"Fine. Just the sandwich and water."

After I paid, he handed me a glass and nodded at a pitcher sweating on the counter.

"Am I paying for the glass or the water?"

Ed pulled a black skillet from a drawer below the stove. "You're paying for my time. Serve yourself and we call it even at three."

I drank half a glass, refilled it, then turned to Memphis.

Memphis looked up from his mug at my heels, legs, and face. Indifference. He had the eyes of a man who carried the weight of the world but had gotten used to it. Welcomed it. His mama wasn't born free, so he would understand my struggle. Had she run while pregnant with him, or fled with him after he was born, hoping for a better life? Had he left her behind and started a new life?

I took my glass of water and slid into the booth across from the stranger.

CHAPTER 15

THEN

I WALKED ON POLISHED SIDEWALKS, MESH LAUNDRY BAG SLUNG OVER MY SHOULDER. We had a laundry room on-site, but it was crowded on Sundays. The abandoned damp socks and panties pressed to the sides of the washing machines' drums annoyed me.

The laundromat between the library and the oily-smelling doughnut shop was empty except for Francesca, the receptionist from the Capitol. She rolled her eyes at me when I walked in the Capitol each morning and wanted me to answer to Annette, though we looked nothing alike.

Francesca engraved on a gold name tag because her digital ID through Source wasn't enough. She fiddled with it while speaking to the men to draw attention to her chest. Butt pressed against her desk to stretch her hips against her navy pencil skirt, she used the collection of teal vases on her desk as a conversation piece. She pointed out their origins, how she found them, how expensive they were.

Shock registered on her face when she noticed me. "Don't they have washing machines in your building?"

"You can use them if you want." I dumped my clothes in a three-loader, pressed my thumb to the digital reader on the front, and watched it siphon six dollars from my account. I saved six by not separating them into darks and lights like Mama told me I better. Three hundred and two dollars left. Still rich.

While I waited on my clothes, I walked to the crosswalk signal and pretended I was waiting to cross the street. I squinted at the water rushing through storm drains and wondered if the official showered in the morning or at night. He smelled . . . crisp. Like Dallas in January. He wanted to help me. That meant he was more like James than Bouchard, didn't it? I wouldn't mess this up the way I normally did. I would keep my mouth shut and never leave his side, so Bouchard wouldn't bother me. Sit right there in his office and watch the way he commanded the world. Did he think I was pretty? Black men did, but what was pretty to a councilman? Not five foot nothing like me. Probably blond and skinny like Francesca, with her teaspoonful of tits and booty.

I was light-headed imagining myself walking in heels and a navy pencil skirt and smiling instead of silently counting to three when meeting his eyes.

THE NEXT AFTERNOON, I WALKED THE streets, through the electric buzz of people excited by something looming. Everywhere was the flicker of screens with a talking head discussing the unrest in Georgia and Louisiana. No one noticed me in my jeans and the ball cap James slung on his replica of *The Thinker*.

I sidestepped puddles on sidewalks and glanced into glass store-fronts. I saw the women who had all we didn't, and yet it wasn't enough. They sat on park benches, absentmindedly nudging a stroller with their foot while staring through a child gliding head and belly down a slide and at another pumping his legs on a swing, wind stirring blond curls. When they looked at the little one in its stroller, the smile didn't reach their eyes. Young women with eyes made old from following the flow of power.

In MVs where they sat bruised-cheeked or glassy-eyed next to their husbands, they didn't know where they were going and didn't care.

Manicured fingers fluttered to lips when the executioner's truck crowded with insurgents in death hoods passed. Turning to find impatient husbands advancing down the sidewalk without them, they grabbed at the hems of sleeves and asked about dinner.

When they thought no one watched, they checked lipstick smeared over broken lips in vehicle side mirrors, wineglasses, or anything that shined.

Hundreds of women, and I didn't know any of them. I didn't understand them. Hadn't they stared up at the black sky and been burned into dreaming by its silver? Why hadn't they withered away in this world?

They didn't understand us. They couldn't understand why my ancestors cried out from swampy burial grounds that stank of the Mississippi when I'm lulled into contentment. They didn't understand why I hadn't accepted my station in life when they had. Separate but equal. Gray sky and silver waves.

On the train back to my dorm, I saw her in a window seat three rows away. She leaned under the arm of a distracted man with dense black waves and an official's emblem on his coat sleeve. Her auburn hair was the same, but she'd tinted her eyebrows brown. Was it my gaze that lifted her eyes from the man's hand on her knee?

The train rumbled, shifting us in our seats like mirrored doubles. We exchanged polite smiles before lowering our eyes, drifting apart like the future and the past.

A question lingered when I exited the train and stared back at it from the lonely platform. When had Joy's eyes become old?

THIS ROOM WAS FOR WAITING. WAITING for James. For Mama's calls. Waiting for something unnamed to fill the lonely and empty.

James said to write when I felt empty, but my thoughts wandered to Dalena. How far had she gotten in her plan to live as a nonrestricted woman in New Orleans? I typed and deleted four messages to her before pressing *Send message*.

SOLENNE: How is Atlanta?

I'd been asleep for an hour when Source vibrated. I dropped it, scrambled for it, and let the lights bend the shadows away from me. One message from an anonymous handle instead of Dalena's.

A stilled image of the official on a shore somewhere foreign. In his palm lay a pearl so deeply gold, it was almost the color of my skin.

I wanted to be the first to show you.

CHAPTER 16

NOW

"NICE HEELS," MEMPHIS SAID.

He was young, five years or so older than me. Nails bitten down to the quick, knuckles reddened from repeated brawls. Rough and handsome, he reminded me of Harlem, a young man I hadn't remembered I forgot.

"What's your name?"

"Memphis, but you heard that," he said. "They don't sell shitty cheese sandwiches in Texas?"

I pretended to think, and he laughed.

"How did you know I was from Texas?"

He twisted the gold band hanging from his leather necklace. "Good guess. You staying for the parade tonight? And what did you say your name was?"

"I didn't, but I'm Henriette." Saying it felt natural. "I haven't decided about the parade yet."

"You came from Texas but haven't decided whether you want to watch the parade?"

"Circumstances are moving targets."

"Truer words . . ." He drank from his glass.

We talked about home, and I relaxed, slipping into dialect, forgetting about the rapidly burning fuse five hundred miles away. Memphis frequented the Julia Festival in Texas, and he knew as much about Dallas as a native. He visited Mama's shop once because he heard of her beard oils and twice more because she was gorgeous.

He worked security from time to time at a club called Bourbon's in New Orleans, and Mama was prettier than the women fifteen years younger. It was true. Mama looked the same at thirty-eight as she did at twenty-one.

"So how are you able to travel so much?"

It was uncommon for border patrol to allow anyone from Louisiana to enter Texas.

A pretty, older woman passed outside the window and waved. He pressed two fingers to his lips in acknowledgment. "I know business."

Everything about this man spoke to me. So relaxed. This is what his life should be, not lying bloody and chained on a train platform.

"Do you know about Immigration?"

He raised an eyebrow at Solenne, who morphed from a content officer's wife visiting for Mardi Gras into a woman escaping life as a soldier's wife. "I know they're only open tomorrow from eight to twelve."

"Do you know if they remove applicants off grid?"

"I know they deactivate chips after the application process is complete. That's twenty-one days in."

"Do you know anyone who can remove me from the grid earlier?"

It wasn't a matter of whether these people existed, it was whether anyone would risk giving me the names.

He shook the remaining ice from his glass into his mouth and planted his hands on the table to stand.

I slipped a hand over his. "Wait. Can I buy you another drink?"

"I know the brass froze your account. You have four dollars to your name. If Ed has to refill that pitcher, you'll have one. So no, you can't buy me a drink. Good looks don't buy anything here."

"Then tell me what does. How much will it cost for information?"

Ed placed an oily sandwich the size of the plate in front of me, grunted, and walked away.

I cut it, took half, then slid the plate across the table. "A few more minutes of your time. Please."

"No thanks. I actively avoid headaches. I don't have time to joust with a patriot."

I waited until he met my eyes. "Patriot?"

"*The* official."

"So that shit about visiting Dallas was just that. Shit."

A half shrug. "Mad you can't bullshit a bullshitter? You stay free by learning who to stay away from. Solenne, the official's concubine, made the list two years ago."

I followed the emptiness in his eyes as he pulled himself to a stand. "Don't call me that."

"I was trying to be respectful. You prefer bed wench or belly warmer?" He waited in vain for a response before grabbing a duffel bag from the booth. "Good luck with this experiment."

"This isn't an experiment. This is my life. You don't know what I had to go through to get here."

There would never be another storm, glitch in the system, or a chance to decide not to love the man I'd loved for five years.

He looked out at the scene that played through the window behind me and shook his head.

"I have jewelry. People still value stones, right?" I held up my thumb, imagining Bastien and Julian staring at my location, respiration, and elevated heart rate on a screen. "I need to get off grid *before* I get my papers. I can't live with this any longer than I already have."

"As much as I'd get a kick out of watching the official lose, I can't touch this. Even if your entire bag was full of treasure, I still wouldn't get in the middle of whatever you're trying."

"Your mama probably went through this. You can't understand what I'm going through?"

"I'm not trying to change the world. I'm trying to disappear into it." He swung the bag on his shoulder. "I have my way. Find yours."

Find your way. Instead of including me in her plans for freedom, those were Dalena's words. I would never understand how it was so easy for some people to leave people behind.

From the corner of my eye, Memphis shifted his bag from one

shoulder to the other. "Look, he's a government official, so the system of checks and balances puts him at a disadvantage. One, he can't come into the state whenever he wants. Two, you're on nonrestricted soil. He has to petition for extradition, and he needs a good reason to get it approved. Never heard of that happening. Politics is a game, and he'll want to play it right or risk pissing too many people off."

"You don't know Bastien."

"I know Admin. Why do you think the official isn't here right now? I heard Admin is reviewing his injunction to enter the state. The first he sent requesting approval to enter with two jets and sixty staff members was denied without prejudice."

These legal terms jumbled together meant nothing. I spent the last five years with Bastien, and this was still a foreign language.

"What does it mean?"

"It means the official has to change the injunction to something Admin likes. They'll go back and forth. If he doesn't get approval before tonight, he likely won't be approved for three days. Admin doesn't work through Mardi Gras. Use that time to find an underground Configurator to get off grid, then . . ."

"Then what?"

"Then he'll use his advantages. I think you know what that means . . . Good luck."

I thanked him without looking at him.

He took a step, then paused. "Hey. If I could be more help without—"

"Don't worry about it. I'm used to hypocrites."

The bell over the door announced Memphis's exit.

CHAPTER 17

THEN

ACH MORNING, I SLIPPED PAST CONCRETE-FACED GUARDS INTO THE OFFICIAL'S office. I didn't need more than the pale-yellow light slivering from underneath his door into the dim hallway.

The official drank tea, not coffee. Coffee was a gateway into addiction rife with nasty headaches if you didn't keep your caffeine levels up, the official said. Addiction was for the weak. I didn't admit I'd loved coffee since I was eight.

I sat on the sofa, bare feet tucked under me, watching him carry the mug my fingers just touched. Listened to him speak into his device and sipped every one of his words from the air and made them mine.

He pointed to each destination before approaching it so his movements wouldn't scare me. He didn't need to anymore. After his digital meetings, we'd talk about things that seemed random until he somehow tied it all together with such precision, I felt satisfied, like I'd finished a good book.

I loved handing him fresh tea and watching his hand dwarf the mug. He held it from the base instead of hooking his fingers through the handle like a regular person. When I was this close, I could see the order of him. The side part in his hair, the peaks in his eyebrows, the meticulous beard and mustache lines. Did he do it himself, or did someone have their hands close to his lips?

He sipped, then lifted his eyebrow and the corner of his mouth.

"Too sweet?"

"It's perfect." He leaned back in his desk chair. "You should be aware I won't be in the office for the next two weeks."

The words caught me off guard. I shifted my eyes to the collection of firearms hanging on the wall behind him to hide my disappointment.

He followed my gaze. "Twenty years of gifts. It's a tradition for Traditionalists to give me a signed firearm after meetings or banquets."

The white scrawl on the firearms hanging behind him wasn't random. They were signatures. Inked proof they had been in the official's presence.

"James said—"

"Do you begin all your sentences that way?"

I chewed a thumbnail until he tapped my wrist. "I meant to say younger men are usually Modernist. You said you're against the assignment system. How, if you're a Traditionalist? And Modernists are . . ." I stopped before saying "better."

"There is a difference between Traditionalist and Modernist, but not one that makes them better. Traditionalists have done more for your population than Modernists." He paused to lift my chin the moment the three-second rule forced my eyes to the floor. "Where do you think funding for your schools and health care comes from? A Traditionalist drafted the legislation that created the monthly stipend for DoS. You're too young to remember the times when the stipend didn't exist."

"So you're Traditionalist because you believe they do the most good."

"Partially. I spent most of my time with men thirty years my senior. My beliefs were formed in the Legislature Chamber and at my father's dinner table. Beliefs don't exist on either side of a spectrum. It's never that neat or simple in our country." He frowned like the criticism-adjacent words tasted bitter. "And still, this country is better than it was when it was the United States. An economy outpaced by the rest of the world, the racial unrest, the increasing crime and abortion rates, no, we couldn't go on with so much death."

My daddy was killed in action in North Carolina. His paperwork said he died in a riot of fifty thousand that spanned two hundred miles. Who was the Order better for? The official saw the question in my burning eyes.

"Maintaining peace and order in your country is an honor," he said so gently, it was enough to scrub his quotes on the undisciplined from my mind. "He died an honorable man."

Abandoning my training was becoming easier. I did what he wanted and kept my eyes on his while he told me stories that weren't in the history books. He was born a triplet, but his older brother and sister died at birth. His father told him this at eight during a camping trip in the Santa Monica Mountains. He turned his back for a few minutes, and Abraham was gone. Abraham left him there for four days with nothing but what was in his backpack and his rifle. Again, he survived. His back stiffened when I asked why Abraham would leave a child in a forest with the cold, snakes, and bears.

"We do difficult things, things we don't necessarily want to do. We master the impossible and emerge a better version of ourselves. All that I am, I owe to my father."

At ten, he and his mother saw his father off to France. That night, she put him to bed. The next morning, he found her dead. Undiagnosed heart arrhythmia.

No woman was adored more than Genevieve. I watched recordings of Abraham and Genevieve—her sitting behind him on a stage while he addressed the Order, jewel-glitzed hands wrestling with the wind to keep her hair perfect, springing to her feet in applause at the conclusion. *I'm not human without this woman*, Abraham said. When she died, the Texas flags flew at half-mast for three years.

"My mother. Gone without warning." At the window, he stared out at a city that always moved on. That was when he understood the pain of the unexpected and unpredictability, he finally said.

I knew the pain of sleeping unaware while the person you loved more than anything took their last breath alone. It had been almost five months since my daddy died. I didn't want to talk about it now, but I told him I understood that pain.

He nodded once, his face sympathetic. "I guess you do, don't you?"

"Why don't you have a wife?" I blurted. That question had burned my chest for at least a week.

"What do the published articles say?"

He knew I'd read everything about him. The history records said he wouldn't choose between sacrificing a family for the Order or vice versa. It was why he was so good at what he did.

"The last time someone wrote about it was eight years ago. You were only twenty then. James said . . . I read Traditionalists believe in maintaining the values the Order was founded upon. Morality. Structure. Family."

His gaze became too heavy. I felt consumed—chewed and swallowed to join the part of me that was already inside of him. No one should have eyes that changed so quickly from nothing to nothing else.

"I never quite figured out how to hold on to anything. I've been alone for a long time."

Every word was unintended. I knew because he pushed his hands in his pockets and looked away as if he embarrassed himself.

But I understood him.

JAMES WAS GONE. INSTEAD OF THE bitter scent of coffee meeting me at the elevator, there was nothing. He didn't answer my messages or calls. I considered calling his husband, but what if James was with Albert? He would hate me for the rest of my life if I ruined things for him. I started a pot of coffee, washed his mug, and replenished the diffuser on his desk with lavender oil.

I browsed the rows for books on Louisiana. On a shelf I had to use the step stool to reach, I found two books on the economy from 1800 to 1850. Wealthy from cotton, sugar cane, and the bodies of the enslaved, more millionaires lived in Louisiana than any other state. Henriette belonged to one of them.

Without realizing it, five o'clock had come and gone, but James hadn't. I dumped the coffee in the restroom sink and walked back to my dorm, shivering in his blue windbreaker.

I WAS IN BED WHEN JAMES called from an airport.

He raised his voice over a digital announcement. "I wasn't ignoring your calls. I've been so busy preparing for the retreat."

Who knew a word could be so heavy? *Retreat*. This mystical place in Oregon he was supposed to take me to where everyone would see me as their equal.

"You didn't tell me it was in November. You didn't say it was this week." It was all I could manage to say.

He rubbed his temple. "It never occurred to me that I should. God, I'm no good at this."

"No good? Try terrible."

"I won't argue, but you know why I can't apologize."

He told me once he was learning to be free. No longer would he apologize for who he was or become weighted down by someone else's expectations. That's how he saw my disappointment. A claim on his time that he never seemed to have enough of. In a basement, looking into his kind eyes, he said he could bring a plus-one on the writing retreat. What he didn't say was that if he had to choose between me and spending eleven weeks with Albert, unimpeded by his marriage, he would choose Albert every time.

"What do I do while you're gone?"

"They don't really give us instructions on that, do they?" He fidgeted with the strap of his bag, and for a moment, I thought my question was enough to make this all go away. Albert inched next to him with a brown leather travel bag hanging from his shoulder. "I have to go, Solenne."

So dismissive, so hurtful without intending to be. I searched for something that would give me a few more minutes with him, but found only his eyes favoring digital signs and Albert's hand settling on his shoulder. He was already gone.

THE COLD CAME EARLY, BUT I found no difference between now and the summer that took everything. Time didn't matter. For two weeks, I slept too much and awoke not knowing what time of day I would find. Apple juice grew warm in my paper cup. The canned soup congealed in my bowl. I scrolled Source for public images of Brookings, Oregon, and when that hurt too much, I queried images of Dallas. The storefronts, homes, and brown people gathering for neighborhood block parties. Officers home for a season grouped around barbecue smokers. Their eyes smiled at a calm sky, at their wives dancing to music swelling from speakers shoved under white folding tables, at their little girl sitting under the safety of the sweet gums calling, *Daddy. Daddy.*

An incoming message saved me from the sullen memories.

ANONYMOUS: Meet me in the courtyard at the Capitol at 7:00.

IF I COULD WATCH FROM THE night sky, I would see us following the graphite pavers framing the courtyard—breath streaming in white clouds, elbows brushing. I would hear myself saying things were never fair. I would hear confusion in his silence when I asked him to be my friend and see myself stop short of telling him it was lonely on that stretch of road between the Capitol and my dorm. Memories of home burned my eyes.

"Things will remain as they are," he said, looking at me with haunted eyes. I told myself those words were enough to temper the silence that never ended when I was alone.

He told me a story about Thomas Jefferson and Louisiana and what that acquisition did for the United States. I hung on to every word, subdued by his knowledge. He said I looked like Jefferson's Sally. How he imagined she would look with a deeper skin tone.

Exquisite, he said. That meant I wasn't pretty to him. I was something more.

My shoulders curled in on themselves to hide the shivering, and he adjusted the collar of James's windbreaker so the slip of cold couldn't find its way in. My hand was warm and enclosed in his where I put it. Somehow, we walked to the front of the Capitol that way. Yellow floodlights led us. The cameras whirred from lampposts, warning him to let me go. Then his hand was in his coat pocket, and he was looking over my head at a passing MV, saying he would offer me a ride, but it was improper for me to ride with an official I wasn't assigned to.

I thought he would walk away, but he hesitated. Men speak without words when they hesitate, my mama said. She didn't tell me what the unsaid words meant, whether I should be uneasy or comforted by the sadness in his eyes. Or was it longing?

He descended concrete stairs, passing soldiers lined on both sides like monolithic posts.

I watched his MV until I couldn't see the blue exhaust fading into the gray.

IT WAS DECEMBER WHEN HE PUT a journal in my hand. This one was light blue with *Solenne* debossed on the cover. It held thick pages with that velvety scent of something new.

He twisted the obsidian ring on his finger. "To replace the one James Gibson gave you."

To keep my thoughts from scattering like dandelion seeds. To fill in white pages with black. While I ran my fingers over lined pages, imagining my words there, he reached for me with those large hands, like it was a habit not yet formed, then let them drop to his sides without me in them. He asked if he could kiss me.

"I have more integrity than to ever let it progress beyond a kiss," he was saying from somewhere beyond the journal. "No sitting. No open mouths. I swear it."

His gaze ran from my fingers clutching the journal to my eyes. "Is that what you want?"

I wasn't supposed to, but I thought about him holding my hand in the courtyard—that liquid touch I'd drawn up and injected into my veins. I'd experienced that one other time with a boy at a skating rink, until Dalena told him who my daddy was, but no one had ever kissed me. Could I measure the difference between handholding and kissing by the weakness in my knees?

"Yes?" he asked, standing so close now I could see the threads wound through buttons on his shirt.

The journal was fragile in my arms. I counted the pairs of boots hollowing past his office door that was heavy enough to hide secrets and shame. I nodded.

So he kissed me during that white-gray winter that stunned the catalpa trees outside his office window into silence. When his lips touched mine, I pretended this was as normal for me as it was for him. I was Dalena, who always knew what she was doing.

"My God," he murmured, lips lingering above my eyebrows, on the bridge of my nose, and where the hair curled behind my ear. "As soft as it looks."

I didn't know until then that men kissed this way, lips on all these small places no one noticed.

I stayed later and later each night, until it was normal for the two of us to be the only things moving in the building. It seemed he was never ready for me to go home.

Late one evening the sky churned. Bits of foreign ice pelleted the windows. I hadn't seen snow or ice since the ice storm that shuttered businesses and schools four years ago.

My palms iced against the glass. "Do you see this? But you hear it, don't you?"

He watched me with a pained expression, a brooding silence. He asked me to sit next to him on the sofa—

Please, for a little while.

—and his tongue touched mine for the first time.

My shoulders stiffened. My tongue darted away to familiar places in my own mouth until it rested.

To be watched and seen, to find a rip, to pour yourself inside of a man who would never be involuntarily deployed, never become a starred green flag folded in a glass box, wasn't that what every woman wanted? Wasn't that why the sparrows sang at first light?

Eyes screwed closed, I listened to footsteps approach, the knocking persist, and the footsteps recede because the official and I weren't there in that office. We were somewhere else.

THE COLD CONTINUED TO BLOW IN from somewhere up north. The book of poems that smelled sweetly of stored wood and whiskey preceded his promise to be kind, to be different from anyone else. "I could break you. I could hold on tighter and *break* you, but I won't."

He said to call him Bastien when I thanked him for the red cashmere coat. No one at the Capitol used his name. The name roamed around my mind for a moment before I decided it didn't belong.

"James Gibson made his feelings about you clear, didn't he?" He smoothed a rogue curl behind my ear. "But I will be here."

That night in my room I pulled out the blue journal he gave me. At two a.m., I had heavy eyelids and an eight-hundred-word allegory. In it, on the coldest day ever, two people exchanged pieces of themselves. "You have uncannily innocent eyes," the man told the little girl. "Eyes incapable of judgment."

She exchanged her eyes for his, her hands for his, her heart for his. "What else do you have?" the man asked the little girl, and she wasn't afraid. Time had gone, and so had the lonely. It burned out into embers, ash, smoke. She kept giving, and he kept taking, until she was no longer a little girl at all.

MEN WERE ALWAYS VISITING THE OFFICIAL'S office, needing his signature or his look of approval. He was always gathering things and leaving to meet a deadline. Just seeing Bouchard was enough to sour his mood for a few hours. While I stood at the official's side, staring up at the blade of their profiles, the two argued in the doorways of offices, in elevators, or on Source about Georgia's upcoming election for administrator. The Council's support was divided between Lucas Magnan, a Traditionalist, and Cade Glosen, a Modernist. Lucas Magnan. The man the Order sent Dalena to.

While he paced the office, I asked why he couldn't support the best man for the job. He looked at me for too long, the ropy muscles in his forearms taut, and I knew I'd said the wrong thing. In that question, he saw who I was—a girl from Dallas who didn't understand how the world worked. Razor-voiced, he said I was naive. Politicians have long memories. If he campaigned for Cade and Lucas won, Lucas would never rally the citizens in Georgia to vote him onto the Council permanently in four years. Even if most of Georgia's citizens voted for him without their administrator's support, Lucas was Georgia's elector. He could choose to deny rather than confirm his position.

He left for a meeting in the Chamber without saying he'd see me later. I sat in his chair and shuffled through the boring things on his desk—a stack of papers, a glass cube of gold paper clips, navy pens with *Strategic Services* on the barrel, and a chrome letter opener inside a metal holder. "Careful, that's sharp," the official would say if he were here. I unsheathed it, found a sheet in the middle of the stack of papers, and sliced off the tiniest corner. He wouldn't notice.

I looked up to find Francesca watching me from the doorway. Her hair was pulled up into a careful bun that highlighted the straight line from her neck to her cleavage. In this office where she thought I didn't belong, my fingertips ran cold.

"He's in a meeting," I said.

"I know that. I came up to see if you were still here."

"Why?" I hesitated to ask. If she called me Annette or mentioned cleaning, I wasn't sure I would be able to keep myself from knocking the piss out of her.

She blinked at my gifted coat hanging on the coat rack, blinked at my boots below, the toe of one over the other to hide a scuff mark. "Bastien is taking me to Georgia."

The sound of his name from her lips was a punch to the stomach.

"You know how it is." A tight smile. "I guess you wouldn't know how it is, would you? Officials don't date. They reserve your time. It's sex or marriage, nothing in between. He asked for my calendar and schedule for the next eight weeks."

She was lying. I heard it in her voice. I was with him every day, and he never mentioned visiting Georgia.

"I'll be honest. It used to annoy me to see you following him around like a puppy in your little red coat and swinging ponytail, but then I remembered that's exactly what you are. The boy's not chasing you. You're chasing the boy. You have my sympathy."

I angled my burning face to the desk. It was easier for her to believe I meant nothing to the official. A man like him could never see me as human, let alone as a beautiful woman. But she hadn't seen his lips on my fluttering eyelids, the goose bumps spreading from his wrists to his elbow, his hands reaching for me like a sleeper wave from the Gulf, dragging me to the warm gray sea.

CHAPTER 18

NOW

TIME PASSED ON THAT PARK BENCH TWO MILES FROM ED'S CAFÉ. NEW ORLEANS became the sinking sun and drums in the distance. Soon, it would be dark. I would be alone in a park with nowhere to go, no one to turn to.

I saw his shadow, long and gray on the grass, before I heard him.

"How did you find me?" I asked.

Memphis rested beside me, a duffel bag between us. "It wasn't hard."

"Then why did you find me?"

"Guess I still have some loyalty. I'm from Dallas. Former Code."

"You tracked me down to lie to me?"

I looked into his eyes, so dark like mine. The scars on his knuckles—not brawl scars, battle scars. "You take an oath for life. Why would you leave your brothers in the Code?"

He sighed like a man who just finished a long shift. "A situation happened when I was deployed to Georgia. I spent close to two years in jail because of it."

When he was released, there was no home to go to. He was stripped of rank, his wife had been reassigned, and his two-year-old son had a new daddy who refused contact, which the Council upheld.

"They say the Code are the pillars of our society. We deserve respect and honor for our sacrifice. Where was my respect and honor for the dozen near misses on my life?"

I didn't move. It was best to stay quiet when a man was shredded by anger.

"I came here. Met with the administrator directly to get him to push through my citizenship. Immigration tried to deny it because I was Code." He stood. "Fuck the Order. Fuck the Council. Fuck Abraham. Fuck Abraham's son."

The sun had slipped from view. Music settled in its place, rousing gray ghosts with red paint on their bodies.

Memphis rooted around in his bag and pulled out a silver device, slim and sleek as a pen, while throwing around illegal terms like *configurator*, a person who could delete you from the grid. He held out his hand, and I placed mine in his, palm side up.

"What are you doing?" I asked, though I didn't care. I wanted to win.

"Temporary fix . . . very temporary. I'm rerouting you in the system so we can move. This will show you in a different location than where we're going."

"What about Source? Get rid of it now?"

"Nah. Your chip is linked to it. Wherever your chip shows you are, Source will show the same. That's what we need. Get rid of it now, and he'll be suspicious." He pressed the point of the device to my thumb. An electric-like surge wrapped my thumb and wrist.

He watched me massage the area of my chip implant. When our eyes met, my first thought was of home. Memphis wasn't white, his eyes weren't blue, his hair wasn't sandy, he wasn't more than a foot taller than me. All comparisons to Bastien. He had been my measuring stick for too long.

"So you'll take me to your configurator?"

"I have one in mind, but I'm not guaranteeing he'll help."

THE SPV WAS AN OLDER ONE with cloth seats that smelled like damp bodies. With the sun setting, the air was cool. Memphis handed me a green sweatshirt from his bag, and I pulled it over my dress.

We arrived on Royal Street in front of a cluster of historic buildings with wrought iron and green awnings. Inside the last building, bright lights highlighted broken grout lines between dingy tile and empty glass jewelry cases lining the perimeter.

The configurator finally came from the back of the store. Brown, with arms furrowed with veins like tree bark, Lou was the largest man I'd seen in my life. He also had the look of a man who had no intention to help me.

I looked him in the eye, complimented him on the location he chose for his business, and said I was sure he would turn this place into something great. He was good. I couldn't tell if it softened him.

Memphis pointed me to a folding chair against the wall and whispered he would talk to Lou first. Lou's right-hand man sat in the corner alternating between looking at me and the pages of a motorcycle magazine. *Armie* glittered in diamonds on his oversize belt buckle, and his knuckles were so ashy, I thought of offering the lotion from my bag.

"I'm Armie, by the way." He leaned with his elbows on his knees like we had been in conversation.

"I know."

He grinned, rows of diamonds shining on his lower teeth. "Oh, so you heard about me?"

"You have a name tag." I gestured to the gaudy belt buckle. "And why 'by the way'? When people say that, they're usually adding on to a conversation."

"I been having a conversation with you in my head for the past hour." He closed the magazine after I returned his smile. "You know, getting off grid is the easy part. Y'all usually get tripped up once the search starts. If it was me, and it ain't never gone be me, I'd stick to areas where there ain't nothing but fields and cows."

I looked into his eyes, waiting for him to offer his place. His bed. "Why is that?"

"People ain't in your business." He ran a hand over his cornrows. They had fuzzed and lifted from his scalp so much I couldn't see the parts. "I don't normally look this throwed together. Been working so much, you know?"

"Mm."

"You braid?"

"Never learned."

"You got all that hair and never learned to braid?"

Source beeped, pulling my attention to my messages. Three new from Mama, two from Julian. In the SPV on the way here, there were more than one hundred unread from Bastien. Now there was one. One.

I walked out into a night that wasn't unlike January in Austin when the wind chilled, and the air tasted like confusion.

CHAPTER 19

THEN

THE OFFICIAL WASN'T IN HIS OFFICE THE NEXT MORNING. I WANDERED AROUND, peeking in open office doors, and panicking each time a graying head looked up from paperwork instead of the official's. I waited in front of his office door, testing the handle every few minutes. Maybe he was on a private call and couldn't answer. Maybe he had a late night and had fallen asleep at his desk. Any of that was preferable to what my gut was telling me. He didn't want to see me because I had done something wrong. I let the tea steep too long, whined about James too much, didn't say the right things when he told me stories.

Councilman Russell stopped next to me. Two young men passed us, arms sweeping up into a salute.

The hallway was too warm. My stomach hurt. I had been here before. My voice was a rough whisper. "I'm waiting for the official."

Russell sighed. His hand on my shoulder ushering me to the elevators, his kind eyes, his untethered words reopening a hole in my center.

THAT NIGHT IN MY DORM UNDER my daddy's afghan, silence blistered. Heat breathed through a partially blocked vent, fluttering the flimsy curtains. Source lay silent, a rectangle of useless glass in my hand. It was impossible not to think in silence so perfect. Impossible not to spin memories—the official's eyes changing when he told me about the Indonesian pearl farmer who harvested golden pearls from white-lipped oysters and dropped one into his hand. It shined, he said. The sun was his for a moment. I was a fool and thought that story was for me, that I was the golden pearl.

On the fifth day without him, I couldn't stop myself from calling him using the anonymous handle he messaged me from. No answer the first, third, or sixth time. The endless cycle of refreshing messages, waiting, spiraling. Dying. Jotting down the nonsensical characters of his anonymous handle then inputting them into the girl across the hall's Source and waiting, waiting for him to pick up.

I watched for him. Walking past cafés and peeking in glass storefronts became a ritual I didn't acknowledge until the evening I saw him in front of a restaurant waiting for the valet. Emboldened by time lost and coveted, I rushed through gaps in traffic, cold wind licking my face. I reached for the sleeve of his overcoat. Streetlights unmasked a confused white man I didn't know.

"Can I help you with something?" The man flipped his collar up against the cold.

I didn't stop running until I got to my dorm. The room's nothingness chafed my insides.

"I hate him," I said, slinging one boot against my closed door and the other against the wall.

I messaged Dalena, but still no answer. Was she ever there when I needed someone the most? I lay in bed coming up empty. I decided I hated her, too.

I WROTE. WHEN MY THOUGHTS DRIFTED too far from the page, I wandered, like fog wanders, for days that turned into five weeks.

I stood on Pfluger Pedestrian Bridge as the dark silenced the last bit of sun. Red and green kayaks navigated the lake below. The paddles sliced through glassy water, in sync, never resting. Behind me, bicyclists passed in straight lines linked by an invisible chain. The reflectors blurred orange on the tires. "Right behind you," the leader warned unsuspecting pedestrians. I watched until my exterior was numb from cold. A girl who didn't feel pain.

I walked to Magnolia's, one of the nicer cafés we were allowed to enter. I sat at a corner table drinking peppermint tea and scrolling articles on Source. Then because the universe always conspired to knock me back three paces when I moved forward once, the last article was about the official. I read every word. Six weeks ago, the Council appointed him to the Office of Ambassador. He traveled to Louisiana, Chicago, Ohio, and Georgia to meet with administrators and their cabinets. New York was next. My eyes swung to comments at the bottom of the article. Refreshing for new ones, heart fluttering, mug cold in my hand.

Thank you for your service, Official.

. . . Francesca Lamone . . .

We look forward to your return to Texas.

. . . traveling with Ms. Lamone . . .

. . . Ms. Lamone promoted to librarian at the State Archives and Library building . . .

. . . plans to marry Ms. Lamone?

I guess it had been in the back of my mind, but I didn't want to believe Francesca. If she was right about the official taking her to Georgia, she was right that I was nothing more than a puppy in a red coat.

Outside the café's window, I didn't see the bank's crystal lights piercing the night sky, the couples bundled together in coats and scarves, or the street sweepers lumbering by. I saw a brown girl's reflection in the glass, the sadness that spanned more than two hundred years.

I sent a message knowing it would go unread.

I don't blame you for forgetting about me.

The café's door parted, then closed me on the other side with bitter wind and the dark. I buttoned my coat with lifeless fingers.

On the warmer side of the glass door, the busboy finished my tea before dropping my mug and napkin in a plastic bucket.

Once, I heard the official say no one owes anyone anything. Why had I let the days pass without understanding that applied to me, too?

The grieving night sky pressed down on me, the Capitol in the distance. I pulled up my hood and made it to my dorm without knowing how. The building stood in front of me with its double doors and ragged squares of light cocooning Black girls who knew better than to want a life they couldn't have.

I could stop here. Welcome the familiar and slip back into nothing.

A MONTH PASSED, INCHING ME CLOSER to a visit from Mama. At Magnolia's, I waited for her in a booth near the storefront window. I wanted to see the moment she rounded the corner onto Government Avenue, a familiar sight in the lonely.

Three minutes later, I was in her arms. I breathed in blackberry and manuka honey, the humectants she sprayed in our hair to attract moisture, and asked her to stay with me. I wanted her to help me forget everything.

"Of course, I'll stay."

She looked me over. Grasped the ends of my hair, feathered them through her fingers checking for dry ends in danger of splitting, checked for stray eyebrow hairs, a properly fitting bra. She nodded, relieved.

While we waited for our order of coffee and two maple nut scones, we chatted the way we used to when I was her little girl.

"I wish you'd use your passes to visit home," she said, then looked away. She knew why I couldn't. Walking back into that house without Daddy being there would rip apart the seams I'd stitched together. She changed the subject. "So tell me about James."

James was back, but my new understanding kept me at a distance. He was my friend, I was sure of that, but he had no obligation to press pause on his life to deal with the wants of someone he didn't ask for. I forgave him for the hurt, listened to his stories of golfing, hiking on Indian Sands Trail, and writing for hours in a gazebo with lighted mesh panels resembling the stars.

I spoke to her reflection in the café's window. "We talk about him all the time. What else do you want to know?"

"What you're up to."

"I'm writing. James helped me start Henriette's biography. I decided to write it in five parts."

Her face fell. "You're not showing anyone what you're writing, are you?"

"I'm not stupid."

Mama smiled at the young barista balancing coffee and muffins on a tray. "Thank you" put him under her spell. We could order three of everything on the menu and pay for none of it.

"But you're bold, and that doesn't mix well with working in a building full of government officials. James is a good man, but don't think because he signed off on it, it's okay. You make sure you're not sharing that information with anyone else. Not this type of story."

"I won't, Mama."

While I told her about part one I drafted, she watched me add three spoonfuls of water and hazelnut cream into her coffee how we liked it. Gentle.

"What will I do when I don't have you to make me coffee anymore?" She sipped from the mug I pushed across the table. "I'm turning a profit at the shop. Margaret Ann's ordering supplies for me in her name. I'm getting jars twenty-five percent less now." She looked up from her mug. "She puts the extra money in an account the conservator doesn't know about. That's your Louisiana money. To help get you started when you leave here."

I couldn't tell her I told James I didn't want emancipation yet. She wouldn't understand.

I sipped my coffee. "How is Margaret Ann?"

"Decompressing after the wedding. Joy got married a few weeks ago. Julian Garnier, the official's chief strategist."

I thumbed the end of my braid, thinking of the man with black hair who sat beside her on the train, scrolling through Source. Everything was a straight line for Joy—being pretty in a museum, love, a wedding. It would be a straight line for Francesca, starting with her trip with the official. No one would ever make her feel wanted and then smother the life out of her by disappearing without a word. Shame wilted me. To continuously want to be a part of a world that didn't want me—I was a fool.

Mugs clicked on tiled tables. A group of men leaving the café cast curious glances at us. After our barista handed Mama a pastry bag of complimentary muffins, we stepped out under a sky flushed with sunlight. I clung to her. We could walk in the parks like we used to. It was February, but it was warm enough. We could—

"Your breakfast tomorrow. You love muffins." She pressed the pastry bag into my hand.

Sweets, the substitute for her.

"You said you'd stay."

"I didn't know you meant overnight, Solenne. I can't."

Why was it so easy for her to leave me when it was hard for me to leave her? I was staying here, shackled to the Order for her. The least she could do was not force me to watch her walk away.

Mumbling about getting back to my dorm, I charged through people carrying shopping bags.

Mama spun me around by the shoulder, startling me. "Pick it up."

The muffins lay in a red plastic heap next to a trash can in front of a jewelry store where I slung it. "You pick it up. It's yours."

We argued, her voice even, mine shrill.

Two women craned their necks at us, lipstick-stained mouths in perfect Os.

"You won't act like this in front of all these white people."

"No one cares what they think except you." But I tossed the bag in the trash can.

She flashed her sales smile at a man leaving the jewelry store then glared at me. "Do you think I want to work so much?"

I crossed my arms, shoulders knotted like rope.

"If I have to work night and day to save up enough so you have money when you leave here, that's what I'll do." She pulled me into her arms. Kissed me and crooned like I was a baby. "Why are you still so angry, little girl? He left me, too, you know. I didn't get enough years with your daddy. I can't change that, but I wake up every day knowing I'm still here, and I'm still your mama."

ALONE IN MY ROOM THAT EVENING, sleep wouldn't come. Girls wandered the hallways. A shower started in the room above mine. My thoughts were on my mama in layers. My mama before I knew mamas got tired, sad, or weepy like purple wisterias.

The automatic streetlamps clicked on. Light passed through those plain white curtains too easily, and I missed my bedroom curtains at home. When I was twelve, Mama and I made them by cutting tiny stars into blue fabric and attaching a tulle overlay. Star-shaped sunlight woke me each day. When Daddy's eyes and smile appeared through a crack in my door, I had a constellation.

Clinging to that memory, I dreamed of Daddy in soldier's white, eyes forever closed, fingers laced over his heart where his little girl once pressed her ear to listen to his life.

I AWOKE HOURS LATER UNDER THE afghan, pillowcase damp. Source blinked intermittently on my nightstand. Red light for low battery. Green light for received messages. The pattern made me dizzy enough to grab the device. Nothing from Mama. One message from Anonymous.

I could never forget holding the sun.

....

CHAPTER 20

NOW

IN THE ALLEY BEHIND THE JEWELRY STORE, I STARED OVERHEAD AT THE SAGGING lamppost with one good light bulb, another flickering, and two broken. The shattered pieces lay on loose gravel pleated by SPV tires.

I checked Mama's message.

MAMA: Let me know you're okay. I'm worried.

Guilt was a boulder, heavy and chipped from a mountain.

SOLENNE: I'm okay.

She video-called. Source was the mirror between us—our long black braid and yellow-brown skin. I saw Fulani girls, the milk-maids, our arms curved to balance the calabash of fresh milk on our heads. I felt the warmth of the copper rings adorning our limbs. I heard the wind whipping against the millet and reed mat houses behind us, and in the distance, the Niger river rushing to meet the cattle with swishing tails and tongues.

If this worked, if the configurator removed me from the grid, this could possibly be the last time we saw each other. If this worked, this truly was the end of a story that had lasted more than two hundred years.

"I'm proud of you," she said, voice hoarse. "You know you don't have to have it all figured out right now, don't you?"

Years of fearing what could go wrong with Bastien had changed her. The woman who used to leap first then open her eyes now studied the ground for cracks before walking. She paced the floors, making my sins hers, praying like Daddy used to.

I touched her nose, lips, and hair, warm glass under my fingertips instead of soft skin and the black curls at her hairline. What do you say to your mama when you'll never see her again?

She stared into me, my oracle, my mama, only eighteen years my senior. The words she didn't say weighed more than the ones she did.

CHAPTER 21

THEN

WINTER FADED AND THEN CAME A SUMMER FRAGRANT WITH THE WILD ROSES crowding through chain-linked fences. A cloud cover that made and broke the promise of rain lingered for weeks. I poured myself into writing, finishing part two of *My Henriette* on my sixteenth birthday. I held my journal close while passing through rows of uniformed men, rifles tethered to chests. A rifle could be taken away. An emblem could be torn away with fabric scissors. My story, half on the page and half in my brain, was mine forever. That was proof that what I owned was more powerful than anything they owned.

I was curled on the sofa writing when James pushed a thick, well-worn book into my hands and said one of the officials requested it.

"Chamber," he said. "Leave it on the desk under the Texas flag."

The Chamber's doors stood at the end of the hallway, a good twenty feet away from the elevator doors, but the voices inside grabbed and pulled me. I made out the words over the air conditioner's hum.

"Lucas Magnan's campaign for administrator of Georgia was successful. He won by a clear margin."

The official. Feet or miles between us, I knew him.

"I'm told he's quite attached to my gift he picked up last year," Abraham said, amused. "Dalena Batiste. He called her 'my salt and sugar' in his thank-you letter."

My Dalena. I pressed my ear to the door to capture every word.

"He's fond of her, yes," another man with a silky voice said. "Though she's had a difficult adjustment period."

"At this age, they're naive, temperamental, and unreasonable," Abraham said. "First year away from home, more responsibilities, clashing with the wife. I'm certain he can keep her in line. I've heard encouraging things about his performance in Georgia. A fine young man."

"At our last meeting, his cabinet praised Source's upgrades and tracking capability," the official said. "I wrote the software. Magnan hasn't contributed anything of note."

He spoke to Abraham like he was a stranger, his voice a hard collection of nerves. Why did he speak as if he needed to prove himself to his own daddy?

"I sincerely hope you were more successful at masking your disdain for him than you have been today. Georgia's administrators have a history of being fickle."

"I understand my actions are a step toward or away from securing my position on the Council, sir," Bastien said.

"Never forget," Abraham said. A pause. "Solenne Bonet, these are private matters—"

I knocked through the rest of his sentence as if I'd just arrived and had been planning to all along.

The door swung open. A man with blue eyes and dense black waves filled the doorway. This was Julian Garnier, chief strategist. Joy's husband. The man I'd seen her with on the train.

The official sat at a desk under the Texas flag, tanned, wide-legged, arms crossed over his chest. Julian lowered himself in the chair next to the official's and mimicked his posture.

The book was heavy in my hands. I searched my memory for how DoS were supposed to greet the president. *Memorize his preferences*, Guidry said. *You never know when you may run into him.* Hand and smile out in front of me. Three seconds of eye contact. Most importantly, call him Abraham, his mononym.

"Abraham," I said.

He stood and took my hand in his, the intimacy jolting me. "What can I do for you?"

I held the book up, so he could see the cover.

Abraham frowned at the official. I understood then what he had done. I felt his eyes on me, but I wouldn't look. Nothing is real unless it's written, and I had tried to pen our story many times over the past four months. As if they didn't want to be born, the words blocked themselves from existence. How many times had I hoped, wished, *prayed* for a new message from him? Always silence. Last week, after putting the finishing touches on part two of Henriette's story, I deleted that pearl and sun message he sent me. He could go to the hell he sent me to.

"Official," I said, because it was required to acknowledge him, but I kept my chin to my chest. I stared at his boots, now between me and Abraham. They were different. They were in this place and not our place on the sofa in his office with the world outside of us. I hadn't known that someone could feel a memory—have it sprout arms, hands, and fingers to pull you through time. Bitterness fading, my eyes responded to his orders. They met his.

Abraham dropped my hand and angled his body between us. Julian opened a door.

"Solenne, I'm afraid there was some miscommunication. Speak to James Gibson if you have questions."

The door was between us again. I waited through a long silence.

"I see it," Abraham said. "They taught her to hide it, but I see the insolence. I see the storm."

THAT NIGHT, I DREAMED I WAS drowning in muck, thick and bottomless.

A white sun pressed itself on a slave row, a carriage house, a blacksmith's shop. In the yard, women scalded laundry in iron pots. They slaughtered chickens and carried their bleeding bodies up splintered stairs into a kitchen detached from the big house.

They didn't hear me struggle.

I looked for her, always looked for her, but she wasn't there. My ears filled with water, foamy with dirt and algae. When I opened my mouth, muck filled that, too.

Henriette walked out onto the balcony of the big house, white skirts and apron fighting a breeze.

She spoke a single word floating on the wings of a dragonfly.

Don't.

Before I could rub it from my eyes, the dream was hazy, fading, gone.

I FELT THE SMALLEST OF SHIFTS, like tornado season in Dallas when warm air quieted before a storm. He didn't ask me to come to his office. I went, drawn by the winds, those blues and grays wailing that was where I belonged.

He paced his office listening to my thoughts. Strange, because no one ever cared what I thought. They told me to hush. He corrected me and said it was new, not strange, to have someone who understood me so deeply. He understood I liked creamed honey on biscuits, still reached for mama's hand when we rushed through crowded streets, and churned the meaning of words through my brain at night. Why, in a world where *orphan* and *widow* existed, there wasn't a better word than *fatherless* for someone who lost their father?

Under the office lights like a soliloquist in a play, he spoke about his beginning, the darkness, but he stopped at the descriptions in the slaughterhouses. "No one who lost their father at war should ever hear these things."

He said he missed the way I listened, the way I looked at him like I couldn't wait for the next word, but somehow already understood what he would say. "I came back for you," he said.

No one else ever had. I thought then, that these were moments that defined me. Everything would be beautiful from now on.

In my bedroom that night, the air conditioner wasn't working. Sweating on my stripped-down bed, I wrote.

Forgiveness sliced me open.
All that lay bare inside of me was the lonely.
How could I be afraid of scars?

• • •

"SOLENNE, YOU'VE MET JULIAN GARNIER," THE official said when I arrived at his office the next morning.

Julian Garnier smiled, and here where the men didn't, his lips curving until his eyes looked maniacal. I didn't leave the doorway until the official extended his hand to me.

He handed me a Maya blue case from the top drawer of his desk, nodding for me to open it. Inside on white coffin velvet was a pair of thin, silver-framed glasses. He figured out my squint wasn't artificial.

"Try them on," Julian Garnier said.

I couldn't bring myself to put them on, so the official did it for me, adjusting them behind my ears and on the bridge of my nose.

"Perfect. I'll take you for laser vision correction when you're older."

At first, my discomfort wouldn't allow me to notice the difference, but the emblems on his sleeve were sharper than they'd ever been. I browsed a bookshelf and read titles without squinting. The numbers on the clock didn't have watery edges. The label on a tea bag was crisp and bold. LYDIA TEA in green.

"You can see this all the way from there?" I asked. I scudded from corner to corner, a hummingbird, reading small text on furniture legs and paintings.

Julian Garnier parked his elbows on his knees and laughed. The official twisted his ring.

I circled the room for a mirror until the official pointed to the small adjoining restroom. Muted light revealed octagonal tile, the toilet, both pristine, and a face in the mirror above the sink. The buzz flew away. My shoulders slumped. It wasn't my face. This was Carleen— foggy lenses, bloated face, a grunting newborn between my breasts. Carleen, nursing one baby while another nudged her from inside her belly and yet another toddled around with a pissed-out diaper hanging to the backs of his knees.

Above my reflection, the official's face blurred featureless. "Wear them when you read, at the very least. You can't see it now, but this is a benefit."

He didn't understand I'd seen myself in a cabin lying on the sags of a cornhusk mattress, the cadent snores of the man beside me. The children. I saw their questioning eyes, wanting. I saw all that would be and decided sometimes it was better not to see.

WEEKS LATER, LIFE SHIFTED AGAIN WHEN he asked me to visit him at his house. I waited on the porch of my building for Julian Garnier a half hour before he was scheduled to pick me up.

"Call me Julian. Titles change the dynamics, don't they? They shouldn't. We're one and the same. Our jobs are to ensure *the* official is happy." He smiled at me in the rearview mirror. I didn't smile back, but he kept going. What do you like to read? Favorite book? Favorite color? Favorite food?

I stared out of the window and answered his questions as efficiently as possible, so I could pretend to be sitting next to the official in the MV or meeting his eyes in the rearview mirror instead of Julian's. What would a world look like where it wasn't improper for me to be seen with him?

MoPac Expressway opened in front of us. We passed flashing billboards that announced the route we were on led to the Government District, where only approved vehicles were permitted to travel. Once inhabited by regular citizens, the enormous homes near the lake were where the officials lived.

This was what inspired James's fifteen-minute rants about our Treasury and the distribution of wealth in the Order.

We passed through an iron gate guarded by two agents. The official opened his front door while I was still climbing the stairs. He had relaxed out of uniform but wore a shoulder holster over a black shirt. He stared at me in my plain white baby doll dress. "You look so pretty today."

The door closed behind us, a finality in the click of a bolt sliding into place.

I was the only sound in the hallways we walked—the swish of my dress, my clicking intertwined bracelets. I was near breathless dancing from thing to thing, my socked toes spinning on tiled floors. He didn't say, Be careful, you can ruin that. He asked me questions like he wanted me to handle his expensive books and handmade decor and twisted the ring on his finger when I embarrassed myself by blurting, I wanted everything in his house.

The most beautiful room in the house was a living area, with white linen chairs and mahogany wood overlooking the lake. The vases reminded me of jewelry.

"Everything here belonged to my mother." There was tension in his voice, sort of like Guidry when she passed around Source for the first time in first grade. She cradled her hands under ours as if Source were a baby.

From his frame above the fireplace, Thomas Jefferson watched me. I stared into his eyes. What had Sally seen in him? He brought her to France at fourteen, where she worked, lived, and earned money as a freedwoman. When he decided to return to America two years later, she didn't stay like the French urged her. She returned to America, where she remained enslaved and the babies followed like footsteps. I thought of Sally leaving after Jefferson was buried, with his shoe buckles and reading glasses tucked into her belongings. I wondered what it meant. I worried for the mind of a girl.

In the hallway, a teal vase on a table stopped me. I ran my fingertips over the glossy edges. It looked like it belonged with the collection Francesca arranged on her desk to use as a conversation piece. I imagined her in the rooms I visited, knowing things about the official I never would. Everything inside me *wanted*. I decided then to never ask him about Francesca or why he left without a word. If I didn't think about it, that time in my life would no longer exist.

I avoided his eyes by twisting my braid around my hand. "You know Francesca gives these out to everyone like table candy. It's nothing special."

He didn't blink. "Okay."

It was down the third hallway I met Zeus and Hera. Sapphire

collars jingling, the dogs climbed to their feet on the white fur rug. Their black eyes disappeared into coal-black coats. Beautiful sculptures. Eyes on the official, they flattened triangular ears.

"Can I touch them?" I asked, but I had already wrapped my arms around Hera's neck and nuzzled my face in her coat. "Sometimes I thought we'd never see each other again. Did you ever think that maybe I wouldn't be here when you came back to Austin?"

"No," he said, looking down at me and Hera like a heap of puzzle pieces. "Where would you go, Solenne?"

THE MEN IN THE CAPITOL SEARCHED the official's and Julian's faces for the story in the following days. They found it in the stiff lines in the official's back when they asked if I was available for work. They heard it in the blunt edge of his voice when he said, *This conversation serves no purpose.*

This evening he was uncharacteristically distracted, looking past Julian droning on about Lucas Magnan from across his desk. Outside the Capitol, he looked at me like he was searching for words. Feathered a lock of my hair between his fingers like something foreign and told me I should wear my hair down more often. I flushed because he noticed I'd done it for him—ironed it out with olive oil, parted it down the middle, and pinned it away from my face like Mama's.

He said, I cannot believe how pretty you are. It's . . . disconcerting. Agonizing.

He said, Come home with me.

Officials exiting the building passed us on the sidewalk, saluting.

He didn't let me look away when he asked, Do you know what it means to spend the night with an official? Do you understand what happens?

Dalena would've known what to say, but I couldn't think of any words other than his, the words I hung on to while I slipped into dreams each night: *You know I came back for you.* I remembered the waiting. I thought if I didn't want what he wanted, he would leave again, taking everything with him. I'd be alone with no dose of sunlight, no beautiful words.

CHAPTER 22

NOW

I WAS AT A CROSSROADS. ON ONE SIDE WAS NEW ORLEANS AND FREEDOM. THE other side was the silvers and orange of Lake Travis, the bluebonnets in spring, the night-blooming jasmines at dusk. Mama. Bastien.

Bastien's message was on my screen, the one message that replaced more than one hundred marked urgent. A video. A thumbnail of me from four years ago, hair swollen with curls, standing in the doorway of his home office. I'd stood there hundreds of times, but I recognized this image—the string puppet, a face made of wood, a hollow gaze. The night a girl died and a monster was made. Bastien didn't like talking about our first night together. My words would find only his back, his hand cupping the back of his neck, his head bowed as if the floor was code he needed to solve. But only he understood the us that existed that night. He'd made me who I was. Who else could I go to? Where would you go, Solenne?

"YOUR SKY DADDY IS LOOKING OUT for you today. Lou said he'd take your necklace as down payment."

The back door of the jewelry store banged closed. Memphis's boots crunched on fine gravel until he stood next to me.

"Solenne?"

Our eyes met. He shook his head. I followed his line of sight to the lamppost, now with only one good bulb. The flickering bulb had chosen which direction it wanted to go.

"He got to you, didn't he?" He shoved his hands in his pants pockets and exhaled. "They wouldn't have rank if they didn't know how to manipulate, but whatever he said or sent you is his strategy to recover *property*. Open your eyes."

A rocket of color sliced the night sky in red, gold, and green. Three more followed.

He pulled the jewelry store door open. "You better make sure this is what you really want. You don't back out, then show up for a second chance when you figure out you let this man get into your head. If you want to forget what sent you running, that's on you. You have ten minutes."

The door gave an empty thump, closing Memphis inside.

I hadn't forgotten what made me leave. My reasons were still there, but now they were shaded by doubt. Everything, everyone, my beginning was in Texas. If I did this, I would never be able to go back.

I closed my eyes and found the sweet rush of adrenaline when I boarded the train in Austin, and the new air that filled my lungs when I got off in New Orleans. But it never lasts. Nothing ever does. That feeling was fading away like a lake blighted by drought. I reached deeper, searching for the path that led me to this end. I found only the beginning.

. . . .

CHAPTER 23

THEN

I WAITED INSIDE THE MV ALONE, CHECKING HEALTH DATA THROUGH SOURCE. Guidry said, *Cycle Day ten through fourteen, you better sit down some- where, unless you wanna come home with your belly stuck out or a baby on your hip.*

CYCLE DAY 16.

The driver and back doors opened simultaneously. Julian climbed into the driver's seat; the official folded himself next to me. If this moment was words in my journal coming to life, why did it feel so strange when he draped his arm around my shoulder?

When the MV passed under streetlights, my reflection in the window appeared, but it remained indistinct, emotionless, refusing to show me who I was.

JULIAN OPENED MY DOOR, FACE HIDDEN behind the pure dark, a starless sky. He was Uncle with his oil lamp, lighting Henriette's path to where Antoni waited for her in his bedroom.

"Are you picking me up tomorrow?" I asked, because his silence was unnerving.

"We'll let tomorrow determine what happens." He waited until I followed the official to the porch before backing the MV down the driveway. The gate at the end of the road closed behind the man whose job was to ensure the official was happy.

• • •

I FOLLOWED THE OFFICIAL DOWN THE dimmed hallway leading to his office.

"We're not going to your bedroom?" I managed to ask.

From the doorway of his office, I watched him cross the room and sit behind his desk. "You're afraid."

I twisted my braid around my hand. "No, I'm not."

"Come here."

My feet wouldn't move.

"It's tonight or not at all. We'll talk ourselves out of it. That's not what we want, do we? Fear isn't an emotion." He turned his steady hand palm side up and splayed his fingers. "Stare it down, and it loses its form. It has no shape at all. No hold."

But standing in front of him, my hands shook when I thumbed the white thread at the hem of my dress sleeve.

He said I had no reason to be afraid, he would never hurt me, he had never been anything but kind, and we wouldn't go to his room until I said I was ready, he swears it. His fingertips learned the lines in my palms, the veins in my forearms, and the beds of my fingernails. "One day, when you understand what it means to need, you'll forgive me for clenching my fist with you inside."

I held so still, it was like I wasn't there. "I understand what it means to need."

"You're not old enough to understand." He closed his eyes. It was how he searched for answers. "What would you do if you could prevent anyone from ever leaving you?"

I thought of Daddy, Mama, Dalena, and James. The answer came easily.

"I'd make sure I never lost that power."

He opened his eyes. Found me waiting, withered enough to fit neatly in his palm. "We should go to bed now."

• • •

HE REMOVED HIS BOOTS, HOLSTER, AND shirt, which he folded and placed on the dresser next to my crumpled white dress.

I looked at the blanket on the bed underneath me, embarrassed by the sandy hair flashing from his armpits and lower back.

"I want you to tell me a secret. Something you'd never tell anyone."

"Like what?"

He turned to face me. "How often do you touch yourself?"

I pulled my knees to my chest and wrapped my arms around them. "I don't."

If I stayed still, he would forget the question.

"You're embarrassed about something everyone does."

Him knowing I was embarrassed was worse than the embarrassment itself.

"White girls?"

"Of course."

I knew they did since the nail polish incident in Joy's bedroom, but him admitting it relaxed me. I told him I had done it too, once or twice.

He sipped from his glass of whiskey while he waited for the truth.

"Maybe once a week."

He nodded. Glass still in his hand, he pulled me by the calf until I rested on my back. My stomach and heart spiraled together. The lights were too bright, my face too warm. The bed tilted under his weight. He hesitated somewhere next to me. Gave his reasoning for what must be done. "If you weren't so beautiful."

Seconds passed alongside his inhales and sighs everywhere— under my arms, bra, the unraveling lace on my panties. My body was tight, like it was bound by wire. I told him I didn't want him down there. It's embarrassing. Why can't we do it the normal way? He guided my feet over his shoulders and said I didn't understand what I was saying. He said he had to do this first, and this was normal. Lying there where everything was soft but nonsensical until I couldn't stay still was something women did, and I was a woman. A familiar twinge gathered in one place, threatening to come out all twisted and ugly. I held on to it so he wouldn't see it, squirmed away until there was nowhere to go, until my veins rushed.

He pried my hand from his hair, buckles clicked, a zipper. His knees were rigid posts against my open thighs. He was wrong. Fear was an emotion. The night knew it. Darkness peered through every window but held its silence. Before I could turn away, he burrowed his tongue into my mouth. I didn't want it there because of where it had been, but Dalena said this was how they did it. We weren't children. The blunt persisting, the tearing pain. He moved through my silence, wincing, unseeing. My feet pedaled against the mattress. I pressed a hand to his stomach, stilling him to breaths and twitching muscles.

"I know, baby," he murmured against my teary eye. "Let me have you."

I whispered an apology for doing it wrong, for not having a body that understood the flame of his palm under my hips lifting, lifting, while he sank and took everything inside me was normal. I lay underneath him—burning, crumbling to ash, feeling.

THAT NIGHT IN MY DREAM, HENRIETTE traded swamps for the woods after the runaways abandoned her. A concubine was too risky. Not even the most productive field hand was pursued as aggressively as a fancy girl.

Lying on her back, she saw nests of twisted twigs and leaves high in the bald cypress trees. Something newborn and abandoned lived in one. She'd seen a flap of pink at dusk one evening.

Below the whistle of the wind was a hum that sounded alive, and she grasped it so firmly she didn't hear what she'd trained herself to listen to for weeks. She didn't see the blades of grass bending under footsteps, reaching for her like rope, until they closed around her. Henriette didn't look at me where I stood shadowed behind her. She never did in these dreams.

A shotgun clicked.

Why? she asked, looking past the white men into Royger's green eyes, the runaway who once gave her salt pork around a campfire. *Why?* she asked again, and I knew the question was for me.

I awoke with no answers, limp and ragged, lying on sheets still damp with memories of last night. The sun had softened the sky from black to gray, and I could see my dress lying on the dresser. Strange fabric, alone, in the shape of who I once was. The official was confused by my tears. His hard face was soft with worry.

"Shhh." He pulled me to him and ran his hand over my back. "What am I doing, Solenne?"

That was regret in his voice. I was sure of it. I allowed his arms to comfort me, ready to release the truth that would hurl us back to the days of standing in his office kissing like children. What we'd done changed the shape of me. I was afraid a mirror would reveal the vacant stare of someone who wasn't a child but still unready for the pain of being a woman. He would understand why I needed him to turn back time. Hadn't he been here? He was fifteen in the slaughterhouses and seventeen in Yemen. In both, he stood witness to innocence fading like ink in old books.

First light awakened the sparrows in the bendy oak trees. They were midway through their spring songs when the hand on my back changed from soothing to intentional.

I sighed, such an insignificant sound lingering.

He hesitated. It wasn't long enough. "What am I doing, Solenne?" he asked from inside me, where neither of us was alone.

That was the last time he asked.

WE WEREN'T SUPPOSED TO FEEL ANYTHING for these men. It was dangerous— this paradox Black girls couldn't take the long way around to avoid. But Black girls are not parts created from perceptions. We are human in a world that told us we couldn't be.

I awoke each day pretending we were on our own island. We never left the house. No one visited other than a plump, graying woman who came twice a day to clean and leave protein-heavy meals on warming trays or wrapped in plastic in the refrigerator. He called her Service as if it were her name. This ghost in pink lipstick and blue shoe covers floated around the house never acknowledging me or Bastien.

Bastien.

I never had, but I could say his name now. It wrapped itself around my cells and told a girl that this was freedom.

We didn't have anything to fill in the blanks, so I became who he wanted. Woman, not girl. His beautiful Sol. I ate when and what he ate. Smoked salmon, fruit, truffle cheese, greens, beef, and chicken. Clean, balanced eating. *No, she can't bring cherry chewies*, he said. Sugar led to addiction, and addiction was for the weak. *We aren't weak people, are we?* he asked. He remembered I didn't eat eggs or meat off the bone, so there was an alternative on those days. *No, you can't have a drink after dinner. You're too young for alcohol.*

I was his rag doll, limp and stuffed with cotton, posed how he wanted me. *So, so beautiful,* he breathed, animating me, making me somebody. Sex was him above me promising, *It will be easier next time. Wasn't it better than the first time?* Mama said men need to feel like they're good people. His eyes changed from concerned to relieved when I nodded against his forearm damp with sweat.

Nighttime was his drips of information. He spoke to me as if I were a white man. *I don't know why I'm telling you this*, he said, yawning after talking about leaders from historical relics in such detail, he could've been reading directly from them. He talked to me about the Order. Not about regulations, but about his vision. I smoothed his furrowed brow, listened to his plans, and asked questions that made me sound intelligent enough. In four years, he would be the first councilman to secure a vote from the administrator of all states, including Georgia's. That would make his position on the Council permanent. This successful campaign would clear his path to becoming president within fifteen years.

I drifted to sleep each night, contemplating the ever-present sorrow in his eyes, and wondering why I liked some things he did to me in his bed but couldn't get used to others. Did that make me a woman, a girl, or trapped somewhere in between? I liked everything soft, water against sand, my thoughts spinning like music afterward. Dalena said girls were soft and everything gave way under your fingertips. Everything clicked together for her, familiar, like remembering the lyrics to an old song. Maybe Bastien was my song, and I needed to wait until he felt familiar.

The brown leather journal James gave me seemed so distant, tucked in my bag underneath my scarf. So I replaced that dark truth with pretty words in that pretty blue journal the official gave me last year. Alone, I stretched across his sheets and wrote his words. Where else did they belong? *I've never seen anyone so beautiful. I came back for you. I'll never let you go . . .*

I wrote nothing that resembled the pain or uneasiness of our first night together. Like the forgotten pain of childbirth, the transition from girl to woman was the part of a story that women didn't remember. I thought I could forget it, too.

PART THREE

FOR ADELIE

MY HENRIETTE

THE OVERSEER BOUND HENRIETTE'S WRISTS TO A CYPRESS TREE. HER SKIN BURNED from the rope and the mosquitos' attention. She stared up at the sun filtering through Spanish moss, gauzy on the tree's limbs. She thought she heard a newborn's cry. It couldn't be the boy she left behind. He would be six months old, if he were still alive.

It was evening when Antoni came to her, one of the overseers close behind wielding rawhide in his fist.

—A mulatto boy led patrol to her camp in the trees, the overseer said.

—I'm convinced I've procured the most wicked Negress in all Louisiana, Antoni said.

He recoiled at the sight of her frock hanging from her body, torn and filthy from months on the run. It was once his favorite. She wondered if he would whip her himself. She'd never seen him use the whip, but what she'd done, she now understood by looking at his face, was layered with differences. She belonged to Antoni outside and inside of that strange institution.

—I could snap your neck. Drown you right there in that pond. I could sell you to a sugar plantation where you'd learn real work. But you're wicked. Sinful. You'd be in the planter's bed before the second nightfall.

She screamed for her grandmother when the fleur-de-lis seared into the skin of her shoulder. Darkness overtook her, but it was kind. Her grandmother was there. She sat outside their hut engraving sparrows on a calabash with a heated metal blade.

When Henriette awoke, the black sky burned with stars. Uncle stood between the two pillars flanking the porch. An oil lamp lit his solemn face. She couldn't see Antoni, but the porch swing's chains rasped under his weight. His cigar smoke twisted in the dark.

—Why did you run, child? I've treated you well. Why did you leave your boy? Antoni asked in the soft tone he used with his horses.

—Ain't mine. He your boy.

The oil lamp swayed in Uncle's hand. The porch swing thumped against the wood of the house. The savage dogs brayed and bucked against rope tethering them to the overseer's porch. Antoni grabbed her. She spat at him, clawed at the ground rutted by carriage tires, and threw handfuls of dirt in his eyes.

And Antoni, who had already lost his mother, a brother, and a property to the slave revolts in Saint-Domingue, who swore he would never lose anything else, hung on.

From a window each evening in the big house, she strained to see the slave row where her son lived with Delphine in the cabin she once lived in. She imagined him mewling on a pallet of wool blankets far away from Antoni. She envied him.

IN THE WINTER OF 1803, THE second baby came. A girl this time, small and pale. While mother and daughter slept in Delphine's cabin, Antoni wrote the new baby's name in his record book. Next to mother, he wrote Henriette. Next to father, he drew a slash that erased paternity before the ink dried, that symbol that summed her existence to four words used in polite company: *children of the plantation*. Fathered by a white man who would remain nameless, as tradition dictated. Boots up on his desk, he stared into the light from a smoking tallow candle and thought of fire as he had for a year. The night a quarter of his crop mushroomed in flames, Uncle and the overseers howling at his bedroom door woke him. He shook Henriette awake and told her to fetch buckets. When she yawned and handed him his breeches, he wasn't certain if it was turpentine he smelled on the little wretch's hand, but he was certain he'd seen a ghost of a brazen smile before she rolled over and pulled the blanket to her shoulders.

THE NEXT TWO YEARS BROUGHT TWO more crop-destroying fires and dysentery that ravaged the enslaved population at Verreaux. Antoni was away often, leaving Uncle to run the big house. Henriette found freedom in seeing his office shuttered, his bed empty, the dining room abandoned. The cook, Mary, stood by the stove twisting her hands while Henriette peeled stalks of Antoni's sugarcane.

—Where I tell Master his sugarcane gone to?

—He ain't here, is he? He ask behind it, tell him go look for it in the swamp.

She sat on Antoni's porch swing so often, the enslaved people asked if she thought she was the Queen from up there in Washington. *You want a cool drink, Missus?* they taunted, but they wouldn't go further. She was who soured or sweetened their master's mood. She was who they talked to when they needed a pass to leave the property or a day off because of illness. She swayed on that swing, chewed sugar cane, and watched her children play with a cowhide drum. When they sat side by side, the boy tapping out a rhythm the girl followed, she didn't see her children. She saw her brother as he was in Africa, guiding her hand over a cow's teat, smiling when milk streamed into the waiting calabash. She saw him as he was in the port of New Orleans, teary-eyed when a doctor in all black pried his mouth open and inspected his limbs for deformities. *I'm not afraid*, he reassured her. *I'm just tired.* Love—it reached back through time, arranged itself in these little bodies before her to remind her love would always be.

A carriage turned off the main road, and Henriette cursed. She spat the sugarcane's fibrous flesh on the porch and slipped the rest of the stalk in her apron pocket.

Antoni helped a bashful woman out of the carriage and introduced her to the lines of bowing and curtsying enslaved people as his bride.

Henriette hid her trembling hands behind her apron. On Sundays, she did more than watch the enslaved dance the calinda at gatherings. She spread rumors that Antoni was unmarried because he was a sodomite.

—Whisper it in your master ear before you fill his bowl and before he go to sleep, she told the concubines. —You know how to make him believe.

It took only six months for Antoni to yield to this rumor that spread from planter to planter like a field fire.

With her new mistress in front of her, Henriette curtsied, gratitude bending her knees. She would do everything right for the new mistress, so she would never go back to Mobile, not even for a visit. High-waisted muslin dress in white, blond hair arranged to Antoni's liking—he would never leave her side. Henriette smiled at her replacement. *Now it is done*, she thought. *Now I am free.*

IT WAS A MISERABLY WET WINTER when Henriette settled into the understanding she had been naive.

—Mister Toni, her son said at the sound of drumming hooves.

From the window, she watched a lantern swaying through the dark over a horse and saddle, the shudder of light hastening down the slave row. The part of her that was still a girl prayed it was anyone else. The woman in her knew before her cabin door scraped across the wood floor behind her and before she smelled grass and leather, it would always be Antoni. The slave row she rejoiced over moving to after Antoni married wasn't far enough away. The only difference now was she had a partner in her misery, a timid wife who felt Antoni slipping in or out of their bed at sunrise. She whispered her displeasure only once. From the doorway, Antoni told her if being a planter's wife offended her sensibilities, she could go back to her parents in Mobile. Henriette understood she had been a fool to think replacing herself would work. To get rid of one white man, you needed a wealthier white man.

—Tell him to sell us, she told Mistress in the carriage headed for St. Louis Cathedral, where Mistress prayed for her marriage.

Mistress pulled her draping shawl around her bowed shoulders.

—Think of the children, Henriette. God will see us through.

—I know two gods. Both have closed eyes. Both have closed ears.

They passed white men and women on the streets, drifting as insignificant as clouds. Her body was filled with a hatred so raw, her hands shook, but it wasn't at them. It was Antoni. The day patrol brought her back to Verreaux; she thought she hated Royger, the runaway who turned her in. But then she understood some men were merely tools for others, which was no different from how Antoni used her. She sat with her hatred. Turned it over and studied it like the muslin she used to make dresses for Mistress. Why did she hate Antoni instead of everyone who stood idle while this hateful system existed? It wasn't the fleur-de-lis he had branded on her shoulder; indeed, he paid for that injustice three times over. It wasn't how he raised his linen handkerchief to bid on her at the auction, how he brushed his hair until it nested on the top of his head, or the anguish he caused Mistress. *What?*

—I could kill him, she told her weeping Mistress in the garden, the air thick and cloying with star jasmine. Mistress forbade her to ever speak those words again.

I could kill him, she thought while Antoni snored under the quilt she'd washed to rid it of his smell.

He left her cabin before dawn, yawning and folding a biscuit in his mouth. From their bed, her children watched her kindle a fire, their eyes large and green like stinging nettle, green like their papa's. She kissed each eye until it closed again, said a prayer for them, and whispered what she would do for love.

—I could kill him, she told the children.

CHAPTER 24

NOW

I WATCHED THE FIREWORKS, IMAGINING HENRIETTE TIED TO A CYPRESS TREE AT Verreaux. I imagined Dalena in a denim smock, painting images of freedom. I imagined myself, withered without wings under a glass jar.

Before me lay a state of strangers. Behind me, the man who vowed to never let me go. I didn't know Bastien's reason for sending the video of me in his office from four years ago, but I didn't need to relive what I said or what I believed that night. I didn't want to be that peculiar girl anymore.

An empty SPV crunched through the alley's loose gravel. I threw my Source in its path and watched the tires churn it into the pebbled ground.

Memphis, Lou, and Armie stood in the main part of the jewelry store. Their voices coasted into silence when they noticed me.

Memphis nodded his approval.

I placed my bag on the glass jewelry case and opened it.

Lou caught the sapphire necklace I tossed with one hand.

"Meet my conditions and we can do business," I said. "First, you'll take me off grid. This is not down payment; this is *the* payment. That necklace is worth enough that I shouldn't owe you anything else."

Lou held the necklace to the light overhead. "Done."

"Second, you'll make sure I'm not captured—"

"I may be big, but I don't do security."

"—by keeping your mouth shut about me. The moment I go off

grid, he's going to redouble his efforts to put boots on the ground. I don't need you going around New Orleans bragging about your part in fucking the official."

Armie stood, rolling the magazine in his fist. "Your brass is *the* official?"

"Was."

He tugged at his beard. I hoped this was the last time I saw that hatred on anyone's face.

"Boys in Dallas don't rank high enough for you? That's why I can't stand you slave-born bitches. Opening your legs for the first white man you see instead of telling them no, you ain't with it, and moving on to a nonrestricted state. We should be building nations."

"Hey, man, don't talk to her like that," Memphis said before I defended myself. "Some things won't make sense when you're born free. She had no choice."

"She's standing here now. She had a choice. What, you're telling me she was crated and imported like wine or oranges?"

"He's not telling you anything because I don't owe you my life history or anything else. Are you the configurator? I didn't think so."

Armie threw his magazine in his chair. "I bet you talk like that to everyone except that white man. That's who you shoulda—"

I said what would shut him up. "Hey, let me know when your money is as long as that white man's, then we talk respect."

Lou looked from Armie to me, then Armie again. His eyes darted to the door.

Armie grabbed a leather jacket from a chair. He rescued a hand-rolled cigarette that tumbled from the pocket. "Gimme your lighter."

Lou slapped a flash of yellow in Armie's hand. The door crept closed after Armie, allowing in pops of firecrackers or gunshots. Memphis pulled it the rest of the way and locked it.

"Don't worry about him," Lou said. "He's a hothead, but he's harmless. Don't worry about me either. I keep a low profile."

I glanced at Armie's chair. "Last—"

"It better be."

I was in my backyard at home again, Daddy mumbling about the electrician who had me in his truck, Daddy handing me his firearm, Daddy behind me, his hand supporting mine to correct an aim too wide. "I want a firearm before I leave here tonight."

AFTER LOU REMOVED ME FROM THE grid, Memphis gave me the rules. Don't look for him. Don't talk about this. Don't ruin it for the next person. He gave me an address of a woman in Lower Ninth Ward who rented rooms to women like me and said good luck.

The army green duffel bag disappeared into the crowds in the French Quarter, along with the vision of the two of us teaming up. I wouldn't let it bother me he was leaving me to fend for myself. It didn't matter that had we chosen different paths, he could've been my doctor, my dentist, my child's pediatrician. We could've been assigned to marry each other.

Without money, I had to walk instead of taking an SPV. Miles became the edge of town where space opened between buildings, the streets cracked unevenly, the crowds nonexistent.

It was midnight when I reached Lower Ninth Ward. Streetlights uncovered Ventura, a street of detached houses behind chain-link fences. Overgrown trees leaned against boarded-up windows, leaned over what once was. Red construction dumpsters, bicycles, and a series of SPV charging stations lined the curb in front of all except the house at the end. Freedom was that cream, two-story house with an iron-railed balcony. A corrugated plastic sign in the yard read

ROOM FOR RENT. ASK FOR BUTTER.

I rang the doorbell, listening for a chime that never came. After knocking twice, the semi-darkness beyond the curtains shifted to white-yellow. Curtains swept aside, a flash of eyes and nose, curtains again. Bolts scraped—one, two, three, and a chain rattled. A woman peered through a crack in the door.

"Why are you beating down my door like that?"

"Do you accept short-term rentals?"

"How short term?"

"Three days."

"Come in."

A foyer of peeling floral wallpaper and blue carpet welcomed me. My heels sank into the high pile, and I wished they would keep sinking until the pain in my feet disappeared.

The woman snapped two buttons of her housedress closed over heavy breasts with one hand and slid the bolts on the door with the other. "I can do three days. I'm Butter."

Of course, she was. Sixty if she was a day, but her skin rivaled the smoothness of the mango butter Mama whipped and jarred.

"Henriette."

Butter kept her eyes on me while fishing a cigarette from her housedress pocket. "Pretty little thing, ain't you? A doll baby. Where's your man? Why he let you walk these streets alone?"

"I don't have a man. I was told you rent to . . . women like me."

"Can't even say it, can you?" She laughed and poked the unlit cigarette between lips darkened from years of smoking. "What will you do for money for the next three days? I bet he froze you out."

"Yes ma'am, but I have jewelry to trade."

"Let me see what you got."

It took longer than it should've to take the sapphire bracelet from my bag and hand it to Butter. My empty hand fell to my thigh, free.

She held the bracelet up to the sprayed-gold chandelier with lopsided lampshades. "I can work with this. Three days. One room, private bath, clean linens, hot water. I make two meals a day, breakfast and dinner. If you need lunch, figure that out yourself. I'm not your mama, so don't expect me to clean up after you. Nobody will bother you here. I don't run that kind of place. Right now, ain't nobody here but me and you anyway, if you decide to stay." She looked at my bag. "Now, what else you got?"

"If you can work with that bracelet, anything else I have is my business."

The sapphires disappeared into her pocket. "You ain't fooling nobody, girl. I saw the bulletin. That crazy-ass man put a bounty on your head an hour ago. He put our Black asses on notice. Three hundred thousand for any information on your whereabouts. A million-dollar fine for anybody caught harboring you. Said if it's a man stupid enough to keep you, fines plus twenty years in Huntsville prison. Day for day, hard time. Translation? The official will break his foot off in the hind parts of any man who gets the notion he likes what he sees. Ten years in the fields upon release, if anything's left of him."

Threats and incentives were advantages Bastien had at his fingertips.

"He can't enforce that."

She sucked her teeth. "You told him that directly?"

The door was behind me, but it was so far away. Beyond it was endless walking and fatigue.

"Where you going?"

"Sorry to bother you at this hour." I fumbled with metal bolts on the door, got one of them loose. "Will that bracelet buy your silence for a few days at least? Give me a head start."

"I won't turn you in, Solenne. I want a little extra for risk."

"I may be tired, but I'm not stupid."

"If I was going to turn you in, I would've kept my mouth shut, let you go up there and get comfortable, and then called that man. Go if you want to go, and you can have your bracelet back if you do. But I'll tell you. Nobody sleeps in my bed but me, and I couldn't sleep with my own self if I helped that man steal you away from your home. When it's all said and done, he may get you, and he may get you good, but it won't be nobody here that helps him. That's why the penalty is more than the reward. He knows what he's doing."

I paid for her inconvenience with my earrings. She flipped to the end of a flat, leather-bound book she kept on her kitchen counter and handed me a pen. I traced a finger down the page.

Veronique Marsh
Tiffany Carl
Simone Harris . . .

And now, Solenne Bonet.

Butter led me up a staircase that pattered on as much as she did. We traveled a long hallway on a clear plastic floor runner.

"When the bulletin came through, I told my friend, 'Girl, the official stole that child from Dallas. Snatched her right from her mama's arms and won't let her go home.' Well, she said it, but I was fixing my mouth to say it. You called your mama and told her you're all right?"

She didn't wait for an answer. She chattered on as she unlocked the last door on the right. Four-poster bed, white bedding, white curtains. Beyond the curtains, moonlight shone on the rickety balcony, the stairs spiraling down to the front porch, and an SPV drifting past.

"Get you some rest. Tomorrow, get down there to Immigration. Apply for asylum."

Asylum. A person fleeing danger.

"It's probably best if I skip Immigration and go straight to Admin."

"Immigration handles applications. Admin handles escalations."

That night, sleep didn't come easily. I lay on stiff sheets thinking of the winter of 1806 when a Fulani girl made a life-altering decision. My fingers ached for a pen.

WHEN I AWOKE, I WAS ALONE. No legs and arms vined mine until muted. No one breathed me in then exhaled what was left. No one urged me to stay. Arm outstretched, palm up, I reached for the coved ceiling. Closing one eye made the brass light fixture disappear.

Like my digital presence and profile.

I ran my finger over my thumb where my chip lay somewhere inside, empty. That's when I understood. The knowing was sharp, but distant, the kind of knowledge that gifts itself through low-lying fog.

I missed him.

I ran five hundred miles away, resisted his messages, killed his software in my body, walked to a stranger's house in the dark, and I still missed him. Why couldn't anything ever be easy when it came to him?

Damn him.

"This is my new life. I'm here."

The sun agreed with that. Henriette agreed with that.

The faucet whistled and vibrated under my hand before sending water like it was in pain. I took another shower more out of habit than necessity, brushed my teeth, and managed to create a braid without a comb or oil.

I sat in bed with the contents of my bag in front of me. Journals, hairbrush, a silk scarf, lipstick, and two pieces of jewelry—three, if I counted my promise ring. I wouldn't. On the bullet train, I'd looked at the diamond clip in my hair, my rings, bracelet, earrings, and necklace, and it looked like so much. Now what was left looked like a week of shelter. Less, if I needed to trade for supplies. I put everything back in the bag except for the firearm. That hid under the mattress.

I followed the smell of bacon down to the kitchen, where Butter stood in front of a gas stove, alternating between arranging bacon on a plate of paper towels and flipping hand-size pancakes. It smelled like Daddy's breakfasts when I was too small to reach the tabletop without bed pillows in my chair.

"Did I sleep with you last night?" she asked. I hadn't walked into an older Black woman's kitchen in so long I forgot not being first to say good morning was akin to declaring war.

"No ma'am. I'm sorry. Good morning."

"I hope you plan on getting yourself down there to Immigration. The earlier the better."

"That's one thing on the agenda."

I'd go into that office and beg if I had to. Off grid or not, it meant nothing if I couldn't stay in the state.

She nodded to a cherrywood table in the middle of the kitchen. A wooden gate to keep a small child or animal out swung open against my knee. I saw why Butter didn't offer lunch. Grits, pancakes, bacon, fruit, nuts, biscuits—she cooked enough for five people, and she was still at it. She wanted me to watch while she cooked and listen to her talk about life and Bastien. Mostly Bastien. "Chile, they really don't smile? So you're telling me, that's not just a public thing." The more she talked, the worse Bastien became, and the more she gave me. She started with a plate of food heaped with three servings then gave me an unlinked Source loaded with three hundred dollars. The way she saw it, the jewelry covered it.

"You don't like bacon?"

Grease bubbled on top of crisp curls of meat. "No ma'am. Bastien doesn't eat pork."

"I don't recall asking what he eats. I asked if you like bacon."

After breakfast, I mentioned going shopping for clothes and hair stuff. She shook her head. We sat on porcelain tile sorting through a trunk from her attic clothes, right next to the table with dishes still piled on it. Jeans, pants, skirts, hooded shirts, flat shoes, all mine and it wouldn't cost me anything extra.

"What, you don't like the clothes?"

"I appreciate them. I was thinking about how I have nowhere to go and how hard all of this is. It's been one day, and I'm tired already."

Sympathetic faces usually felt patronizing, but I needed it today. "You ain't tired yet. You're still breathing." She held up a dress two sizes too big for me then shoved it back in the trunk. "Whereabout your people come from? Can you trace your lineage back before the second civil war?"

I pulled out a tan hooded shirt, worn soft. "Louisiana. The hurricane pushed them into Texas a year before the United States became the Order."

"Terrible timing. You wouldn't be sitting in front of me now had that not happened. That water takes and takes, don't it? Last one took every house on this block except mine. I'm still here. The Order cut off funding to rebuild, saying these neighborhoods ain't worth much, like my family ain't lived in Lower Ninth Ward since 1875.

Still good people in this world though. Somebody up north started a program to rebuild these houses. That's why you see those dumpsters lining the blocks." She grunted, planted a hand on the table, and pulled herself to a stand. "Knees are louder than the firecrackers from last night."

She laughed when I did.

"And where did the official tell you his people come from?" She pressed a button, and the gas stove ticked until blue flames circled a burner. The tip of her cigarette flirted with the blur. "History books say his people come from Germany and France. Descended from Officer Nicolas Martin himself."

Officer *Nikolai* Martin. His grandfather's portrait was framed over the fireplace in our dining room.

Butter handed me a dress from deep in the trunk and released a cloud of smoke. "Those patriots . . . faces don't move, hunting folks, taking girls from their homes. I don't think they come from Europe at all. That type of evil is not of this world."

Staring out at the vacant street beyond hazy windowpanes, I waited to feel something. Shame for still loving Bastien. Anger at Butter for speaking about someone she couldn't understand. Frustration for not fully understanding him myself.

I felt nothing.

CHAPTER 25

THEN

I WONDERED ABOUT HIM SOMETIMES. WHY DID A MAN WHO HAD EVERYTHING look sad so often? Why couldn't he find a reason to smile? What was he thinking when he stood at the window wall looking down at the lake when the sky was near black?

I wondered when he replaced my hand with his on the buttons of my dress, that ever-present conflict in his eyes. "If you look back at this moment one day and see your hand unbuttoning your dress, you'll hate yourself. You never forgive the person who made you hate yourself."

How could I blame him for anything when I knew monsters? Men with greedy fingers. The electrician who waited for me in his truck behind my school. My ancestor Antoni Dubois whose grip shrouded the branches of my family tree in confusion and heartache.

"I'm not like them. We're not like other people, are we?" he said when I was naked from the waist up. Goose bumps stippled his arms, round like teardrops, mine or some other lonely girl's.

I COULDN'T SEE THE END, BUT it existed. Eventually, he would move on and marry, and one day, when I was a nonrestricted woman in Louisi-ana, I would tell the story of a man who was good to me. No one would understand the real story, so I would create one they would. I would change his name to Phoenix or Khalid. He would have locs, scars on his hands, and a tragic ending—one where the only reason we weren't together was because he was killed overseas.

Then they would understand me.

I watched him pack for a trip hundreds of miles away. "Why do you have to go?"

He unzipped a black suitcase that lay next to me, peeled it open, laid the starchy suits and ties inside. "I'm meeting with Lucas Magnan, the administrator of Georgia. Riots have gotten out of control over the past week. He's asking for military assistance."

The man they sent Dalena to. I would never tell him I knew her. Black girls were judged by who they considered the worst among us, and I'd overheard Julian say Dalena was difficult.

"But you meet with him on Source all the time. Why can't you keep doing that?"

"I'm ambassador. Did you assume I would never go back into the field?"

I hadn't thought about him being ambassador. Since he returned to Austin, that position had become separate from him, something I viewed as the past.

He lifted my chin and saw my fear. Men didn't go into war zones and return. "With government officials, it's different. I'm not on the ground, policing. No gunfire, no combat. Just meetings."

"Take me with you."

"I can't work and monitor your safety at the same time."

"I'd be on base," I said. "I'm sure there are enough soldiers there."

"I can't leave you on a military base."

"Take me to your meetings. I wouldn't say anything. I'd sit quietly in the corner and read a book. No one would know I—"

"No. Final." He zipped the suitcase. "You shouldn't press that way. It makes you look weak. Like a child."

"I didn't really want to go. I don't care if you leave." I shoved against his chest and stood. Knocked his hand away from my body. Ended up caught in his grasp anyway. "I want to go back to my dorm—"

He grasped my chin, catching me off guard. "*Never* speak about leaving me. You'll stay here"—he pointed at the floor—"four days. Confirm you understand."

I left him there, my fists so tight they ached, and sat alone on the porch watching the boats drift, the Texas flags streaming from poles.

His hand on my shoulder. He opened his fist and showed me a string of oval-cut blue jewels. His mother wore a similar bracelet in her portrait that hung in his office.

"They're sapphires," he said, responding to the confusion in my eyes. His fingers looked strange fastening something so pretty and small onto my wrist.

"I can keep this?" Twisting my wrist under the lights created its own. Nobody from home had anything like this.

"I had it made for you."

My arms vined his like sweet pea tendrils. If I clung there awhile, I could absorb everything inside.

ONCE, A POWERFUL MAN PINCHED OFF a section of clay from a slab, sprinkled it with water, and kneaded it into the shape of me with the warmth of his hands. He whispered, and the creation came to life. He left me on a shelf enclosed in glass to sun dry. When he returned, he would study me. That crack he created at the breastbone, was it so he could seep inside and fill me with himself? Would he still hold the soles of my feet to his lips and say he'd never seen anything more perfect?

I rolled over in bed and looked into Jefferson's eyes. On the dresser below him lay a stack of nightgowns and dresses.

Service slipped around the room wearing blue shoe covers, polishing glass, and removing nonexistent dust from furniture. Her sterile gaze rolled over me like something else she needed to rub clean.

"He would've taken me with him if he could've," I told that old bat. "He wants to keep me safe."

She raised her eyebrows and turned away as if she'd heard a lie.

I pulled the sheets over my head and sank back into solitude.

I waited for him there. But I didn't dream of Bastien. I dreamed of Abraham addressing the Order on stage. Behind him, wearing a sapphire bracelet, was Francesca.

FROM THE CEILING, THE BLACK GUARDIANS hummed every few minutes. Ten, lined like soldiers, sending a digital feed of my activity into the unknown. I wandered from door to door, depressing handles that didn't budge, staring out of glass panes. I was alone, locked inside this glasshouse. The feeling wasn't unlike the days rebellion brought agents to Dallas, and we hid from muddy men in the school's book closet. Guidry didn't have to hiss for us to hush. We sat still as portraits, watching spiders bury themselves in cracked brown linoleum. We waited for the screaming sirens to quiet.

Nightfall brought racing thoughts. Was Bastien asleep, or did he lie in bed next to Francesca, doing what he did to me?

Peeling apart rectangles of underwear and undershirts in drawers revealed no secrets. Everything was uniform. No small, lacy things lay tucked underneath undershirts. The closets filled wall to wall with black had no dresses hidden between. Arms stretched deep into the vanity cabinets, I found no secret feminine hair products among the carefully ordered shampoo, conditioner, and lotion bottles.

But the vase Francesca gave him was right there in the open. I wrapped it in a cleaning towel I found in a laundry room cabinet and pushed it to the bottom of the trash bag that Service would take out tomorrow. The knot between my shoulder blades loosened by the time I got back to the bedroom.

Source was buzzing on the nightstand. My heart skipped when I saw the random string of digits from an anonymous handle.

"Why are you still awake, Solenne?"

Hearing his voice, I was the rag doll he stretched out in bed next to him.

"I can't sleep."

He sighed, weary. "You haven't tried."

"I have."

THE BLUEPRINT | 165 |

"Try again." A pause. "I'm waiting."

The cameras forced me back into bed, where I pulled the sheets over my head. "Can you come back? I hate being here alone."

Before he could answer, I was shoved into his background noise. Voices, glasses, laughter. The lilt of a woman's voice, sitting-distance close.

"You're tired," he said, and like hypnosis, I was. "And I have things to accomplish before I get back to the base."

He disconnected, and my thoughts became quicksand.

I got out of bed and poured a trickle of whiskey from a crystal decanter at the bar. Facing the cameras, I sipped. It grabbed my mouth and chest into a hot fist.

Source remained silent. He wasn't watching me anymore.

Outside the bedroom, I found the other giants that lived there. After a minute of protesting over leaving their rug, the dogs followed me into Bastien's bedroom. They would go no farther than the foot of the bed, but at least I wasn't alone. Hera settled her head against my feet. I liked to think she sensed my disquiet, and this was her way of soothing me.

Zeus slept while Hera and I lay awake watching the moon and lake interlock in a thread of silver. My fingers danced over the sapphires on my wrist. I was here in Bastien's bed. Not anyone else. That meant something, didn't it? With the stones of Hera's sapphire collar cool against my feet, dreams opened, and I fell into them asking the leaden sky to lie to me once more.

• • •

SOLENNE: Good morning.

SOLENNE: Are you still asleep?

He couldn't be. If he were here, by now he would have eaten breakfast and gone into his office.

SOLENNE: Are you working?

He would be having lunch by now, polishing off a plate heaped with seared chicken and greens.

SOLENNE: I haven't heard from you all day.

SOLENNE: I know you're working, but it only takes a second to reply.

SOLENNE: OK. Since you hate me, I won't bother you again.

I didn't want to talk to him anyway. Starting part three of Henriette was more important, and I hadn't been able to write anything since I'd been here. I traded the blue journal for the brown one and stretched out in Bastien's bed. The window walls and white sheets and cameras faded until I was in 1805 on the front porch of Verreaux Plantation.

The sounds that drowned out the scratch of my pen weren't horses whinnying as the coachman led them away to be watered. It was Hera and Zeus. I left the bedroom and found Service in the kitchen, placing silver bowls licked clean in a plastic bucket. She didn't look up at me as she led the dogs to the door. The dogs did what I couldn't. They shot out of the door, bellowing down the stairs and already at the water's edge before she straightened her stooped back. She propped the door open with the bucket. It bowed under the door's weight, seconds away from slipping away and locking me inside this glass jar for another long night. When her motherly blue eyes finally met mine and she nodded once, I understood she wanted to set me free.

CHAPTER 26

NOW

THE WAITING AREA OF THE IMMIGRATION OFFICE STANK OF LEATHER, TOBACCO, and onions. A dozen men sat on leather sofas or stood shoulders and heels against oak-paneled walls. Their eyes slid over me before darting to boots or nail beds, both laced with half a day's work. One held a boy on his lap, crossing a bulky arm over him to prevent him from climbing down.

An officer sat at the security desk with business-size Source screens suspended from the ceiling. His lunch leaked from a plate covered with wrinkled aluminum foil.

"Name please?" he asked, eyes still on Source.

No point in lying. Once he saw me, a hooded shirt wouldn't be enough to hide who I was.

"Solenne Bonet."

That got his attention. "Reason for your visit?"

"A private matter. Can you tell me if someone can meet with me? It's imperative that I speak with someone today."

He tapped the white patch on his chest with his name etched underneath. Officer Steed. "That's above my pay grade. My job is to sign you in. They'll get to you when they get to you." He nodded toward the bank of empty seats in the women's section of the waiting area. "You can either take a seat or come back another time."

I jerked my bag onto my shoulder. "I really can't wait. This is urgent."

He lifted the foil and pulled a plastic fork from his top drawer. "Do you stay or go?"

Number fourteen was printed on the ticket the dismissive bastard passed across the desk. "I'll get you logged in." He stared at me until I faded into a seat.

The men were statues, stationary and brooding. None spared me so much as a glance, except the toddler balancing on his father's knee, wetting the frayed edges of a blanket between his teeth.

"Ms. Bonet?" Officer Steed stood, frowning.

I grabbed my bag, trying to disguise my surprise that I'd been pushed to the front of the line within seconds. "Yes."

"*The* official is connected. He'd like an immediate word with you."

WHEN I BEGAN WRITING *MY HENRIETTE* five years ago, I dissected her words. They were muddied by emotion. She grabbed at random times and events and trying to sequence her life kept me awake some nights. I needed the straight line from girl, to concubine, to mama, to woman. I understood now why that line didn't exist. We never truly leave any part of ourselves behind, no matter how much we change.

I wasn't a woman, nested between mannequins in a boutique called Hammer's. A woman would've taken Bastien's call in the Immigration office, stood her ground, and explained why she was ending what should've never been. I was a child who feared being broken by his voice passing from one device to the other, the depth of him stealing my air. I was a little girl scanning those streets beyond a storefront window, expecting Bastien, Julian, a convoy of MVs, jets, drones, and rifles to appear out of nowhere.

Bastien wasn't here. He couldn't jet into the state with staff anytime he pleased. Whether I ran from buildings and refused to talk to him, he couldn't do anything about it. There was a system of checks and balances. I still had two more days before he came in from Texas. Two more days before he got me good.

"Are you actually going to buy anything?" the salesgirl asked from behind me. "If not, it's best you move on. You've been here an hour."

I ran my fingertips over the mannequin's deep V-neck minidress with a peacock print. "I'll try this on."

With the dressing room door latched behind me, I sat on the tufted bench to think. Bastien knew where I was now, even without my chip feeding information into Source. When Steed logged me into the system, Bastien called to put me and probably Immigration on notice. There were no women in that office. I was the only dummy who strolled in there instead of having a man apply on my behalf. I couldn't go back. There was no telling what Bastien or Julian threatened them with.

"How does it fit?" the salesgirl called impatiently.

I bought the dress I hadn't tried on and a makeup kit for one hundred and five dollars. By the time I made it back to Butter's, I was down to eighty dollars.

"It goes fast," Butter said from the sofa. "That man's zeros have you confused. First lesson: What's his ain't yours."

"I know that. I have one bag to my name, and I'm here paying for everything in jewelry, right?"

She propped her socked feet on the coffee table, preparing to dress down a child. "While you don't have a man taking care of you, you have to learn how to conserve. How much you have left?"

"Two hundred," I lied.

She sucked her teeth. "That man didn't do you no favors, did he?"

"Ma'am?"

"Had you thinking you could have it all—freedom, money, the whole world, long as you made him call upon the Lord every night." She hoisted herself up, using the arm of the sofa. "If you have any sense at all, and I know you do, you'd return whatever is in that bag and save the money. You'll need it."

In the kitchen, she removed a mauve oven mitt hanging from a hook over the stove and searched it. "Here. Try to sell this to get you some more money."

"No ma'am. I paid what we agreed to. I can take care of myself."

"Chile, doing what? Ain't nothing free except Jesus, especially in New Orleans." She slapped my sapphire bracelet in my hand. "Take it. You don't take it, the official won't have to find you. You'll be begging him to take you back by the end of the week. Now sit down at that table so I can fix you some lunch."

FOR THE REST OF THE AFTERNOON, I cycled between watching for Bastien through windows and helping Butter clean empty rooms. While we hung vinegar-smelling sheets on a clothesline, I told her about Bastien trying to reach me at Immigration. She waved it off and said New Orleans was a big place. She called me Tati without noticing. The second time, she caught herself. Her fair skin flushed with embarrassment that she called me her daughter's name.

"Does Tatiana live nearby?" I asked later, while sitting at the table chopping sweet potatoes for dinner. Butter shook seasoning into a roiling pot of chicken thighs.

She nodded toward the foggy window as if Tati stood there now. "Ten miles down the road. I don't see her and the baby much anymore. I fell out with her husband. Said I was overstepping boundaries and putting things in Tati's head after the baby came. He never did like how independent I was."

"Is that why your second husband had your marriage annulled?"

"What makes you think he did?"

"Earlier, you said you were single because you need to be the boss."

"Oh no, baby." She threw her head back and laughed. "He up and died on me. My friend said I stressed that man out so bad the only way he could get rest was to lay down and die. But after my first marriage, I wasn't taking no mess."

"What happened with the first?"

"I met him when I was too young. A tall, blue-black man. Loved him as soon as he smiled, but that man didn't love me. Never did, never would. Hate and one-way love hurts the same. So I can sympathize with you. I know how quick being with a man who could never love you breaks you down."

Because she saw me the way I saw Henriette. Broken from trusting Rousseau, who sent her and her brother to the New Orleans shore to be sold with the rest of the inventory. Destroyed when she learned Antoni could hurt her far worse than the evening he had her branded with the fleur-de-lis.

I stayed quiet through the rest of her chatter, focusing on slicing sweet potatoes in perfect eighths. The slip of the knife through flesh, the thump of the knife on the wooden cutting board.

"I say something that bothered you?" Butter asked from the sink.

I tried but couldn't talk myself out of asking. "Is every story the same? How do you know he never loved me?"

Butter sighed. "You girls come through here, half of you hating him, half of you still thinking it was love. Somebody smile and throw you a life preserver, and you call it love when he was the one drowning you in the first place. You have the same trains and vehicles there that we have here. Same feet to run. Most of what keeps you in chains is up here." She tapped a finger against her temple. "It can't be love when he holds that much power over you."

I set the knife down, trying not to take her words as condescension. "So you're telling me I've been stupid for five years?"

"Not stupid. A girl *child*. So your birthday passed, and they say you're a woman now, you're ready to take a man, you're ready for everything he's ready for when he done lived his life and got fifteen or twenty more years of experience than you do. That don't make it true. Can't tell a man what you want when you're still a child, and you can't make heads or tails of what love is when you don't even understand who you are. He knows that. Always did. Now what you gone decide you know?"

I LAY IN BED THAT NIGHT listening to Butter's measured steps in the kitchen below and replaying her words that Bastien could never love me because he had power I didn't. Did that mean that no man in the Order, Black or white, could love any woman? My daddy held power over my mama, and I was sure they were in love.

Was the desire for freedom our crossroads? When a woman chose the path of independence, did that mean everything behind her was ugly and existed only until forgotten? No, pretending the beautiful didn't exist was as flawed as pretending the bad didn't. No one, nothing, was all bad or all good. Life was too complex. Had it been nothing but bad, leaving would've been easy. Butter wasn't there the nights I was on my knees begging God for the strength to leave. After years, I had done it. Why couldn't I decide what I was leaving behind?

Mama once told me you love from your origins. Since people were made up of different experiences, none of us get to decide exactly what love looked like. I asked to be loved. Searched for it. I found his soul, loved it even though it was gray, then became the woman jolted awake in the middle of the night by knowing. Knowing he held my life in his fist, but knowing I wouldn't have been better off with anyone else. At some point, that knowing took form and existed outside of me. I could only peer out of a dark place at it, stacking and cementing a brick at a time until I was sealed inside where nothing made sense. We had never been like other people. Those words—were they Bastien's words or mine?

Love, it could be nothing else, Bastien reasoned on nights our arguments exhausted him. Eyes closed, he asked, *What besides love or death pins you to the ground to rub pain into your skin?*

Like a little boy abandoned to wander in the mountains where the golden dusk was indiscriminate from dawn, everywhere I turned looked like confusion.

I AWOKE TO A SOUND IN the dark. Moonlight sliced the room in half, my half was the darkest.

"Butter?"

Silence, but in the distance, movement. The old staircase creaked under someone's feet. Two sets of feet. Julian? One of my shadows? I tiptoed to the bedroom door and tested the lock, not that it would do me any good.

Muffled voices in the hallway. "I make two meals a day, but I won't clean up after you."

"No ma'am. I don't expect you to," a man said.

"Then why are you here? Already tired of chasing women all hours of the night? I never let my girl rip and run the streets during Mardi Gras when she was young. I told her, ain't nothing open that late at night except hotels and your legs."

"Yes ma'am," the man said, sounding weary of Butter's chatter. "But like I said downstairs, I don't need a room."

"You didn't tell me that."

"Yes ma'am, I did. You talked over me."

"Don't tell me what I did."

"Didn't mean to disrespect."

"You don't need a room, then what do you need?"

"I'm looking for the belly warmer."

"The who?"

"The bed wench. You seen her?"

"I don't know nothing about that, and if your name ain't on the deed, you won't talk like that in this house."

The floorboards right outside my door interrupted them.

"Yes ma'am. Thought she came this way."

Through the gap in the door that didn't lie flush with the frame, Armie stood in the hallway next to Butter, glittering belt buckle and pistol at his waist. I closed my eyes. This sweating-in-the-winter, ashy-knuckled, stupid-belt-buckle-wearing bastard.

"You seen the updated bulletin? Updated the reward to five hundred thousand dollars," Armie said.

"Lord have mercy on that poor child. Some of those men won't quit."

"Nah, he won't, that's why I need to get to her first. We got somewhere in Metairie we can move her to."

I was sinking again, water above and below. This was my new

life, wandering in the dark, wondering who to trust, searching for a place to hide until there was none.

"Well . . ." Butter said, wavering.

Henriette trusted a runaway named Royger around a campfire. He turned her in for leniency after he was captured. Knotted muscles and stomach, I pulled on my jeans and hoodie that still smelled like outside and Butter's old trunk. Everything else went into my bag, the firearm from under the mattress first.

"Have you seen her or not?" Armie asked impatiently.

At the window, I lifted the curtain with one finger. Porch lights dashed white over the lawn. No MVs. No soldiers waited for me. The SPV that brought Armie to the house idled at a charging station. Its lights lowered while it powered down.

The window was old but opened fluidly. Thick, damp wind. Palm fronds rustling. The final hum of the SPV's engine. Behind me, the house shuddered like ghosts walked overhead in hallways. Heat poured through ceiling vents.

I climbed out the window, slid it closed. I swore those old stairs swayed under my feet while I tiptoed down. The SPV powered on when I slipped into the backseat. The digital screen on the dashboard showed a balance of thirty-two remaining. I pressed *Confirm* and buckled in. Butter's house behind me, I acknowledged what I knew the moment Bastien tried to reach me at Immigration. Butter's house was too good to be true, and if I wanted to win, I had to keep moving until I no longer felt him in the air.

CHAPTER 27

THEN

LEAVING A BIRD'S CAGE OPEN WILL COMPEL IT TO STRETCH ITS WINGS. SERVICE knew that when she propped the door open for me. So I opened my wings and flew away from the Government District to James's house in Round Rock.

The house didn't feel like James. Dark walnut floors, exposed beams, and rich reds on wall tapestries. Out of place in this house, Baby, James's black and white rabbit, hopped freely from room to room. I reached for him, but he moved faster and hid under the end of a throw blanket pooling from an ottoman. James scooped him under his arm.

After a brief tour of living areas and the kitchen, he led me to the backyard and down a flagstone path to a greenhouse. Inside of the structure was greens, bursts of red, and misty air.

"Robert can have every room in that house. This is my place." He ushered Baby into a wire cage in a corner. "He never comes out here."

He walked me through, pointing out flowering plants and red and spotted green strawberries hanging in white pots. I stretched on my toes to reach them, asking "Can I" but not waiting for the answer. I had to know if something so perfect could be real. He handed me a small plastic bucket, and we pinched and twisted dozens from green vines he called runners. We washed them in a deep porcelain sink housed between two potting benches.

James switched off the water and handed me a towel. "So do you plan to tell me where you've been for twelve days, and why when I tracked your location after lying awake panicking you were on the side of a road, dead, Source said 'user does not exist'?"

I couldn't lie to him. "I was with the official."

His face changed as if readying himself for a speech, but he only asked, "And where is he now?"

"Delta Base, outside of Atlanta. He won't be back for three days."

I couldn't read his eyes.

He opened a wicker deck box and pulled out a blanket and a stack of relics wrapped in plastic. He smiled conspiratorially. "They're reprints, but I saved these for you." He knew how to put a smile on my face. He walked around humming and pulling weeds while I lay on the blanket, leafing through old fashion magazines with strawberry-sticky fingers.

After some time, James settled next to me on the blanket. We studied the bruised sky through glass. It was then he said Albert ended their affair because he wouldn't end his marriage to Robert. He couldn't, he said. He remembered those low days when Robert was taking two thermoses to work, one full of gin, the other to secretly vomit into while he sat bleary-eyed in the cockpit of the planes he was paid to operate. Bound by something that resembled love, how was he to trust that a divorce wouldn't send Robert spiraling again?

"Suddenly, he's too tired to deal with my issues, when I patted his back and said 'Okay honey' for two years before our affair started. I asked nothing of him, and maybe that ended up being our problem. You can't imagine experiencing this level of pain while trying to hide it from the man you're married to." He never spoke about Albert and Robert at the same time, keeping his two worlds from colliding. I wanted him to know I understood. I knew what it meant to want and lose, to wait and lose. I told him everything about Bastien, starting with the day he held my hand for the first time. It felt good to finally release our story to someone who would understand.

But he climbed to his feet like he needed distance. Said my story was disturbing and that this couldn't go any way but poorly.

"You thought it could work with Albert."

"It's different for men like us. He needed me. You need someone, anyone, when you're figuring out you're different in a place like the Order. My God. I can't explain it."

"Not without telling me how we're different."

He rubbed his temples with a forefinger and thumb. "You know they do this to Black girls. They don't rape. No, gentlemen don't do that. They promise and purchase gifts. They make sure they never hear no. Pettit did it five times that I know of. You can't have freedom while lying in the bed of a man who writes laws to oppress you." He searched my body with his eyes. "What did he give you before he left? A necklace, a bracelet, pretty dresses to placate you while he travels with a white woman on his arm?"

"He's traveling with Julian," I said, because I needed to be right.

"Sweetheart, *no*. They also take women to meetings with heads of state. They work over dinner or drinks. Networking."

He'd taken away my ability to lie to myself, and at that moment, I hated him for it. The woman I heard last night, Bastien ignoring my messages—James made it real. The pit of my stomach opened like a box, and everything I held inside spilled out at my feet.

From somewhere in the greenhouse, James said, "I blame myself. I should've stood my ground for once in my small life and never sent you to him. I'm sorry. I'm sorry that they're all like this."

THE RAIN STARTED. JAMES COAXED ME into staying overnight and taking the train home in the morning. He rushed me through a tour of the room off the kitchen, kissed me on both cheeks, and apologized for the heat of the discussion in the greenhouse.

"You're young. You have so much ahead of you."

"Like what?"

What exactly did I have in this world? More ways to find out how worthless I was? I was tired thinking about it.

His hands settled on my shoulders. "Like Louisiana. I can sign your document. If you're ready to go now, say the word."

I nodded. I would spend the week with Mama, pack, and do what we all wanted: Start over. Find our way in a place where our presence was welcomed. More than five hundred miles from Bastien's heartbeat would be my cure.

Source beeped in his shirt pocket, catching him off guard. "I'll start the application now," he said before leaving.

Robert needed him, but I needed someone, too. The image of Dalena in Georgia sitting on a sun porch with Source in her hand, huffing until her bangs danced against her forehead was so vivid, I believed she would answer my call this time. The line rang endlessly.

STANDING UNDER THE SCALDING SHOWER FOR too long wrinkled the pads of my fingers and toes. Air drying, I held the drapes back to watch drizzles of rain become tiny rivers that flowed downhill to the iron gate. My thoughts raced between Bastien and Frank Pettit, traveling the distance from my brain to my stomach like lightning.

Was I plucked from dozens of others like wenches on a slave ship to fulfill some fantasy? I thought of girls with sweeps of black curls like mine—brown skin dewy from Pettit's sweat, flattened under his blond-dusted chest and promises. Had Bastien done to me what Pettit intended to do?

"I'm *stupid*."

I walked around making a fool of myself, pretending I was more than I was. He could never want anything from me except sex because that's all I was. It's all we ever were. Every cell in my body screamed until it had no voice. I hurt everywhere.

Source beeped from the nightstand, and a stupid little girl rushed over and picked it up. Alert: Torrential rains until . . .

I powered it off and arched it at the farthest wall. I unclasped the bracelet and let it join Source. The meaning of it had changed in the greenhouse.

I wrote our story in my head. When I got to the parts I couldn't unknot, I pictured an ivory box with a hinged lid and a silver lock. Let the pain flutter inside, entombed. The rain pattered on around me like it never wanted to let go.

• • •

THE WEIGHTED SOUNDS SURROUNDING ME WEREN'T part of my dream where I stood on the shore watching a military ship sail away during a storm.

I sat up in the dark, fumbling for the lamp's switch.

Another sharp sound pulled me from the tangle of blankets. I stepped into the darkened hallway as James swept past, white silk pajamas and Source a flash in the dark.

"What's going on?"

"Nothing. Go back to your room, sweetheart." He didn't sound like it was nothing. A series of knocks echoed. James pressed his thumb against a keypad on the front door, then threw it open. Sweeping rain, a convoy of lights stretched at the bottom of the driveway, hooded tactical windbreaker that made all but Julian's and Bastien's eyes disappear.

"She's a child," James said. His lips moved with no sound, a dry run to say something else.

"That you intended to send to an unstable state alone," Julian said.

Robert emerged from a hallway, tugging a white undershirt over his head, confused. Julian spoke to him, but I couldn't hear it. My ears were filled with rag doll cotton.

He approached Bastien, shoulders so low he was nearly on his belly. "Official, please accept my apologies. I missed the call from your strategist."

"You missed eighteen calls," Julian corrected.

Robert gaped at James. "Pardon my confusion, but James said the girl is assigned to him."

Bastien walked around the living area in muddy boots, pausing to study art on the walls and tables.

"My apologies, but I can assure you, James and I operated with full integrity. Dinner. Protein, vegetables, bread. No alcohol. They talked, and then I gave her a spare bedroom." Robert nodded to the tiny cameras on the ceiling I hadn't noticed. "I'd be happy to turn over my feed for verification."

"The upload is processing," Bastien said, accusatory eyes on me. "I made a transfer to your account for her dinner, linens, and room."

"I got the notification. The amount is excessive."

"For your time," Bastien continued, "the floors, and your gate. For the Order."

Robert turned to Julian, desperation for acceptance in his eyes. "You work at the Mexican border? Drone pilot? I did some drone piloting myself."

"*Former* drone pilot. Your intel is behind by about three years." By his tone, he was annoyed to be reminded of where he came from. He cocked his head at James. "Have we met?"

"No, I don't believe we have."

The men stared at each other until James looked away.

"Can James and I offer you men a drink? I bought a good bottle yesterday."

Bastien shook his head once. "We're leaving as soon as Solenne gets dressed."

James held out a hand to me, but Julian stepped forward, partially blocking James from my view. "Now I remember where we met. Albert. The two of you were at the writer retreat in Brookings."

James wilted, hearing Albert's name in front of his husband. I hated seeing James like that, my articulate friend, fumbling for words. Robert scanned faces for pieces of an untold story.

"I was with him in Brookings. No one named Albert was there," I said to my hands, and I waited for the James who said he regretted ever sending me to Bastien to appear.

"I was in Brookings," James said. "Solenne was with me."

"Ah. The mistake is my own." Julian smiled at James, pearly and chilling. "You don't have the face of a man who makes many mistakes."

James looked between me and Robert. He closed his eyes and exhaled. With Robert at his side, he left me. Their bedroom door closed like silent lips. Time passed with only the beat of the rain on the roof, the rhythm of water rushing through gutters.

"You know nothing of men," Bastien said, because I was still waiting. "James Gibson is unstable. One dysfunctional relationship after another. He will never care about you more than himself."

I rested my forehead against the brass on Bastien's shirt. My thoughts were so cloudy when he was in Austin, in a room with me, beside me, breathing. My brain was coiled too tightly. The ivory box was opening on its own.

"Anyone who can leave someone behind so easily is heartless," he said.

My body was weary from being no one. I needed my mama.

"I want to go home."

"We're going home."

"No, back to my dorm, then home to Dallas."

He lifted my chin. "I'll take you back to your dorm. Take your train to Dallas in the morning."

I should've declined, but because I still didn't truly understand him, I looked at the tremor in his fingers and said, "Okay."

CHAPTER 28

THEN

THE MV'S ENGINE ROARED ON I-35. I COULDN'T IGNORE HIS ARM AROUND MY shoulders. It had the same effect as him telling me I was tired last night over Source. My eyes didn't want to stay open.

The MV ticked to a stop. Red brake lights for as far as I could see.

Julian checked the map on the dashboard. "Traffic for eight miles."

"ETA?" Bastien asked, impatience in his voice and his fingers now almost completely encircling my knee.

Julian's eyes met mine in the rearview mirror. "Thirty-two minutes."

That was long enough. I could memorize everything about him and have this ride as our final memory instead of him in Georgia with a woman, or that strange look in his eyes standing in James's foyer, or the low blend of his voice with Julian's when they called James an idiot who should be in jail for trying to send someone so young to Louisiana with those people and a hurricane watch.

"You will never be safe in Louisiana, Solenne. You'd have no one to look after you. There is nothing there for you."

I yawned. "Nothing here either."

He had a face now. A bead of light from the door panel uncovered the underside of his chin, the sharp point of his nose, one of his eyes. "I would worry about you."

"Worry?" He didn't say he would miss me. *Worry*.

The MV jerked to switch lanes, pushing me deep into the seat and away from him. He pulled me back under his arm. "Worry, despair, agonize."

Despair. The word was full in my mouth. Despair. Spair. Speer. Like a dagger to the heart. I traced it on his chest with my pointer finger, rubbed my cheek against the threads of his shirt until it hurt, and drifted to sleep that way.

THE IRON GATE CLANGED SHUT AFTER a line of MVs, their red orbs of light startling the dark, the tires grinding against gravel—this was what I woke up to. Julian and Bastien stood in a wedge of light seeping from our MV's open door, not in front of my dorm, but in Bastien's driveway. Bastien reached for me as if everything was normal. "Let's go inside and get some rest."

He hadn't listened to a damn thing I said earlier. "I'm not going in."

"I have three hours until my next meeting. Get out of the MV."

Why didn't I see it? I should've known he was lying at James's house. He agreed too quickly.

"You lied to me. You said you'd—"

I scrambled farther into the MV when he grabbed for me. Clutched the ceiling handle and became a flurry of leather boots he couldn't catch. The jumbled shouts followed. Him shouting at me to get out of the MV, *I'm tired, Solenne.* Me shouting that he was a goddamn liar, I hated him now, and he had no right to scream at me.

He paced behind Julian, hands trembling. "Get her inside. It's four o'clock in the fucking morning. I don't have time to deal with a tantrum."

"I've been working on it for the past eight hours," Julian said calmly.

They argued like exhausted idiots, melting out there, mist flattening their perfectly styled hair and running off their windbreakers.

They ignored my accusations that both of them were lying, psychotic bastards, until I closed and locked the door.

Face red and misty from rain or sweat, Bastien spun on his heels and stomped up the stairs to his porch. My bag hung from his fist like a sack of trash.

Julian unlocked the door, poked his head in. "Mind if I tell you a quick story?"

"Take me back to my dorm."

He climbed in and closed the door. My hands tightened around the ceiling handle in increments when he grabbed a bottle of water from the minibar, adjusted the pistol at the small of his back, and drank, staring out into the night. He swished the water in his mouth audibly, as if it was delicious. I reminded him there was nothing but plain water in that bottle, so he didn't need to be so dramatic. He ignored that.

"When the official was—"

"I don't want to hear a story."

"You'll like this one. It's the story of perseverance." He used the heel of his hand to swipe rain from his forehead. "May I continue?"

"You will anyway."

The interior lights faded one at a time until only the dashboard map lit us in electric blue.

"When the official was eight, Abraham took him camping."

"He already told me this story."

"The vague story where he praises his father for instilling strength in him at a young age during a camping trip? You're smart enough to understand how a story is told is just as important as the story, aren't you?"

I had to nod. Julian could stare eternally, like Bastien.

He spun a vivid tale of a camping trip off the beaten track in the Santa Monica Mountains. On the second night, while Bastien cut cord to hang the food bucket from a tree, Abraham disappeared. Bastien spent the first night terrified, wandering the woods, slipping deeper into danger. Hunters found him in the cold dawn four days later, dehydrated, using his backpack and brush under a fallen tree for warmth. Abraham told him this was a lesson, that if he conquered his fear of being alone, he could conquer anything.

My hands loosened from the handle. "Why are you telling me this? To feel sorry for a liar?"

"Because everyone has a story that makes us who we are. Because he loves you." He repeated those words while I searched for truth in the sky that no longer seemed as dark.

Bastien had never said it, instead whispering words vaguely shaped like love that I scribbled in my journal. Now they released themselves from the page where space was finite and became real. As real as me and the shape of Julian washed in the blue light.

"We all have a role to play. Who stands next to him in a restaurant means absolutely nothing. He's doing his job, creating perceptions, serving the Order." He pointed to the house with the closed water bottle. "He's the next president of the Order. He doesn't know how to lose."

"JAMES WILL RELEASE YOUR CONTRACT TO me tomorrow," he said from the bed. Source was in his hand, but his eyes were closed. "I cannot send you to Louisiana right now. It's unconscionable. When you're older and can handle the instability of Louisiana, I'll write your emancipation papers."

"When?" I asked. "Seventeen?"

"Yes, when you're seventeen."

"Swear to me. You swear it," I said, but I believed him. He had no reason to lie to me. Mama said you only lie to people who have power over you. I had no power over him.

"I swear it. You know it'll kill me right there, but you'll still leave because that is what everyone has always done to you. You don't know anything other than cruelty." Those were his web of words before he fell asleep. They stuck to me like the other collection of words that replayed in my thoughts constantly.

Solenne has poor decision-making skills, Guidry wrote in my last end-of-year report. *Temperamental. Impulsive.*

I fell asleep wondering if I'd be cruel enough to leave someone who loved me. How was I supposed to know which way to go when I'd never been in this place before?

MONTHS PASSED. EACH SUNDAY, I WATCHED the delivery truck back into the driveway. Tires stopped then lurched, spinning too close to sunlit rows of irises and lilacs. Two men unfolded themselves from the truck, knees and rifles emerging first. They paused with a fist over the heart to honor the Order and Texas flags snapping on flagpoles flanking the driveway. Mechanically, they stacked bright red boxes on the porch. The dresses. Ivory, oat, nude, or clay. Dozens to fill the space in the closet between Bastien's thick black uniforms, like beautiful works of fiction. Stories with untidy endings, the unresolved, the lingering questions.

THE COUNCILMEN SAID A NATION WAS only as strong as its hold on its women. They had to squeeze the life out of women's liberations movements, give it no air, they said. It begins at home with the wives.

Swaying in an office chair in the corner, I watched this battleground of reddened faces, the thickened middles pressed against meeting tables, glasses slamming against wood.

They looked across the table at Bastien who had been silent throughout the meeting. What did he think about the increasing number of women petitioning the Council about abolishing the assignment system? What, in his opinion, should they change to maintain the order?

Bastien watched me sway, fatigue and restlessness in his eyes. "I have no thoughts at the moment."

The councilmen frowned.

Mama said men were beasts, and the map in their brains never changed. But last night I watched Bastien sleep, and the beast was only skin and hair and a little bit of whiskey. Soft flesh under the eyes and chin. Same as mine.

Maybe this was how it was done. Change one man at a time.

I swayed.

BASTIEN TOOK MEETINGS THE REST OF the day in the Chamber, while I worked in his office, toggling between journaling and braiding my hair. I wanted to walk the courtyard and sit in the café that James and I once visited. Write while the men passed, tight smiles, assuming I wasn't capable of writing more than a grocery list.

I stepped inside the elevator. An arm snaked across the glass, and a manicured hand wedged the doors open. Joy walked in, and for a moment, I saw her with a twiggy ponytail and bitten nails. I'd always thought she was pretty, but as a woman, she'd figured out how to create the illusion of beautiful. Lush, perfectly curled hair, perfect makeup, alabaster dress contoured to her body.

The childish hopes came in snapshots—hugs, hazelnut coffee in a café, shopping downtown, Bastien and me having dinner with her and Julian at their house.

She studied her heels, the distance between us. "My mother's a lobbyist for DoS. Margaret Ann, the woman who doesn't quite fit into either world. Did you ever think of what that was like for me growing up? Pulled in two directions. Living in two worlds. You live in one."

The elevator hummed under our feet, but I wasn't there. I was in her backyard, laughing, running through parched grass and twisting sprinklers, my hand in hers. It would never be again.

She continued, suspending us in the air like the elevator we stood inside. "The wives in my neighborhood found out I know you personally. They asked me to speak with you."

"About what?"

"Bastien Martin is a patriot," she said, pleading. "The next president. Following him around everywhere, attending his speeches. This isn't good for you. You're going to end up hurt."

"Say what you came here to say, Joyce."

She flinched, hearing her full name from the little girl who once adored her. "They said—"

"Who?"

"The wives. They said he's hurting Francesca. He doesn't return her calls."

I jabbed a thumb against the floor-one button, as if that would speed things along. My heart was a hot thump in my chest. I remembered my last conversation with Francesca, the spiteful way she called me a puppy. "Tell her . . ." I took a breath. "Tell your friend she has my sympathy."

"Do you ever listen? You don't know these men and this world better than I do. This isn't just about Francesca. This is about you. I'm trying to do the right thing."

I shrugged her cold hand off my arm and told her not to speak to me. I sounded like a child, but at that moment, I didn't care.

Outside the elevator, her voice stopped me. "Julian says when they were on the ambassador tour last year, the official was obsessed with you. Viewing your images. Tracking your location. He wrote articles about his travel and planted comments about marrying. He tracked how many times you accessed the articles and compared it to your health data, looking for surges in cortisol and adrenaline. Stress hormones. How many times you slept in. How many times you ate. He wanted to know if you were heartbroken."

I turned, and my eyes met hers. "So?"

He hadn't done that to hurt me. He did it because he loved me. He loved me before he could even articulate it. I would've done the same thing if I had access to his data, to hold proof that he loved me, too. Born just right with museum passes and friends and fucking nail polish and her perfect white blanket, Joy didn't understand because Julian didn't crave her—spending two days a week at home, declining her calls, and referencing a visit with another woman as "having a taste for wine instead of whiskey." She didn't care about me. Her rushed, rehearsed words were for her and her world. Not for my benefit. She wanted me in my place, not in Bastien's office, but put up like a toy, tucked away unseen while Francesca sat in the wives' gossip circle, wineglass in hand, knees stacked on the same side, shrugging off Bastien coming to me twice a week, and me, opening my door, my heart, my legs for a splinter of him because that's who I was. When Francesca came to my apartment a crying distance from her husband's office, they could imagine me standing silently, envious of her position because I could never have what she had. But that wasn't my story. I could make him happier than Francesca could.

Joy's eyes watered, startling me. The only time I had ever seen her cry was when she was afraid. I thought but didn't ask, *What on earth could you be afraid of?* "The Solenne I knew said she'd find someone who loved her like her dad loved her mom. A man who'd never hurt her."

Once, I wanted Joy to unsheathe her sword and threaten the sky. I didn't need saving anymore. I'd found my own way, my own beautiful skies. The up arrow above the elevator glowed white, and the doors reached for one another.

"I did."

CHAPTER 29

THEN

JULIAN LAID A SERIES OF FIREARMS ON BASTIEN'S DESK. THE SOLDIER INSPECTED each, fingers gliding across the different parts. He picked up a large rifle and pressed the stock against his shoulder. His eyes met mine, questioning.

Bastien noticed. From his desk, he glared at the soldier's loose, shoulder-length locs. "Do you know her?"

"Sir?" the soldier asked.

"Do you know her?" Bastien exaggerated the space between each word.

"Never seen her before today."

"Of course you haven't." He crossed his arms. "That's the answer to any question you have about her. Keep your eyes on the weapon."

Julian's eyes darted between the two. He directed the soldier's defiant gaze away from Bastien. "You may recognize that rifle. It was manufactured in San Antonio."

The soldier nodded, then placed the rifle back on the desk.

The desk chair slanted back farther under Bastien's weight. "You're not interested in that firearm."

"No," the soldier said, then met Bastien's eyes. "Sir."

"You sound certain."

"I am certain."

"You tested one with the same action a month ago and wrote a favorable report."

The soldier crossed his arms, distressed by the presence of a white man with rank.

His discomfort pulled me to a stand.

"You're standing," Bastien said without looking at me.

"I need the bathroom."

"You'll sit right there."

I sat.

"Explain why this firearm doesn't interest you," Bastien said.

"I prefer the one assigned to me."

The two men stared at each other, breath rising over the intrusive click of someone's timepiece.

"The one assigned to you is no longer an option. Your choices are limited to what's on my desk, General. Make your selection before you leave the building today."

"Confirmed, sir." He saluted before leaving the office.

I WAS AT THE VANITY IN the first-floor bathroom, finger-combing my hair, when the door swung open behind me. Annette stood next to me and placed her hands under the faucet. Water splashed over her hands in timed spurts.

"I'm Annette."

"I know."

Her eyes were troubled like she needed to release something but didn't know how. "You're from Dallas?"

I smiled, embarrassed I hadn't taken time to download the digital ID of a DoS I saw so frequently at the Capitol. "Where are you from again? I forget everything."

"San Antonio," she said. "Me and Quinton. He's in the Code. Operational contact. I . . ." She frowned at her reflection, the fear within capturing our attention.

My Source buzzed on the countertop, the excuse I needed to leave this awkward conversation. "It was nice talking to you, Annette."

"Quinton," she continued, as if I'd said nothing. "He's been saving up so he can beat the algorithm . . . buy my assignment. You met him earlier."

The soldier who met with Bastien about the weapon. Running into Annette in the bathroom instead of the café wasn't random.

"I saw him."

"You know how it is, don't you?" she asked, pleading. "My contract here is up next month. The algorithm assigned me to marry a forty-year-old man in Georgia. I can't go to Georgia. Me and Quinton been loving each other since we were six."

Wasn't this the story for all of us? Wanting to choose someone outside the confines of the algorithm, or like Dalena, not wanting to choose someone at all.

"I can't do anything about that."

"But I see you with the official all the time."

Her mirror image revealed all she'd seen—those late nights vacuuming hallways and watching elevator doors close on an official who rested his hand on a Black girl's shoulder and leaned to kiss a center part, or that place above her ear where a sapphire clip rested. Mirror Annette believed I could change her life if she could get me alone.

"Can you?" she asked.

IT WAS LATE THAT AFTERNOON WHEN Mama called.

"What happened with James?" Mama asked, her voice almost nonexistent over Source. The call came minutes after Source updated her assignment tab, with Bastien as her conservator.

I sank onto the couch in Bastien's office and pulled a throw pillow over my head. Listened to the air conditioner shudder into a start.

"He didn't want me around anymore."

"I don't believe that. Do you think I'm stupid?"

There was something in her voice I'd never heard in her before. I strained to understand it. "Why can't this be good for us? You won't have to deal with that man anymore. You won't have to worry about him closing your business."

Or his disgusting threats disguised as warnings. *You're only thirty-four. Too young to think the only hand in your panties should be your own.*

"You have no idea what you've done." A long, weary sigh. "Let me guess. He promised to write your emancipation papers."

I shifted Source to my other ear. "Next year, when I turn seventeen."

"Seventeen," she said, then laughed. "My Lord. Had you been seventeen, he'd say eighteen."

"I believe him."

"Why?"

"Because he has no reason to lie, that's why. He didn't have to become your conservator or help Annette."

I asked him to show me the back end of Source before asking him to reassign Annette to Quintin. He refused, sighed, then relented against his chair. Typed the eleven numbers into his device that changed a woman's life forever.

"Who's Annette?"

I closed my eyes. Everything sounded ridiculous now. "Nobody, Mama."

Outside the window, the Order's black and green flag snapped against a flag post. "He doesn't want to leave me here alone. He's taking me with him to New Orleans next week," I offered as proof that Bastien was different. He wouldn't take me to a nonrestricted state if he didn't intend to sign my papers.

"I don't care where he takes you. That kind of man will never give you what he has for himself, and there is no taking, not from him."

That night, I awoke in an empty bed. My heart beat too quickly, and I sat up, pulling the sheet around me. Bastien stood against the window wall, a dark figure lit by an overbearing moon, looking out over the lake still devastated by drought. The rain hadn't been enough.

"It's not change that feels threatening. It's the unknown. The uncertainty," he said, and then I understood why he was drawn to watching this thing he couldn't control while darkness obscured it. He didn't want to see what it had become. Then I understood what I'd heard in Mama's voice when I spoke to her. It was fear.

CHAPTER 30

THEN

I WASN'T NERVOUS WALKING WITH BASTIEN TO THE JET, BUCKLING IN, OR BRACING myself for my first takeoff. I was nervous when the aircraft stabilized with the flow of the wind. Nothing made sense. I was disembodied, leaving my destiny to some technology I couldn't understand.

I gripped the arms of my seat, trying to ignore the plane jerking like it was navigating a hill of rocks while Bastien, Julian, and Bouchard discussed Bastien's upcoming speech in Louisiana. Votes were won by standing before your base to show them you were the everyman, you shared their interests, and you wanted for him and his family what you wanted for yourself. Safety, liberty, and freedom from tyranny. Who did he imagine when he said those words?

Dr. Bouchard huffed about the administrator from Arkansas and his concerns about the drug abuse crisis in rural areas.

Bastien spoke over him. "Lack of discipline and intelligence. The education system is well funded. Thirty-four percent of boys in Arkansas dropping out of school before seventh grade to work is a personal choice that leads to drug abuse. Involving the Council would be government overreach, and, as a man, the administrator of Arkansas should be embarrassed by his request for assistance. Men find their own. Cover their own ground."

Julian and Bouchard agreed. But two of Bouchard's sons went through treatment for addiction. Only days ago, I'd heard Bastien and Julian praising them for their bravery, for confronting the weakness that addiction causes.

Bastien looked at me. "Is something wrong?"

I didn't have an answer. I would never be able to make him understand that everything was wrong.

WE DESCENDED AIRSTAIRS ON THE BASE into a heat I recognized. It sank down into me and curled my hair at the root. Two graying men in crisp uniforms saluted. From the conversation that followed, I learned they were strategists from the Alpha Base, they'd be attending the speech, and they weren't expecting me.

A strategist surveyed my wind-rumpled hair, the hands that floated from here to there, not sure of where they should be. His eyes were kind but impatient. "We don't show a woman listed as approved staff."

Did they have the power to send me back? Bastien outranked these men, and yet, they questioned who he brought on base. Feeling out of place, I took a step back and became a shadow, the secret Solenne. Solenne behind office doors.

"You have my approval. Analise. Wardrobe."

The men led us across the pavement toward a building. Bastien disappeared inside it while Julian guided me into one of three MVs parked out front. The locks engaged, closing me into a bulletproof capsule smoothed with leather. A masked driver clutched the steering wheel.

"Entertainment?" the driver asked.

"What?"

"Are you on base to entertain?"

It took seconds of eye contact for it to sink in. He thought I was a prostitute. My lips begged to report my status. I lived in Austin and slept in Bastien's bed every night. I had my own towels, silk pillowcases to keep the ends of my hair from splitting, and my pink fuzzy socks were folded in drawers next to Bastien's dress socks. But I had no title to give, and in the Order, you're nothing without a title.

"I don't entertain."

In the distance, the jet lifted its nose in the air. Did the soldiers assume Francesca was a prostitute when she traveled with Bastien, or was my presence questioned because I didn't look like I belonged?

JULIAN SLID INTO THE SEAT NEXT to me. The MV's engine surged, whisking us to a gate flanked by soldiers and the Order's eleven Black Flags of Rebellion.

I reached for the door handle. "Where is Bastien?"

Julian motioned for me to buckle in. He wasn't like Bastien, who believed his arm draped around my shoulders functioned better than a seat belt. "He'll follow in a different vehicle. For security purposes, he won't ride with you through this visit."

The MV paused at the gate. A guard leaned inside the driver's gapped window. His eyes lingered on me before waving us through the gate.

"He hasn't destressed yet. He hasn't had his fruit or water."

Julian smiled. "He's fine. He's made these trips more times than you've had years. He'll have water in his MV."

"I didn't want to ride with him anyway. I don't want to listen to those strategists talk for the next thirty minutes." I relaxed against the seat, watching the city through the dome-shaped windshield. Clusters of new and old. Buildings scraping against the skyline. Buildings tiered like wedding cakes with columns and fondant white paint. This was New Orleans. A thrill I hadn't felt since leaving Austin drew a line down my spine to my toes. Henriette was once here, and now, so was I. This was nonrestricted soil.

"We have things to go over before we arrive at the site," Julian said. "When we arrive at the Parliament, you'll sit in an overflow area until the speech's conclusion. If anyone asks about the nature of your business, you're a staffer. Wardrobe."

"They all know about me. I saw the strategists' faces."

"Outside of the base, you are *staff*. Divulge no information about the official."

"I don't need to be reminded." I didn't mean it to sound so sharp.

"And why can't I sit in the audience? I bet if my name was Joy I could."

"If your name was Joy, you'd be at home planning my lunch for the week, not traveling across the country."

"You hate this, don't you?" I asked.

"Pardon?"

"Me being here. Me being with Bastien."

"The opposite is true. He shows more restraint when you're around."

The buildings were a blur. I twisted in my seat to watch a Ferris wheel with dangling feet and hands waving against the skyline.

"Take route M," Julian said.

The driver's eyes flashed in the rearview mirror. "Are you sure?"

Julian smiled, edges hard. He repeated his instructions and opened a bottle of water from a minibar. "Joy tells me you're acquainted."

"Ancient history."

"She wonders aloud sometimes if things would've been different had the two of you lived in another country. 'Just two girls, wandering around Switzerland,'" he said in a mock tone. "Joy can be so ungrateful at times. This is the greatest country on earth. We're fortunate to be citizens of this nation, and Texas, the finest state in the Order."

Deeper in the city, the scene deteriorated. Shotgun houses platformed on faded bricks; bottles and paper littered unkempt grass in front of apartment buildings; people huddled under leaning electric posts or sat in plastic chairs in front of buildings with sunken roofs. Buildings that should've been abandoned.

A toddler with a wide-legged, stiff-arm gait got tangled in his shirt and fell next to a brown-skinned woman and boy, sitting on a curb. The woman waved a man down. After a quick exchange, she pulled a piece of fruit from her dress pocket and handed it to the boy. The man followed her behind the building unbuckling his belt.

I wasn't naive; I knew about prostitution. But women were forced into it; they didn't lead men behind buildings.

The outline of my reflection in the window hardened under a bridge's shade—sapphire in my ears and hair, fuchsia painting my lips. Only glass and metal separated me from these lives that seemed worse off than we were in Texas.

Julian pulled me away from the window, and I finally breathed. "The official told you it wasn't pretty. He didn't want you to see this."

"Why is this happening? Is it the hurricanes?"

He gave me a sympathetic smile and shook his head. "They've had years to rebuild their state. Texas sent forty-eight million dollars after the last storm, but they squandered it. Solenne, you're smart. You can see there is nothing good here. But you never need to worry. The official will keep you safe from these people."

CHAPTER 31

THEN

THERE WERE WOMEN IN THE PARLIAMENT'S OVERFLOW ROOM. THEY SAT ALONE AT wooden poseur tables. They twisted the ends of goddess braids over their shoulders. They studied me with a mourning kinship in their eyes. I sat alone at the bar, refusing to allow *they* to become *we*. I measured the empty space between us and told myself I was different. I didn't need to address how.

I watched the entrance doors, heart pounding each time it opened. Men in black uniforms, men in military fatigues, then Lucas Magnan, Georgia's administrator. Black shirt, army fatigues, and a rifle poking over his shoulder like an extra limb—he was dressed like a soldier, not an administrator of a state.

When he noticed me, he paused. The toothpick jutting from the corner of his lips rolled from one side to the other. A thin white woman with ash-colored hair snaked an arm through his, urging him behind the State Room's double doors.

In the MV, Julian said women didn't sit in the audience. Julian had left out a descriptor. He left out the word *Black*.

The Parliament doors opened again, and my heartbeat quickened again. A woman with pale skin and a gray cap of curls made a beeline to the bar. She poured a drink from a crystal decanter, held it up in offering to my detail, and chuckled when she received no response. The black lining the room rippled when she plopped on the stool next to me.

She twisted her body to look at each man. "I'm safe, I promise." Then to me, "I'm Penelope. Lucas Magnan's aunt slash assistant."

Julian hadn't told me how to handle this, so I sat idiot-silent. Should I say my name? Was I Analise or Solenne?

"Nice to meet you."

"Oh, thank God. He lets you speak. Heaps better than the ones the rest of the concubines belong to."

"I'm not a concubine."

Henriette was a concubine. Bastien said that's not what I was.

Penelope smiled around the rim of the glass. "You waiting on someone? You're staring that door down like your long-lost love is on his way."

I glanced at the doors to the State Room that separated me from Bastien. "No."

"Not that door." She nodded to the double doors she had just come through. "The entrance doors."

"Not waiting on anyone."

"So you don't have a name, you're not waiting for anyone, and you're not a concubine. Why are you here?"

"I'm on the staff."

"What do you do?"

"Wardrobe."

Penelope laughed and clapped loud enough to pull a soldier a foot closer. "That's what they're calling it now?"

I fumbled through the words, knowing I would reveal more than intended. "I've been the official's assistant for almost a year."

She nodded to the bracelet on my wrist. "Does he pay in jewels? Ain't never seen an assistant wearing jewelry worth more than everything in this room—that's not an exaggeration—and a ten-soldier detail. I got stiffed. I don't have a single one. You must be really good at what you do."

"Why does it matter to you what I do?"

"Don't at all. You want a drink?"

I declined and glanced around the room. Eight pairs of eyes

were on us now. Their bodies had shifted forward like they strained to see something on a stage.

"The administrators trot the concubines out at these speeches as proof of how well the Order's system works. They don't let them talk to each other anymore though," Penelope said, "so I'll do the honors." She pointed an age-spotted finger at each woman, rattling off states from as far east as New York. "And now I'm meeting Miss Texas, first of her kind. You must be special."

I could've ended this by moving to one of the tables, but I couldn't walk away with her believing Bastien was anything like those administrators.

"He's a good man," I said brusquely.

"Oh? Tell me exactly how he's different from the other tyrants and racists."

The public only had one side of him. They created an image by stitching together a Frankenstein composed of men who came before him. There were layers to him, like a complex story written over decades. I saw the softer side. The man kissed my feet every morning.

She leaned forward as if she were a psychic medium, siphoning memories from me. "Now after you finish thinking of that pretty picture, tell me how hard he cringes when he thinks about you with a Black man. Next, tell me how many soldiers had Black women and Black children at home but marched off to fight for the Confederacy. If sex ended racism, racism wouldn't exist. In the dark, they can forget who you are. But if a sunrise don't do anything else, it brings the truth every day. The men tell the sun this is their world, then they close their eyes and do it all over again like their great-grandfathers."

I stood. "Can you excuse me?"

"I could, or we could talk. Did you notice we're missing Miss Georgia, or did you think there was no Miss Georgia because Lucas is a decent human?"

I sat again, unable to deny I was curious about the man they sent Dalena to.

"Dalena Batiste."

"You know her?"

I nodded. "Where is she?"

Penelope glanced at the State Room doors. "She ran. She's a non-restricted woman now."

My eyes trailed from Penelope's face to those heavy oak entrance doors. There I saw Dalena, her hair in two rust-colored poofs, her black leotard a second skin, her high-waisted jeans smudged with a thumbprint of white paint. This image was why my heart paused each time the entrance doors opened. This was what I wanted when I demanded Bastien take me with him to Louisiana. Dalena, here with Lucas Magnan, apologizing for never answering, never returning my calls. We wouldn't have had long together before the tether shortened, but we would've had something. But those oak doors didn't open, they were closed, the threshold sketched in daylight. She'd done what she'd always done, painted an image of freedom without me in the background.

"The official says he can find her, and with his technology, he can guarantee Lucas never loses her again. *If* he supports his bid for a permanent Council position. So what do you think? Can he find her?"

"I don't know," I finally said, not missing the worry in her gray eyes.

She poured another drink. "You sleep next to him every night. You should know everything he knows. Learn to open your ears and not just your legs."

"Where do you think she went?"

Her gaze slid to my detail. "Why would I tell you that? So you can run your mouth to the official?"

"If you don't know, just say that," I snapped, because I was done with her, Dalena, and this day.

"You have a smart mouth."

"So does my mama."

She chuckled. "Coushatta, about five hours north of here. Keep it to yourself, but remember that location."

A question climbed up to my lips, one that gave me a glimmer of hope that I missed something.

"Did Dalena send you to help me?"

Penelope looked at me, innocent from knowing her next words could make me whole or tear into me.

"Other than stories about her twin brother, she never mentioned anyone from home."

My body felt weak, everything suffering under heavy stones. Being left behind. This was the familiar.

She reached for my hand over the bar, urgency in her eyes. "Listen—"

The dramatic click of a round being chambered in a rifle echoed. "This is your warning, old woman."

She held her hands up in surrender. "I know, I know. Hands off the property." She downed the rest of her drink. "You're nonrestricted here. *Free.* You're a fool if you go back to Texas with him. Slip into the Creole town house with blue shutters on Decatur Street. They'll get you your papers, and then there ain't a damn thing the official or his guns can do about it."

A SOLDIER SHOWED US TO A room on base in the ten-story housing unit. I followed in a daze. The door opening, the stark white walls, the chemical stench of blue nylon carpet, the hand on my shoulder, my arm, the small of my back where sweat slicked my shirt.

Bastien hovered. I saw myself in his eyes, small and insignificant. Someone you leave behind. "Solenne, are you listening to me?"

This couldn't be true, this was make-believe, the backstory of the heroine from a 1950s movie. Friends didn't create a new life in a small town while their friend struggled in quicksand. They pulled them up before the ground swallowed them whole. All those nights I'd called Dalena with no answer. She had already started her new life.

"Leave her be," Bastien told Julian, who had asked me a question I missed. "She has her moods."

Bastien and Julian settled in chairs in the sitting area while the soldier stacked white pillows on top of a folded blanket at the foot of the bed. Crisp movements and quick replies to questions to impress his superiors.

"The sheets will have to go," Julian said, removing a stack of papers from his case. "Unless you expect the official's woman to sleep like a soldier."

The soldier blinked at me still standing in the middle of the room cupping my elbows.

"Not *her*, Marshal. Did I give you any indication this is the official's woman?"

Bastien twisted his obsidian ring.

"No, sir. My apologies, Official."

"I don't need apologies. She needs sheets, Egyptian cotton." He glanced at my hair, hanging lifeless over one shoulder. "And a silk pillowcase."

While the men worked, I paced the room peeling an orange. Pierced the flesh with my thumbnail unintentionally. Juice ran like tears. Bastien handed me a napkin, but still, I didn't stop. Ten paces from the bed to a blue modular sofa. Twenty paces from the balcony to the door. Again. Again. I needed something new, to grasp the unfamiliar, to walk the streets Henriette once walked, even if for an hour. I needed the door to this cage open.

"I saw a Ferris wheel today," I said.

"There is a carnival fifteen miles from the base," Bastien said absently.

"I want to go. I saw a video once on—"

"Dirt, viruses, prostitution, sixteen murders in seven years, frequent mechanical failure," Bastien said. "This state is destitute. Crime-ridden. Unsafe. Did you read the book I gave you on New Orleans?"

Shops and clusters of two-story buildings were visible through the balcony doors. "Then I'll go for a walk. I want to look around."

Bastien rubbed the back of his neck, nose still in his paperwork. "No, you will not wander around a military base of undisciplined men."

"You never say yes to anything, Bastien—"

"I don't have the patience for—"

"Do you even know the word?"

"You're speaking when I'm speaking." His tone warned me not to press.

Julian's eyes traveled down my body, stopping at my bright pink toenail polish. "Did Lucas Magnan mention Dalena Batiste?"

"He saw her forty-three days ago," Bastien said. "Forty-three days in a state full of predators. No money, nowhere to sleep, no protection. I suppose my twelve years in government and combat isn't enough for Solenne to trust me. An old woman who spends more time drunk than sober is a more trustworthy source of information."

Now two sets of tired eyes were on me. They knew this wasn't just a mood. They saw the ache, the stretch of my fingers toward Dalena. Henriette.

An hour later, the soldier returned. Our eyes met underneath the top sheet he snapped open and let flutter to the bed. Saluting, he left with the trash bag containing my orange peels and lipstick-stained napkin. I was in this cage, but if I hadn't pressed my fingertips to the glass balcony doors, it would've been like I had never been here at all.

THAT NIGHT, I PACED IN THE silence of the room. I wanted to sleep alone. At the very least, every human should have that as a choice, but he said no, and urged me to tell him what was bothering me. He rolled on his side and dented my pillow with a fist the way I liked it.

I wouldn't turn into liquid. I told him I would rather stand all night than to sleep with him. Told him I couldn't stand to look at him, and he was a criminal keeping me locked in a room. Pervert. Bastard. Racist. Hypocrite. No wonder you're not married. No wonder your daddy ran off and left you in the woods when you were eight. He couldn't stand you either. I said all those things from my corner.

Sad eyes set in a hard face. A wounded animal shredded by a woman's weapon, and I was happy to do it. I had holes in my interior. He should have the same.

He folded his arms behind his head and said that was fine. Neither of us would sleep. If he wasn't as sharp as he needed to be at his meeting tomorrow morning, so be it. None of it mattered anymore if I couldn't even stand to look at him. Since I didn't need him, he could go back to the infantry with bullets flying past his sleeping bag and skinning squirrels in forests for meat and burying the entrails. When death came, it would be a mercy. He looked into my terrified eyes and said his soldier's directive stated his burial flag should be sent to me because I was the only person in his life, the only one he ever loved.

Once he had me, he kissed the corner of my mouth where tears I'd been holding back all day ran. The lone crease in his forehead deepened, and in his eyes was an exhaustion I had never seen in another person. He asked why I was so unhappy, why I tormented him. How could I make him understand when we spoke different languages? I wanted him to hold me like he used to when there were parts of my body that were unknown to him, but he was already nudging my knees apart with the flat plane of his forehead and calling himself a fool.

My forearm barred against my eyes, No, formed on my lips but it was drowned dark, lifeless. I was the girl who had never been there at all and, yet, had nowhere else to go.

Bastien sighed, warm against everything he wanted. The taking, like the ocean shaping rock until the original no longer existed. The hush of fading waves. *Hush*. Be quiet and soft. That was how it was done.

Whispering, he asked why I had made him wait so, so long.

CHAPTER 32

NOW

Lᴵᴷᴱ ꜱᴼ ᴹᴬᴺʸ ᴰᴬʸꜱ ᴵᴺ ᴹʸ ᴸᴵꜰᴱ, ᴵ ᴴᴬᴰ ᴺᴼᵂᴴᴱᴿᴱ ᵀᴼ ᴳᴼ. ᴬꜰᵀᴱᴿ ᴵ ᴸᴱꜰᵀ ᴮᵁᵀᵀᴱᴿ'ꜱ, ᴵ boarded a train that circled New Orleans and contemplated my next move.

"Fifteen minutes to French Quarter. Station Six," the electronic voice said. The reminders came every few minutes like a cruel countdown. Each one twisted my stomach, urging me to search for somewhere to empty Butter's sweet potato cornbread.

I grabbed my bag and barged into the restroom. I held it together long enough to flip the lock. Using the sink was rude, but I couldn't bring myself to stuff my head in the same place where thousands of people sat their bare asses. Lemon from the automatic scent diffusers could erase smells, not the image.

I rinsed my mouth and the sink with lukewarm water until nothing clung to the stainless steel. The dispenser ejected a paper towel. My cue to leave. I dampened it and blotted my cheeks. The woman in the mirror was nervous and unsure.

Bastien had a plan. He had money. He had time. How had I gotten this far?

Disorder.

The storm, the glitch, the insurgent escape attempt. The unexpected was the only way I'd ever been able to knock *him* off balance. Like Service four years ago, freeing me from Bastien's house by propping a door open and taking the dogs on an unusually long walk while I climbed in her vehicle and let it take me past the unsuspecting guards at the iron gate.

He designed his life so he never had to guess and could always see the end. He would pay for certainty, for absolutes. He had the means and influence to do it.

I could leave New Orleans and hide in a rural area, but that would buy me days at most. I was in a city that had the highest concentration of nonrestricted Black women who had fought a battle identical to the one I was in now. They won. If it was true for one of us, it could be true for me.

I pulled the makeup kit and dress from Hammer's from my bag. Two peacocks printed on the dress, preening and bold. I didn't know how to get in to see the Louisiana administrator before Bastien closed his fist around my world, but I knew the man who did.

THE STEADY MUSIC LED ME TO the front of Bourbon's, a two-story white building with green shutters. The line was long, but I had no intention of waiting in it. At the entrance, two men argued. I stepped out of harm's way but stayed close enough to see how the men here settled things. One had a finger in the other's face. He could knock his ass out, he told the crowd, but his shirt cost more than a month's rent and he wasn't ruining it.

The bouncer folded his arms over his massive chest and looked at me instead of intervening. "The taxman's woman."

Word traveled faster than I thought. I moved close enough to see the shine on his bald head. "Former."

He lifted his eyebrows in amusement. "The bulletin said always. What you do to make him so crazy about you? Bastards love nothing but their dogs, war, and money."

This wasn't a man interested in turning me in.

"Yeah, he has enough of that."

"So what you doing here?"

I stretched a leg out and pointed my toe. "I came all the way from Austin to show you my shoes."

His laughter was deep. "What is this, mama?"

"What does it look like?"

"Like twenty years in a box and my great-great-grandchildren working the crops to pay off my debts. You going inside, or you wanna hang out here and watch these fools embarrass themselves?"

I reached past him and ran my hand over the gold rope blocking the entrance.

He unlatched it from the pole and waved me through. Flashing lights, odorless vapor, and music from a jazz band vibrated my bones.

Misty bodies weren't easy to squeeze through. Some danced, some stood frozen with glasses of dark liquid or electronic cigarettes pressed to their lips, glassy eyes hawking women on a stage in vintage chorus-girl costumes. Feather skirts and fans, fishnet-clad thighs and glittered arms intertwined—this was freedom.

Outside of images in magazines, I'd never been anywhere like this. I was good at pretending. Not letting my eyes linger on any one person or thing, I subtly rocked to the music.

A waitress in a 1920s flapper dress handed me a glass of champagne from the tray in her hands that sparkled like the rhinestones on her eyelids. "It's on Cairo." She nodded to a man sitting in a bank of chairs by the stage and leaned in close enough for me to smell the champagne on her breath. "The women's section is over there."

Across from Cairo's box, a small platform with white sofas, bistro-style tables lining the perimeter, and no women. In the flashing darkness, I made out what led me to this club in the heart of the French Quarter, what led me to mix in public instead of hunkering down in the swamps like Henriette once did. A gray beanie—askew and ill-fitting like the doors in Butter's house.

Memphis's eyes met mine. Even yards away in the dull light, the surprise on his face was concrete, a man zapped by a taser. Without hesitation, he climbed the stairs to the platform and dropped onto the sofa next to me. He leaned into me, lips near my ear, the closest I'd been to a man other than Bastien. His scent was deep, like coconut oil and tobacco. Like his voice in my ear. "You pretend to be clueless, but you're not."

"What do you mean?"

"You got me talking at Ed's. I dropped enough for you to figure out where I worked."

Over his shoulder, the strobe lights spun over Cairo and a woman with waist-length braids sweeping against a dark blue kimono, loosely belted at the waist. Underneath, everything curved on her like a sculpture. Despite how flawless she was, Cairo and his men sitting behind him looked up at her, eight pairs of dismissive eyes, heads tilted the same. It was the way they told us we had nothing important to say. They were no different from men in Dallas.

"I swear I'm not stalking you."

"So you just happened to be in my place of business after I made it clear we go our separate ways?"

"You think I wandered around in the middle of the night because I wanted to see you?"

He pulled away so I could see the smirk that already defined him. "Yep."

"Far as I knew, you don't put down roots and don't have a place of business. Coincidences exist. It's Mardi Gras."

"I'm a sucker for pretty feet and long hair, but I'm not dumb. Why are you here?"

While I gathered my answer, the woman laid a stack of papers on the table in front of Cairo. She folded her arms under her breasts, and I knew she was pissed. I couldn't see her face, but I imagined the defiance there.

"Going through Immigration won't work. I need an appointment with Admin, and I have nowhere else to go."

Seconds passed. If he said no, I had no other plans.

He leaned into my ear even though he didn't need to. The drums quieted. "I'll send a request."

After he added my handle to his Source, he left me there to watch the scene unfold between Cairo and the woman. Cairo stood when Memphis approached. The woman looked between the two of them, grabbed her braids in a painful grip, and knotted them into a top bun with the hands of a master. I'd watched those hands work before—lining rubber-smelling hair glue on Styrofoam wig heads, sweeping paintbrushes on mini canvases, tacking swaths of fabric to mannequins.

Without trying, I found Dalena Batiste.

CHAPTER 33

THEN

THE NEXT DAY IN THE PARLIAMENT, I SAT AT THE SAME BAR DRINKING SPARKLING water from a wineglass and viewing images on Source. I swiped through dozens—Bastien and me on the shore, in the bedroom, in his office. One taken of Bastien from behind, shirtless, palms on the vanity, his overnight stubble and parted lips visible in the mirror. I couldn't remember his question. I paused on a picture of me and Dalena lying on a blanket under a shade tree, arms twisted together, up and out in front of us, brown skin joining like different shades of paint on a canvas. I remember thinking that day there was no way she'd leave me behind, no way I wasn't part of her. I clicked delete.

Permanently?

I pressed *Confirm* and stood, causing ten pairs of eyes to shift.

"Five minutes before departure," a soldier warned.

The bathroom was right outside the overflow room, but they'd follow me anyway. Two soldiers swept the bathroom, opening every stall and the cabinets before flanking the door. My cue to enter.

I was washing my hands when Penelope walked in. We'd never been here before, but déjà vu overwhelmed me. The old people in Dallas said déjà vu was misnamed, that experiencing the familiar was the ancestors communicating with you through visions. If they were right, what were they trying to tell me about Penelope?

"They let you pass?"

"They don't run anything here except their boots. Besides, this is the only women's bathroom in the building." She stood beside me at the vanity. "I see you can keep your mouth closed."

So Coushatta was a test.

"Is Coushatta even real?"

"It is, but I don't know anyone there. Just know Dalena is safe. Happy." Penelope narrowed her eyes at me. "You can have that, too."

I ran damp hands over my hair, smoothing a center part. In the mirror was no one, broken and unable to see a way. There was nothing here for me. All I had was the man who rested his face where my heart beat, listening to its twisting hum, its drift as I fell asleep—in his words, the cruelness of it. "I won't leave him."

There was concern in her eyes that small and sad was an identity. "I usually see it in the eyes, the ones who don't feel the chains around their wrists. I thought I saw something else in you yesterday, but he's really done a number on you, hasn't he?" She pulled a ball of fabric from her purse, laid it on the countertop, and unfolded it. "If you're hellbent on staying . . ."

Inside the scrap of fabric, eight white tablets. I knew, but I asked anyway. "What's this?"

"Progesterone blocker. It stops a pregnancy from growing. You can't get this in Texas, and you don't want his child. Dear God who sits high, not the official's." She folded the fabric in sloppy fourths, then pressed it into my hand. "Catch it early when it's still just a bag of water. Take one before bed for two nights. It'll look no different from your period when it starts. The official won't know the difference. The pig bastards never know."

Boots patterning past the bathroom froze us in place, reminding us a closed door didn't equal privacy. There was a confused shuffle of the fabric between us, ending with Penelope as its possessor. Her fingers tightened around the fabric—harsh words visible in her eyes.

The footsteps faded until there was only one set approaching, then pausing outside the door. Bastien. Deliberate, intimidating, commanding—I could sift through and isolate the sound of his footsteps in a stream of one hundred.

She forced the bunched fabric against my palm and waited until my fingers curled around it. "May not need it now, but you will. If you have his child, no matter what you do, you'll be stuck."

HE LAY ON TOP OF THE blanket that night to stay cool, so unknowable beside me, like the mouth to a dark cave.

"What is this called?" He ran his hand over the braids patterned against my scalp.

"Cornrows. Canerows." While he worked at the small table in the room, I had spent an hour on parting, oiling, and braiding my hair.

He tested their tightness and sighed, long and dissatisfied. Just as he did most nights, he talked about history. This was the first time his story sounded wrong. His facts aligned with all I knew, but it was the way he told the story. The millions of Black people who fought and died in Civil War II were absent from his words. Bystanders. His grandfather was a hero who ended a war and saved a nation rather than becoming a wrecking ball that led to the collapse of a system with a weak foundation.

He twisted the end of one of my braids. "Civil War II was about federal rights versus states' rights. States wanted the ability to enact laws that the federal government believed interfered with economic progress in the country."

I nodded against his shoulder. He always needed to know I was listening to him. I didn't tell him Guidry told us the civil rights movement and protests against Jim Crow laws sparked the war. When the United States government turned its guns on Black people and their allies, it divided the country, and the unrest led to martial law. They said a military authority would restore peace, but citizens fought back for seven years.

As if by magic, my braid gave under his fingertips and unraveled to my nape. He captured another before I could pull the hair away to safety.

"Seven years of militias, fragmented state governments, and

millions of deaths. We're fortunate the Founders of the Order had a vision for the country. Their sacrifice ended the war."

I didn't tell him my great-grandfather sacrificed his life in that war. My daddy said he was too stubborn to die right off. Over two months, infected wounds rotted him from the outside in while he lay in a medical tent marked COLORED watching an extremist group use the weakness civil war creates to overthrow the US government. In that unseasonably warm January of 1960 in Metairie, Louisiana, he witnessed a military dictatorship seamlessly replace the civil government. *Where did these men come from?* he asked his nurse. She couldn't have been more than thirteen. *Nobody knows,* she said. *They came from nowhere.* But that wasn't true. They were military officers, police officers, senators, governors, a World War II veteran like Bastien's grandfather. While my great-grandfather slept, Black and white men stood in offices letting the ink dry on treaties. In those documents, women had fewer rights than they did before the war, and Black women caught the worst of it. *Your men sold you out,* the Order's history books told us. *In the treaty, the Order gave 862,000 Black men Louisiana. It was their responsibility to relocate what remained of their population to Louisiana before 1962. Whoever remained must accept the Constitution in their existing locale.*

There was no mention of the Order designating the one state devastated by two major hurricanes in fifteen years, war, and the strain of overcrowding as the only nonrestricted state.

Face in my hair, now free and loose from every cornrow, Bastien exhaled. "Those men left their people. They had no sense of duty and loyalty. They still don't. Look at the condition leadership allows their people to live in. If you need to place blame, place it appropriately."

When he was quiet and the floorboards in an upper room stilled, and the headlights in the parking lot faded enough that I didn't have to remember glass jars of murky paint water, the blues and orange of the French Quarter on a canvas, or a girl with rust-colored coils, I slept.

CHAPTER 34

NOW

I TILTED MY HEAD TOWARD THE DOOR AT THE END OF THE HALL. LAUGHTER. WOMEN'S voices.

A dancer answered after I knocked once. She left me at the door and flopped on a sofa. Another dancer crouched in a corner and picked through a plastic plate of nachos. Two women in a corner fluttered reddened tongues stretched like taffy against each other's. I tried not to stare.

"What do you need, sweetie?" An older woman met my eyes in the vanity mirror she sat in front of. *Grace* was written in purple lipstick in the mirror's corner.

What did I need? What did I expect to happen by trying to talk to a woman who hadn't cared enough about me to call once in five years? My silence brought everyone's attention. Eight pairs of eyes turned on me at once.

"A waitress said I could find Dalena here."

"Have a seat. She'll be here in ten minutes to make sure we're working."

I perched on the end of a settee. This was their domain. A bank of lockers, vanities with makeup strewn across them, sofas, a small bar. They smoked e-cigarettes and sipped from wineglasses. Louder than women at home, they counted money and mocked the men who paid them. All things that would rack up refractions if they weren't nonrestricted women.

A woman wearing a tiara and a gold flapper dress stripped off her heels and shoved them in a locker. She flopped on the chair across from me, draping a stockinged leg over the chair's arm.

"Who's this?" she asked someone nearby, though she kept her eyes on me.

"Taxman's woman," a woman at the bar said.

"Solenne." I rose from my seat and offered her my hand.

The woman glared at it before flipping her hand over and studying long black nails.

Like an intruder from another planet, I sat. I looked like these women, but there was a deep disconnect, a divide that reached further than being born and raised in different states.

Dalena walked in, and I was in sixth grade again, following her around. She circled the room checking costumes, wigs, and makeup, and going off about Cairo refusing to pay for thirty dancers unless thirty dancers were on the floor at all times. On cue, the women cleared off a high-back sofa. Dalena sat, crossing her legs so her kimono parted. Someone handed her a martini. Dalena's eyes met mine over the glass and silver skewer of olives. The shock was electric, the face of someone finally seeing home after a long trip. She freed her breath.

In the hallway, she put her back against the door to seal the voices inside. There was only us, the years that hung between us, the curve of our shadows on the wall.

"So you made it out," I said.

"So we finally have something in common."

"I'm here."

She fiddled with a narrow black ribbon, knotted and hanging limp from her right wrist. "But it took you five years. That's not how I told you to do it. You were supposed to gas him up, get the signature, then get on a train when his back was turned. Not run off in the middle of the night, dodo bird."

"It wasn't the middle of the night—"

"Still stupid. Didn't your mama teach you which ones you can play as a joke?"

"I can write and wear the hell out of a dress. Never said I was smart. Never could listen."

Disarmed, she laughed, and we wrapped our arms around each other like our mamas used to—leaning into each other, chattering at once, leaving smears of lipstick on cheeks. We were the women now.

She stepped back to look me over, grasping my hips. "Girl, look at you. You're not giving this dress mercy."

Everything about her had changed, and I hadn't witnessed the transformation. Strange that, back then, we stared at our reflections in storefront windows and saw our teenage bodies as permanent. Strange that we thought our bodies couldn't move beyond the new curve of breasts and hips. We didn't understand what it meant to be women, so we tried it all on. Backs arched, hips swinging like a dance, arms loose—we chastised boys for looking, then smiled into our hands. This woman with fluttery eyelashes and the full lower lip snagged between her teeth was solid, like she figured out who to be on her own. I was manufactured, shaped in Bastien's hands. Still worlds between Dalena and me. She didn't understand who I was. Her last memory of me was standing in a train station, relieved about going to Austin. She hadn't seen me heartbroken, my despair. She hadn't seen me become a woman because she hadn't bothered to call me a single time in five years. I wanted her to know I was no longer that little girl who was afraid of katydids and dark fields and being alone.

"I'm applying for asylum."

She shook her head like I was an idiot, light mood gone. "You ready to go toe to toe with a patriot and his property? If you think I whooped your ass when you were fifteen, you have no clue."

STORIES COME FULL CIRCLE, AND THE irony in this story was that Dalena lived in Chalmette, where Verreaux Plantation once stood. The land was now subdivided into small lots of two-story homes, but Dalena's house was surrounded by trees and tucked three miles off the main road. She renovated the home, keeping only the original hardwood floors. She'd even refused to remove the ones under ceiling vents and windows that were warped and pelted black from water damage. The tired sounds under her feet reminded her of the floors back at home. A navy velvet chair was the focal point of the living room—Twin's chair, a replica of the one her brother loved.

Floodlights, strategically placed exterior cameras, and security screens with a checkerboard of footage in each room made her feel safe. "You know what's crazy? Lucas wasted so much time and money trying to void asylum papers for a woman he doesn't even *like*," she said while showing me a digital feed of the perimeter of the house. "It's the principle for him. That's how he is. He'll be damned if you take anything away from him, even your own body."

She grew tomatoes, basil, and rosemary in her kitchen in bright red plastic pots under LED lights. Her outdoor garden failed. The squirrels and rabbits got to it all before she did. I studied everything, every rug, every curtain, every drop cloth splattered with shades of blue in the garage she had converted into an art studio. This was all hers. I handled the tomatoes on the vine, thought of Daddy's plants on the windowsill in Dallas, and labeled the heat in my belly as jealousy. She saw me struggling and addressed it like she had lived decades longer than I had rather than two years.

"You grew up thinking pretty meant everything—"

"Heffa, you did, too," I snapped, following her to her bedroom.

She opened her arms. "Difference is, I know you still think that will get you out of this mess. You think you'll walk into that administrator's office, squint, and look cute—"

"I don't squint anymore. I had my vision corrected."

"—and get him thrashing at your feet to help you. Folks here are all about business. You need to learn that."

She was right, so I argued about petty things. The tank top she let me borrow from her dresser was too thin to sleep in. The scarf she tied my hair up with wasn't tight enough.

"Pretty worked against you," Dalena said while we moved decorative pillows from a four-poster bed into a mountainous stack in the corner. "Had the official never liked what he saw, you wouldn't be in this mess."

I shoved the peacock dress in my bag and hung it on her closet's doorknob. "You know everything, don't you?"

"You have nothing in common with him. Why else would he keep you for five years?"

"Four years."

"*Five.* You think he didn't start planning the moment you got off that train in Austin? He probably sat at his desk sorting through every girl who came in that day until he found one who looked like you. And you can be mad at me if you want to—"

"I'm not mad."

"Then why are you snatching my blankets back like that?"

"Because you're talking to me like I'm stupid. Like I wanted a man who . . . Look, he was good to me. He took care of me and my mama."

"Good to you? Chile, please. Nothing about the way they treat us is good. We knew the assignment system was bad, but you really see it for what it is when you're out. They brainwash us with that system. Ruin our entire lives."

"Bastien used the assignment system once, so he could be with me. He's not like the other men who use it."

Dalena studied me as if seeing me for the first time, synthetic eyelashes fluttering. "You don't even sound the same. You have all these excuses that you've been parroting so long they feel real to you."

We lay with only the sound of our breathing. When it evened, she asked me about Dallas, the Corner Store, Harlem and Kingston. I told her even though I lived only two hundred miles away from it, I was no better off than she was. I hadn't been home in years. The craving to see the streets of Downtown Dallas faded over time into nothing.

"That's how he wanted it." She shook her head against the pillow. "He designed it that way, so you know nothing but him. The earlier, the better. That's how they hurt you."

"We hurt each other. I can't sit here and act like I was perfect."

He was imperfect, hurtful, jealous, selfish, but what did that say about me? I dug into him. I never let him pull away. Never let him leave me behind. What existed inside of me that made me want a man like that so fiercely?

"That's him talking right now, not you."

On the way here in the SPV, Dalena said I needed to get mad. I needed to do more than apply for asylum or put distance between us. I had to *hate* that bastard; it was the only emotion that would give me forward momentum.

Could I hate him? How long had I promised myself one day I would? There would be peace in that freedom, but there would also be a void, the emptiness I would never know how to fill. Each line had been created and sharpened in the shape of Bastien.

But if I didn't love him, I would be free from the words I wrote in that blue journal when I was sixteen, stretched across his bed. He tore a page out, leaving tatters against the spine where my feelings for him once lived. I didn't see that page again until last year when I found it, creases worn and translucent like a spider's web, locked in his lower desk drawer. Maybe that drawer embodied us, and it was those words that kept my soul chained to his.

"We have history. You can't erase relationships overnight."

"It's not a relationship. Never was. Never will be. He was something bad that happened to you. Something unfair, like your daddy being killed in action or like Twin never being able to read above a first-grade level." Dalena yawned, deep and gusting. "You sound like a woman in love, but I don't understand how you could stand him."

I counted the peaks and swirls in the ceiling's texture over the bed. Twenty-two. I counted them again and again until my eyelids grew heavy and I breathed more truth. It was easy in the dark.

"Sometimes I didn't think he wanted to be the way he was."

"Then he should've changed."

"Into what? He doesn't know who else to be."

CHAPTER 35

THEN

T HE SKY WAS HEAVY THE WEEK BEFORE BASTIEN WAS SCHEDULED TO LEAVE FOR Georgia. He had to be filled with me all day—working from the porch, sorting through paperwork then looking up at me like I was what he was searching for all along.

While he soaked sore muscles after an interrogation with insurgents, I sat on the edge of the bathtub where he wanted me, trickling water up his chest with my toes.

"My brain is sore, love," he murmured through the damp washcloth plastered to his face, arms draped over the sides of the tub, fingertips trailing water on the tile where it would stay until New Service he hired arrived in yellow shoe covers and red lipstick and no motherly gaze behind the fake one she created for Bastien. "Tell me how you feel about me."

This was my cue to turn to the most poetic passage in the blue journal and read aloud the words I wrote about him. A grown man, needing those words.

"I want to go with you to the Delta Base," I said instead.

His hand encircled my foot under the soapy water, the pad of his thumb rough. "You don't know how good you have it. You sit in rooms few women enter. I've taken you places few Black women have gone, and still, that isn't enough for you."

I said the only words that had ever been able to change his mind. "Then I'll go home. I'm not staying here waiting for you."

Washcloth pulled from his face, he stared into me, mustache and beard slick with water. He wanted me to delete my words from the air, to show him his word was my world. "You've been starting arguments before bed. You'll refuse to let me touch you. Yesterday, it was about attending a meeting. Tonight, it's Georgia."

I looked into the exhausted eyes of this man who was saying I was pulling away from him; he could see it. He was right. I couldn't find what I'd seen in him during that white-gray winter last year.

"Tell me why you're never satisfied," he said when I pulled my foot from his wet grasp. I stood at the picture window, cupping my elbows, and squinting at a gray sky stealing the sun. He always demanded I speak first, my thoughts spilling around us like seawater. For reasons I couldn't understand, that was exactly why I ended up drowning. I never won.

My silence stole his peace. "Goddammit. Every day, something else to show your discontent. I don't know how long I can go on like this. Why can't you just be?"

HE TOOK ME TO GEORGIA. LOCKED in a room on the tenth floor of a housing unit, I saw little more than the tops of the tiny heads of masked soldiers lined on the sidewalk below. I let a drop of tea dribble from my mug over the balcony's edge. A test to see if a toy soldier would look up. They didn't.

Only the sun moved, skimming behind the tangle of highways. The trucks carrying lumber. The brothels I mistook for large hospitals.

Before he left for a meeting this morning, I lay in a bed that wasn't mine, head pounding, childhood tucked in the buttoning of his shirt, the looping of his tie, the zipping of his pants. "You're just like the rest of them. Yes, you are. Then why didn't you find a white girl to do all these nasty things to every single day? I hate being here. Send me back to my dorm when we get back to Austin."

But then at night in the dark, who would I be? One of a million nothings in twin-size beds in nondescript buildings repurposed as housing for DoS.

He stared at his reflection, but he would never see what I saw—

the incessant taking, near frantic, of the time I could never rewind. He saw only duty, the sharp lines of a suit, each hair perfect and shaped with sandalwood pomade.

"You're ready to move on to ruin someone else?"

Everything was always my fault. I was never happy. Even in my dreams, I was reaching for something hurrying away from me.

I pressed fists to my bleary eyes. "I haven't ruined you. I'm tired of doing these things."

"Things you ask for. Things you like," he stressed, and I couldn't tell if he was asking me or telling me.

He used to ask, plucking the words from me, satisfied by the way I hung new details in the air like globe lights. Was God listening the night I said those words without Bastien asking? What kind of girl couldn't determine the difference between things she liked and things she pretended she liked?

"I don't like how I feel afterward. I want to be normal," I said. "I want to be with a good person."

But I didn't know what that looked like. I thought I knew back when I was an uncomplicated girl in Dallas. Now I was in the twisty dark, foraging for proof that men at home were any better than the man standing in front of me.

"You don't know what you want, do you? If you can't see the good in me, I'll let you go. That's what you want? Yes? Then I'm done with this." He slammed the door behind him, then seconds later unlocked it and folded me in his miserable arms. "Why are you never happy, love?"

Because we were waking from this dream in color and rubbing it from our eyes. I could see it then. There was a less disturbing version of us that existed in another life. There was me in New Orleans writing *My Henriette*, the sun rising over palm trees, crimson houses, the sepia ground my ancestors once walked. There was him at his wedding, him at a dinner table with administrators and their wives offering him their cheeks to kiss. Lipstick smudges on water glasses. No soldier assigned to hide it from a contemplative God.

. . .

THROUGH PAIN AND UNDERSTANDING, THERE IS writing. At a table on the
balcony, I opened the brown journal I hadn't touched in months.
Part four of Henriette's story poured from me. I had entered her
time, and she was guiding my hand with a whispered story. If I
could hear her, could she hear me? I turned to the last page and
wrote:

Tell my daddy his little girl still hears his footsteps in the dark . . .
Love, Solenne

The sky was lusterless, and the air had chilled by the time I lifted
my eyes to where Henriette's soul had surely gone. Once on a ship
called *L'Aliénor*, once on a plantation where she loved and lost a boy.
My Henriette. My blood. My compass and map song.

A knock at the door disturbed my thoughts. I didn't move until
the lock clicked. Bastien had unlocked the door remotely.

I tied a robe over my cami and answered.

A soldier craned his razor-burned neck into the room. "I have
your dinner."

I stepped aside so he could enter, but he pushed a silver tray into
my hands.

"My orders are to remain outside of the room." His gaze shifted
nervously down the hallway. "How much does it cost?"

"What?"

He gestured to what he saw as nothing more than an exotic pool
he could pay to dip himself into. Black girls couldn't get angry. Black
girls let it roll off their backs. Tell yourself it doesn't matter, doesn't
hurt, doesn't rip you apart at the seams.

I kept my voice even. "How much would you pay?"

How much would he pay to remind me of exactly who I was?
How much was that worth?

. . .

THINGS SUBMERGED EVENTUALLY RISE TO THE surface. It was in the stiffness in my body when Bastien returned to our gray-dark room and gathered me in his arms. He smelled like a dinner table I'd never be invited to— wine and tomato sauce.

"Exhausted," he said with his face resting in my sleep-shuffled hair. "What did you do today?"

I rolled out of bed to stand and look down at him. "What can I do in a locked room other than wait for you to come back?"

He closed his eyes so he wouldn't see me. "You understand this is for your safety."

I didn't see him either, I saw the soldier with a tray of mediocre food and his offer reducing me to nothing. I fisted my robe at the thigh.

His eyes looked so old—veins trickling from eyebrow to eyelash, the lower lids rimmed with blood-red exhaustion. A fingertip-sized horseshoe was imprinted on his upper cheek, like he'd pressed a nail there, using the jolt of pain to stay awake.

"No answer. You'd rather stand there fuming, of course, to add on to the rest of the nonsense I deal with daily." He reclined on the bed and, my God, the journal containing *My Henriette* I forgot to hide in the bottom of my suitcase lay next to him. I lunged for it. The first mistake. Bastien read panic as a threat.

"Give me my journal."

He frowned at the nondescript cover. Brown, not blue. The one James gave me, not the fancy blue one he replaced James's gift with. "Where is the journal I gave you?"

"Give me—"

We were on the bed, a tumble of breath and limbs until he peeled me off and rolled away. I kicked at the bars of his back and stomach until he was winded. Standing with the journal above his head, I couldn't stop him from flipping it open, exposing all that was inside. Words meant nothing on their own. It was the *way* the story was

told. On those pages was proof Bastien and I would never understand each other. Time had shown me one too many versions of him.
I'd seen him sitting behind his desk, his hard face, the swipe of his
pen on a document denying Black women all he was born possessing.
I'd seen the worry in his pacing, footsteps falling like prayers before
he pressed a chilled washcloth to my feverish forehead. We lived in
a nation of hypocrites, and I lay next to this man each night, hating
and loving. I was one, too.

"If they're just words and drawings like you say, why are you
hiding it from me?"

"Because you take everything even though you have everything,"
I said, weeping. "Nothing is ever mine."

His face contorted as it had the night he learned my unwilling-
ness to sleep facing an open closet door wasn't me being difficult.
I was afraid of its yawning dark. He exhaled and kissed my empty
hands, the frailty inside. "My God, I forget you're so young. Sometimes I don't remember."

WHILE HE SLEPT, I STOOD IN front of a basin filled with warm water. Once
I made the decision, it really wasn't as hard to do as I thought. The
sheets peeled easily from the journal, tearing cleanly at the binding.
My work, *My Henriette*, dissolved into a blue blur on crumpled pages.
The words were safe now, away from his eyes. The story would remain
where it belonged—with me, my family, the descendants of slavery.
I'd already given him everything I had. He would never take this
from me.

CHAPTER 36

NOW

DALENA STOOD IN FRONT OF THE OPEN REFRIGERATOR. "I SHOULD BE ASHAMED. Refrigerator is so empty it looks like it's for sale. Eggs, it is."

I sipped my coffee. "I'm fine with this. I don't eat eggs, remember?"

"Okay, princess," she said, like I was obligated to love everything under the sun.

"Princess? When I was twelve, I cracked open an egg, and a chicken fetus tumbled out into my cake batter."

Dalena slammed the refrigerator door. "Oh, yuck. Sadistic. Why would you tell me that?"

"If you hadn't disappeared for five years, you would've remembered that story."

She did that fluttery thing she did with her eyebrows when she was annoyed, but she smiled. "Brain like a sieve. I'd hate to see me at fifty."

Source buzzed next to my mug.

MEMPHIS: Admin will see you any day between 8 and 12.

"Why do you look like you saw a ghost?"

In a sense, I had. "Memphis messaged. He got me approval to see Admin."

"That's what we want. We'll go get groceries, you'll go see Admin, then Bourbon's tonight."

"No, I'm laying low until I get my papers."

I told her about Armie.

She held up her hands. "Did anyone bother you last night? Nope. Seen any agents in New Orleans? Nope. That Armie guy probably was really trying to help you."

I sipped my coffee, thinking it over.

"And what if he wasn't? What if he was trying to turn me in for the money?"

"Look, no matter where I went, I didn't get Lucas off my back until I made it to New Orleans. Nobody here will turn you in."

AFTER I DRESSED IN BORROWED JEANS and a black chiffon shirt, I stood in front of the dresser staring at my reflection.

"Ready?" Dalena appeared in the doorway, fiddling with her wrist ribbon. I met her eyes in the mirror.

"This afternoon . . ."

She sighed. "You're having second thoughts about seeing Admin."

I gathered my hair in a ponytail right at the shoulders. "I want to get a haircut before I go."

She folded her arms and leaned against the door frame. "A thousand grandmas just flipped in their graves. DoS don't cut their hair. It's cultural."

Yes, but it hadn't really been mine for years. It had been Bastien's. The cultural significance had been pruned back to one brittle branch.

"I need the change."

Outside the window, there were so many oak trees. Immovable brown with tangles of green. If I stayed here and was nonrestricted like Dalena, I would remove all the curtains. Let the sunlight and earth in.

"You mean you want to take something from the official. I get it, but it won't change the mistakes you made with him. Find another way to leave him behind. Solenne, are you listening to me?"

A black spider crawled from a corner of the window. Its thready legs trembled. "Of course, I'm listening. You're the expert on leaving people behind."

She was beside me at the window, her reflection blurring into mine. "You have something to say to me, speak your mind."

"My mama said guilt guides assumptions."

She didn't lash out like she would have back in Dallas. She smiled, but it took effort. "I've lost so much in my life, but guilt? Never could shake it. It's persistent. It wakes me up every morning. I figured I may as well learn to live with it."

AT A TIME WHEN I'D NORMALLY be in bed for the night, we left Dalena's house in an SPV. We arrived in front of Bourbon's and caught the tail end of the parade. The drones overhead captured the colors of women wearing feathers above and below, strutting in front of a band of drums and brass instruments. We watched until the sounds faded into the next block, then stood clapping with the rest of the crowd.

Memphis waved us through the line, promising me a dance later. Through manufactured smoke and vapor, Cairo sat at a table with one of his men. He tilted his head at us in acknowledgment, lights catching on the ridiculous shades he wore in the dark. Dalena accepted the glasses of champagne he sent to our table and motioned to the waitress for more. I finished two glasses too quickly and felt it rush to my head. "Are we dancing?" I asked Dalena.

She waved me off to join the brown bodies writhing on floors slickened with spilled champagne. Vapor crept between us, weaving us like a quilt, and I laughed at the idea there was an us I hadn't known about until now. Us meant you were part of something larger than you, and after music and buildings were gone, you'd still have the life next to you to say, *Hey, remember that night when?* Eyes closed, I stretched my hands over my head and became someone else. Someone free to feel the sweat from unknown bodies bumping against her and laugh because of it. Someone who forgot she was ever a little girl left behind.

An arm slid around my waist. I looked up into Memphis's face. Instead of recoiling, I leaned into him.

"I made it in time," he said after slipping his lips under the hair over my ear.

The music led our bodies. Champagne-loose lips, I said things I'd only said to Bastien. Things that lifted dark eyebrows. This wasn't me, or was it? Who would I have been had I made different decisions at sixteen? I was here now, under mist and lights and a man's arm who didn't have paperwork stating he owned me. The lights. There were so many, transforming me into a woman with her own thoughts and a body that belonged to her alone.

Someone bumped me, sending me farther into Memphis's open arms. He didn't mind.

"We can go to your apartment," I said when another bump was enough to tap the back of his head against the wall. We checked the beanie; it was safe.

"No, let's get something to eat. We can have dinner," he said, frowning, but that wasn't true. Men didn't give a damn about dinner. They wanted the Black girl's parts, assembled or otherwise.

We left the dance floor fastened together. Everything could change for me tonight. Somewhere along the path to the door, my legs became heavier, pinned by the lights.

"You good?" Memphis asked.

My eyes swept through vapor to find the lights. The champagne swirled in my stomach.

I was paranoid. Multiple people could use Source at once. I'd seen it dozens of times on the train, in stores, at theater performances. Maybe it was the dark and the sway of bodies that made it appear the users weren't aware Source hung connected from their palms.

More green lights flashed then disappeared like lightning. One user, two users, five. Flickered, then closed. Over and over the lights flashed, seeking, creating a straight path that pointed to me like a candescent arrow. Tangles of bodies—dancing, smoking, drinks in hands—I ripped through them all, shoving, and shouting my apologies until I found the back door.

Around me, alley lights swept over shadows, opening everything for drones hovering overhead. I pressed my back against the building to breathe.

Memphis spilled out after me and used his shoulder against the door to press the music inside. "What happened?"

I felt the bricks at my back, the gravel beneath my heels. "The official knows I'm here."

"He can't track you without an active chip. You're working yourself up for nothing."

I slid to the ground, probably ruining Dalena's scarlet silk dress. "What was I thinking, leaving here with you? This is ridiculous."

He crossed his arms, defensiveness lifting the corners of his lips. "Spending time with a Black man is ridiculous?"

"What? This isn't about you."

"No, it's about you letting a white man who ain't even here dictate your every move."

"Like I still wouldn't be in this exact position if he were Black. How many women here are hiding from a Black man?"

"Nah, we're different. There's certain things we don't do."

"Explain that to the one who had me by the throat in front of my school."

He threw up his hands. "Let's make this simple. Do you want to forget about all of this? Do you want to leave here right now and go to dinner like we planned?"

My answer wasn't there in the night sky where the drones flew. It wasn't in the concrete and gravel beneath my feet, but I searched there for words.

"I can't, but it has nothing to do with you."

"Keep making excuses. If that's the life you want, fine. Don't waste my time." He flung the door open, and I closed my eyes so I didn't have to witness him walking away from me.

"Maybe this is your fault," I said.

He paused. "My fault?"

He was my daddy, James, and Dalena, all that the drought and dry winds took from me when I needed.

"Your fault," I repeated. "I was just a girl. I couldn't do anything alone. Couldn't move mountains. Make waves. If those of you who made it out reached back to help us who didn't—"

"How do you know we didn't, because the official told you we didn't?"

"—the Order would look different. You didn't. You go from city to city, hiding your face, worrying about no one but yourself. Like a coward. Like Dalena."

I opened my eyes. Dalena stood in the doorway. I wanted to pretend the music drowned out my words, but her face wilted, denying me that opportunity.

The back door banged shut with Memphis and Dalena inside. They would never understand how I had become who I was, and maybe I never would either.

CHAPTER 37

NOW

IT WAS JUST BEFORE DAWN WHEN THE UNSPOKEN TRUTH LED US TO DALENA'S kitchen table. I tried not to think of the dozen ways Dalena left me behind to become the girl searching for love until the bitter ground swallowed her.

I picked at a muffin while she smoked, ashing the cigarette on a saucer.

"What did you want me to do? Break into the Capitol and drive you to Louisiana? Even if I had, you'd still be in the position you're in now."

I twisted my promise ring, the stone smooth under my fingertips. "Back then, he would've let me go."

"When? At what point would he have released you?"

She watched my face as I cycled through the years. Fifteen in the Capitol, sixteen in his bed, seventeen, eighteen.

"What happened with James Gibson? He was your way out, not me. You got in your own way, thinking you were in love, and now you want to blame everyone else."

"It didn't start with James. It started in your bedroom in Dallas. Why didn't you include me in your plans? You sat in front of me talking about leaving me behind because I was nothing."

I was crying, staring into my mug and crying.

"You weren't nothing."

"I was nothing to you."

She closed her eyes. Words were easier in the dark. "You were everything to me. I talked big like I had plans, but I had nothing but two names to use in New Orleans that turned out to be fake and the want to be free. If you found out I was nothing, I'd have to admit it to myself. You have this way of seeing things in people and making them feel bigger than they are. A mercy or a curse. That's what the official saw in you."

We sat, murmuring apologies, healing, letting tears exist. Here, Black girls could be sad and soft, stories in a brown leather journal. Human.

IN MY DREAMS OF HENRIETTE, SHE keeps her back to me. She moves too quickly, her voice a whisper. I let her guide me through a world where brown girls move without shadows. Right before I awake, she turns to me and says, *Remember. Nothing is just.*

In a just world, Lucas wouldn't have had a wife named Sunny who made Dalena her enemy. She wouldn't have had quick hands, open or clenched into fists, for the girl who didn't go to the baby fast enough, for holding him too long, for existing. Her name wouldn't have been, *hey you, girl,* or *idiot.* Numbing poison from a woman who drank too much to dull the fatigue of being an administrator's wife. Dalena wouldn't have had to sleep on a pallet on Sunny's side of the bed—the weak insurance husbands would remain faithful.

She lay still in darkness until her mind dusted away to nothing. The months brought bitter winds and breathless thoughts of slitting Sunny's wrist that hung from the mattress above her head. She would never do it. She wasn't like Sunny. She was Dalena, empty and cold. So when Lucas slipped out of bed with his sleep-drunk wife, Dalena welcomed him under her blanket and let herself become warm. For weeks, only their breath blended with Sunny's sighs. She never wanted him, but she took him from that bitch because she could, and she kept on taking him until the cold morning he chose to seep into her instead of beating the sunrise to his empty spot in bed next to his wife. They lay, Sunny's white hair haloed on her blue pillowcase above them, and Dalena thought about paints and art room closets and lips soft and full like her own, and she held Lucas tighter and trembled until he put his mouth on hers to silence her. That moment they became Magdalena, a mash-up of his last name and her first, inked permanently on her right wrist and between his shoulder blades. That moment she knew she needed to fade away or lose herself in the ash storm.

DALENA LOOKED UP AT ME AND tightened her wrist ribbon. "The worst thing our mamas taught us was how to be good liars. I pretended every day I wanted what he wanted. What I really wanted was for him to keep telling Sunny he'd send her back to Augusta if she didn't keep her hands off me. But he was never going to have me like that. Never changing me into something I'm not. His aunt Penelope knew a configurator who took me off grid. She found places for me to hide out. He eventually found me. Seemed like he always showed up when I was happiest, too. Got to the point I was scared of happiness. The last time I ran, he found me with Yara."

That name had to hurt for her to speak. Her voice crumbled over syllables. The sparrows in the crown of the oak trees sang their songs, filling the kitchen with all I wouldn't ask.

"He scared me so much when he found me that time, I gave up. Told myself I'd never run again. But then I got pregnant, and the pills Penelope gave me didn't work. It went far enough for Source to detect a pregnancy. Lucas didn't have access to that data, but someone from Austin contacted him. Me and Sunny sat on the porch that night, watching him drink whiskey from his beer bottles, shooting his guns, and screaming at the sky that the official and no man on earth could take anything from him. Not his salt and sugar. Sunny thought he was talking about Georgia, but I knew it was my contract. She was too drunk to care anyway. Later, he came to my bedroom and said I was never leaving Atlanta. When he fell asleep next to me, like he didn't have a wife, I thought about Sunny. I thought about her grandma, that hateful bat, and how both bitches told me every day I was nothing. A whore. Tattoos meant nothing because Sunny had Lucas's only child. She needed that *one* thing I didn't have, you know? To go on every day knowing what Lucas was doing with me. Now that was gone. I knew what she'd do to me and that baby if I had it. I decided right then, I wasn't having it, and that would be the last time I saw any of them."

She fled to Louisiana and found a more reliable way to end the pregnancy. She drifted from place to place after that, hiding until she got approved for asylum.

"A Black girl can't breathe, can she?" I finally said.

"Not in a storm."

That truth punctuated our discussion. After I finished my muffin, she stood. "Let me show you something."

She led me into the living room past Twin's chair to the window overlooking the front yard casually lit by a rising sun. Crouching there, she ran her fingers over the wooden floorboards until she found a groove. A board slid away, then another, revealing a space large enough to hide valuables . . . or a body. "There's another reason I never ripped up the floors."

"We need time," I told the both of us because I couldn't imagine my life hiding under floors like escaped enslaved people two hundred years ago. That wasn't freedom. "He'll see this is good for us once he gets over being pissed off."

"Solenne. Sometimes you're so smart, you're stupid. This is the official, not Lucas. You want to win, you gone need more than a piece of paper from Admin."

Sunlight quickened over the floors and walls and consumed the shadows. It left the truth.

....

CHAPTER 38

NOW

THE WATER FEATURE BEHIND THE ADMINISTRATOR'S DESK GURGLED LIKE A WATER-fall. TROY MOSELEY was printed in bold on his clear desk nameplate, but he said I could call him Troy. Sable skin and dark waves tucked under a black beret, he looked younger than his mid-fifties until you got close enough to see the accordion folds at the corner of his eyes and mouth.

I liked Troy until he stuffed his hands in his pants pockets and jingled keys inside and said, "This could be simple. Have you tried asking the official to release you? That could be more effective than removing yourself without consent."

My smile receded. "I came here for your help."

"And I'm here to provide it."

"Yet you ask if I've tried asking *the* official if he's willing—" I breathed through the wave. "He's not willing to release me. Can we please move on to the next steps?"

Troy was closer, bringing with him the smell of fruit. Probably from the hair grease he used under his wave cap at night to maintain waves so slick.

"Arbitration. Bastien Martin is a councilman, which complicates things greatly."

"I'm not willing to do arbitration. I don't want to see him."

"It's a virtual meeting. What do you fear?"

That he would break me as usual, and I would go limp, rolling back to him like tumbleweed.

"That doesn't matter. He has his strategy; I have mine."

The keys jingled as he crossed the room behind me. "And your strategy is to avoid speaking to him? How long do you expect that to last?"

"I can't talk to him. He won't listen. He makes decisions with no input from me."

"During arbitration, the goal isn't to get him to listen to you. The purpose is for each party to present their positions to me. He doesn't see you; he doesn't speak to you; he speaks to me."

"He doesn't follow rules he didn't make himself."

"If he can't follow my rules, I disconnect and rule without him. You have my word."

His smile and the tune of his keys reassured me. I exhaled.

Bastien answered within seconds of Troy sending a communication request. "You've reached a decision on the injunction."

I was fifteen again, lightning-shocked, counting black brass up his shirt until I reached his eyes.

Troy rattled around the room, Source in his hand. "Not quite. I need a bit more information."

"You're trying my patience, Administrator. First, you dismiss a reasonable injunction, then you go on vacation after receiving the modified request. Now you need a bit more information. I have—"

"I'm here with Ms. Bonet."

"Let me see her." The command was instant. "Solenne, are you safe?"

I closed my eyes as if it could block out the turmoil in his voice.

"Official, she has applied for asylum."

"Which you immediately denied." Not a question, a command. "She doesn't understand what she's doing, Administrator."

"Her application is in consideration along with your request to enter the state."

Bastien's voice hardened. "She cannot file documents on her behalf, so anything she has submitted to your office is illegal. Let me speak to her."

Troy sat behind his desk, his Source painfully close to me now. "Ms. Bonet has requested arbitration. Do you agree to proceed?"

"This is between Solenne and me. We don't need outside interference. We know what we want."

A neat shuffle of paper. A chair rolling. Murmurs.

I gripped the arms of my chair. I counted on Bastien's personality clashing with Troy's but if Julian was there, winning would be nearly impossible. Julian existed to provide everything Bastien couldn't. He was Bastien's voice of reason. The calm.

"We look forward to entering arbitration, Administrator. Before we begin, your brothers in Austin thank you for opening your state and taking excellent care of Solenne. We trust that this will continue for the few remaining hours of her visit."

Fuck.

"I'll guarantee her safety while she's in my state."

He was already buttered.

"You've done an excellent job so far, brother," Julian continued. "You know, it would mean so much to us if we could see her to make sure she's safe. Briefly, of course."

Troy looked over the desk at me.

"No," I hissed. "You gave me your word."

"My brother can be harsh, I admit, but understand the circumstances. That woman in your office means . . . *everything* to him. You're a smart man. You can see she's well provided for." He took a dramatic pause, probably flashing an empathy-inducing smile. "Imagine a world you wake up in where you can't see Sakina's beautiful face for four days. Misery, correct?"

I found the silver-framed image of the pretty woman on Troy's desk, rotated just enough so everyone who visited his office could enjoy her as much as he did. What came next didn't surprise me.

Troy threw up a hand. "Brief. Then we move on to arbitration."

Source opened on the mirror behind Troy's desk. Bastien stood in his office, arms crossed over his chest, glass tumbler in one hand. I couldn't look at his face, but still, it was enough to knock the air from me. Sometime between my body begging for a breath and Julian speaking, Source flickered closed.

Troy presented the arbitration rules. We weren't to address one another directly. We should only say things we wanted entered into consideration. He would make a decision by the close of business today.

Bastien succinctly presented his position. I was only twenty years old, naive, confused, and perhaps influenced by people who were also naive and confused. I didn't understand what I was asking for. I had no idea how to earn money, manage expenses, or find housing. I did not and would never have permission to leave Austin, and as administrator and a man, Troy had the obligation to return me to him without delay.

Breakfast was coming back up. I could parse the coffee's bitterness from the maple muffin on the back of my tongue.

"Ms. Bonet?"

What did I expect in this place where dismissive eyes told me Bastien could never love me because of the power imbalance, and I was only a belly warmer, his stupid little girl who needed no more than locked doors, the drive through slums, the gifts, the accusations that I caused his brokenness, and the whispers, *I love you, I love you*—to keep me from running, to keep me flailing against the truth that I was no different than his dogs or vehicles? Why didn't I expect him to work this process with ice in his voice like he did with any business deal? Bully into submission, and if that didn't work, send in smiley Julian for property recovery. The weight of five years thinned my breath. There was none.

"Ms. Bonet, are you ready to continue?"

My eyes finally met Troy's. "I'm ready."

But I wasn't. My body wanted to curl in on itself. My heart hurt and my tongue was stunned dead in my mouth. I fumbled through questions. My voice sounded odd, like listening to a recording of myself from years earlier. Had the official abused me? Did he provide for me? Did I believe my life was in danger?

"Why did you flee?" Troy asked.

"Four years ago, he promised me emancipation."

"Fabrication," Bastien said.

"I asked him to honor that promise. He said no. Not even in death."

Troy stood, pulled back the drapes so sunlight drowned artificial light, and stared at the street below. "What if he offers that document now? Would you drop your request and return?"

"He won't, Troy."

"Troy? You're on a first-name basis with a man you just met?"

"Let's not make assumptions," Troy said.

"If he did, I still wouldn't return. I'll never return."

It would be a trick anyway. A bending of the truth in his hands that I wouldn't recognize until it was too late.

"I hold your contract. You don't have a choice."

"You're not to speak directly to her."

"Bullshit. I have a state full of choices now. Everything I lost when I met you."

"You had nothing when we met. You were wandering around a basement, chasing a gay man, depressed, until I stepped in. The time I lost, catering to you." He took a breath. "You disrupted my life, and now you expect me to allow you to walk away from me."

Is that what I'd done? The shift in his routines and thoughts, our arguments, my demands. If I had, what had he done to me?

"What did you think it would be like when you decided to be with someone almost half your age? You disrupted your own life. Let me live mine."

"The life of privilege I provide for you isn't living?" His ability to hold it together was dissolving like salt in water. I imagined his fists clenched. "How much are your jewelry collection and wardrobe worth?"

Troy looked over my privileged body—carefully trimmed ends, manicured nails, the jewels on the straps of my shoes. Bastien was winning.

My hands shook, but I spoke before I changed my mind. "Living is going home with a different man every night for three nights."

Glass smashed.

I grimaced.

Troy muted the audio, then shook a finger at me like Guidry when the class got too loud. "You cut that out. Now!"

I caught a breath.

After several minutes of pacing, Troy restored volume.

"Gentlemen, we've veered off course," Julian said calmly. "We're on the same side. Now that we have preliminary discussions complete, let's focus on negotiations. Administrator, you have something the official needs. Your state has needs. Let's discuss how to bridge that gap."

I searched for Troy's eyes but only found his back. "What about my needs?"

"You understand we will pass Proposition 1077, allowing a contract holder to pursue a fugitive. Brother, the incentive to get that pushed through Council yesterday is sitting across from you right now," Julian said, voice soothing like the water in the faux fountain. "Next comes the manhunt. We'd rather avoid that. It's cost-prohibitive and could spiral out of control in ways I don't enjoy imagining."

Troy's back stiffened. "Is that a threat?"

"Of course not, brother. Isn't your policy to put the needs of your state first? Solenne is in your office. I'm merely pointing out we have a more sensible solution before us."

The air changed in the room. Julian stacked bricks against me one at a time like a man building a bridge over a moat.

"What do you propose?" Troy asked.

"Lower Ninth Ward. My records show the area is being rebuilt by donors. They've made progress, but they can't do it all. Accept the transfer I wire to your Treasury account," Julian said, lingering on "accept" and "your" like hypnosis.

"I don't make any decisions without conferencing with my cabinet."

"Troy, let's be honest. Your cabinet defaults to your judgment, as they should. You've never steered them wrong. Approve the modified injunction. We need one hour, one jet, two men if you entertain Solenne in your office until our arrival. This can all be behind us before lunchtime. Now, how soon can you speak to your treasurer to accept the transfer?"

I stood. "I don't consent to this. I won't go back."

"My treasurer arrives in two hours."

"You'll be compensated directly for your time, in addition—off the record of course."

Troy gave his pocket a hefty shake. "I'll follow up in three hours."

When he disconnected, the rotten fruit-smelling bastard spun to face me.

The electronic bolt on the office door echoed.

I HAD BEEN BOUGHT AND SOLD again. I did everything right, and still, Bastien won. Troy looked through me, counting the flurry of dollars on their way to his Treasury.

"So this is it? You turn me over to Bastien without considering my side?"

The coward still didn't meet my eyes. "I heard your side. To be approved for asylum, you need to be fleeing danger. This isn't a case of abuse. This, by your own admission."

"I admit it doesn't look like your other cases, but it's the same."

To the men, it was black and white. No bruises, no torn clothing, no abuse.

Back still turned, he opened Source and sent a message. If he didn't see me, I wasn't real. I was Bastien's thing. Something that slipped from his grasp that he would offer a sizable reward to retrieve.

"I run a state on rules predetermined by the original administrator seventy years ago. That which keeps Louisiana a nonrestricted state."

He had been willing to ignore those rules before Julian. Dalena said people here were all business, but there was more than one way to approach business. I'd watched Bastien and Julian negotiate for years. I needed allies, and I'd have to do it by convincing Troy he had more in common with me, a Black woman, than he had with them, white men.

"Troy, do you have a daughter?"

"This has nothing to do with my family life." He finally looked at me. "My daughter would know better than to place her plans for freedom in the hands of the man who owned her."

Troy was right, and it stung to hear. I was trying to undo what I'd spent years building in days, and the climb was steep.

"I was sixteen."

"You should've known better."

"At what point can we be children? Why do we always have to know better? We were taught that this was our way out. *He* was my way out. I knew nothing else."

He stared at his boots and rocked on his heels. "After the last hurricane, Texas sent ten million to assist with restoration. Reconstructing the levee system cost twenty-eight million. New Orleans is struggling. Now, I can empathize with you, but I'm obligated to settle this with the least amount of disruption to my citizens."

"I'm your citizen. I'm here with you now."

"I think you knew this would be temporary."

"I guessed it. What I didn't guess is that you'd allow yourself to be manipulated. Julian tested you and knew he would win the moment you let them see me. You lost."

His gaze snapped to me. "Tread carefully, Ms. Bonet."

My legs still struggled under me, but I moved close enough to smell the fruit in his hair. "Where was your protection of your citizen's privacy last night? Bastien accessed more than four hundred users' Source at Bourbon's to search for me. I may not know all the laws, but I know a data breach when I see one. That's an illegal use of Source."

The accordion folds around his eyes deepened. "How do you know this?"

"I was there. I saw it. He does it because he knows you'll let him get away with anything. Run an audit, question some of the patrons, or don't. You'll find what I'm saying is the truth now, or when your people vote you out of office next year."

He lifted the corner of his beret, scratched scattered black at his crown, capped himself again.

CHAPTER 39

NOW

W HEN I GOT BACK TO DALENA'S HOUSE, SHE WAS IN A CHAIR ON HER PORCH, smoking. She blew out a cloud of smoke, eyes flitting over me. "I was starting to think you were back in Austin," she said. "You've been gone all day. Troy screwed you over?"

I dropped in the wooden chair next to her, my bag on my lap. I didn't feel like speaking, but she was in this with me. "Still undecided. He let me leave his office so he could meet with his cabinet. He said they'd have an answer in a few hours, so I rode around to kill time. When I called to check the status, his assistant said he left the office."

"You'll go back tomorrow."

"I can't—"

"Twelve rounds, remember?"

"I'm not giving up. His assistant said they'll notify me through Source."

Calling Troy every type of bastard I could think of, I told her about the arbitration and how the only thing that saved me from being sold immediately was the data breach from last night at Bourbon's.

"Bastien owes me my freedom. I gave him everything," I said. "What more does he want?"

Dalena ground out her cigarette on her chair's arm. "He doesn't want to lose."

• • •

I COOKED SHRIMP CREOLE FOR DINNER, and we ate on the porch, plates balanced on our knees. I didn't taste most of it. I ate quickly and let the sound of the wind in the trees replace my thoughts until the mosquitoes sent us inside where the dishes waited. I washed; she dried and worked on a bottle of wine.

Later, I sat in her bed and watched her try on dresses and jewelry and listened to her story about each of her paintings that hung on the walls. They were places she had hidden until Lucas found her. Some were tiny towns with fewer than five hundred citizens, towns made of nothing but fields and sky, nondescript enough to forget. She stared at the ceiling and snapped her fingers when the names came to her.

"Did you meet Yara in one of those towns?"

Sweeping her braids into a top bun one at a time, she gave me the final piece of her story she buried long ago to distance herself from the pain of happiness.

She met Yara on a private beach in Florida. Blue-eyed, sandy hair and skin tone, she looked like she'd been created from the ground beneath her feet. They spent their days entwined under blankets on the floor of Yara's unfurnished apartment and their nights breathing salty air on the shore. Moonlight giving way to sunrise, they sorted through the shared pain of life hidden behind a mask. Yara's mother presented her to the world as the fourth and final child of her marriage. Her real daddy was a Black soldier from Michigan. Yara yearned to grasp those roots, but she never would. Her mother wouldn't name him out of constant fear Source would update Yara as Black and dump her into the assignment pool. Dalena painted portraits of how they thought her daddy looked, using Yara as her model. They named him Samson and hung different iterations of him in every room. Yara never asked about the man Dalena escaped from or the tattoo on her wrist. When she awoke one morning and found Dalena tracing the green ink, indelible both in form and memory, she tore the strap from her nightgown and ribboned it around Dalena's wrist. Dalena looked into Yara's eyes and named that place love. It didn't matter. Lucas found her there, too.

"Why didn't you go back to find her after you got your asylum papers?"

"Yara was a dreamer. She reminded me a lot of you." She peeled off her dress and let it pool at her feet. We both stared at this version of her in the floor-length mirror, naked and honest. "Lucas sucked the magic out of us and ruined her fairy tale. He showed up with his rifle and demands, and she saw what life would've been like had she been born two shades darker."

"You could message her. What if she's thinking of you?"

There were days in my past where even one message from Dalena would've healed me. What if Yara was somewhere waiting, too?

"I looked her up on Social last year. She found a different fairy tale. She married a pilot. A brownstone in New York. A house in Sanibel. A baby girl swaddled in a blanket that matched her blue maternity pajamas. Her baby is the age mine would've been." She stripped off the wrist ribbon, let it join the dress at her feet. "You know me. It doesn't bother me at all. The best way to love someone is to want a beautiful life for them, however they find it."

By the time we finished hanging all the clothes and jewelry she pulled from the closet, it was well after midnight. She lit the dark living room with three taper candles in glass jars on the coffee table. We lay side by side on the sofa, neither of us admitting we worried Bastien would show up while we slept in the back of the house.

Dalena pointed to my firearm on the table in front of the candles. "How good are you with it?"

"Daddy showed me the basics when I was thirteen."

"I can show you more than the basics. We can go right out there in a clearing and practice."

"How do you know how to shoot?"

"Penelope showed me. She overheard Lucas tell me if I ran again, I better take a Sunday dress with me. He said, 'When I find you, I'll bury you in it.' Penelope said if he tries me, I better send that bastard six floors below hell with his daddy. I know he will one day. I'll be ready."

"Wasn't Lucas's daddy her brother?"

"She hated him, too."

Our hands entwined in the dark.

"Tell me about your book. How old was Henriette when they brought her here?"

"Fifteen."

"Was she pretty?"

I had no images of her, but more than brown skin cursed her.

"My mama has her bill of sale. They sold her as a fancy girl. The man who enslaved her paid five times what he paid for a field hand at that same auction."

Dalena yawned and rested her face in my hair. "How did you write Henriette's story and still mess up with the official the way you did? Because he didn't hit you? Because he didn't get married? Because he gave in to those fits you throw?"

Because I wrote when I was hurting. Only then could I look at the truth.

"No matter what happens with Admin, you'll never see the official the same. They know once you get that taste of freedom, nothing will keep you in line. Lucas knew it. I'd already seen the sunset over Sanibel Island in pink and orange. Seeing something like that makes you feel like somebody created something just for you. It was like unwrapping a present every time I blinked. I wanted to keep it forever. Not a piece. All of it."

"You can't own a sunset," I said, yawning. "It wasn't meant to be owned."

"I'm not a man, dodo bird. I know that." She draped an arm over me protectively. We slept.

SOURCE BUZZED FROM BENEATH THE SOFA, waking me. I squinted at the lights.

From the Office of the Louisiana Administrator . . .

I sat up. Now I would learn whether I'd talked Troy into approving my asylum application and if I had outwitted Bastien and Julian, an award-winning master negotiator.

Hands shaking, I reached for Dalena. She wasn't asleep behind me anymore. I clicked the message.

> In a unanimous vote, the Louisiana Council approved your application for asylum. You will receive a . . .

I stretched my fingers to the ceiling. "*I win. I'm* the master negotiator."

Dalena wasn't on the porch smoking. She wasn't in the dark kitchen or bedroom. A slice of light from a crack in the bathroom door stopped me. I moved close enough to hear a forgotten trickle pattering in the sink. Through the vanity mirror, I saw Dalena sitting in the bathtub in a few inches of water hugging her knees. She was there, but her mind wasn't. Eyes no longer slurry from too much wine, she looked immobilized by sadness. You didn't have to be strong alone in the bathtub. You could come apart at the seams. Let a black ribbon float on water. A ribbon that was everything and nothing but a reminder of the woman she would never see again. I understood her at that moment more than I ever had. Time frayed my memories, but some memories remained whole. Alone in a café, in my room checking for his messages, in a bathtub *longing.*

But that was over now. I could leave behind that predawn morning Bastien woke me with his absence, the jolt of seeing him outlined against the window wall, a lake destroyed by drought before him. *It's not change that feels threatening. It's the unknown. The uncertainty,* he said when he knew I was watching.

Maybe that was the morning he understood he wanted the impossible. I wouldn't forever remain Solenne in a café, Solenne waiting for office doors to open, Solenne in a hammock. His Sol. Things always change. I left him behind. Now he could leave me behind, too. Louisiana would force his hand.

I could've told Dalena I was here, but I slipped back down the hallway. Some places, women have to wander into alone.

| PART FOUR |

FOR EVIE

MY HENRIETTE

IT WASN'T FIRE OR POISON, BUT HENRIETTE FIGURED OUT HOW TO KILL ANTONI. A commission merchant sat across from Antoni, wealth stitched in the threads of his pantaloons and waistcoat. The offer of purchase the merchant slid across Antoni's desk: *One Negro woman, 21 years of age. One Mulatto boy, 5 years of age. One Mulatto girl, 3 years of age.*

Henriette read the offer herself. She could now. During weekly visits for a year, her lover taught her letters, and by touching her pointer finger to words in the *New England Primer* and the news-paper, how to read full sentences. *Very good,* he said. *Splendid.*

On a spring morning under an oak tree, he learned of Henriette's desire to find the brother she lost. *No one should live with such torment,* he said. *I'll do all I can to learn his whereabouts.* He quickly discovered that her brother was purchased by a traveling wagonmaker, and the pair may be in the free state of Philadelphia.

Henriette folded her body against kindness and let herself become human.

—Henriette is pregnant, the merchant said. —My generous offer includes the purchase of this child.

Antoni looked up from the written offer to this man who, with all his mercantile skills gleaned from training abroad, didn't know the first rule of approaching a planter in his own house about his own goddamn property. Property he considered himself fond of.

—If gentlemen held such conversations, I would be inclined to ask the gentleman before me if he believed the child to be his own.

The merchant sipped from the glass of brandy Antoni offered at the beginning of the meeting. —That gentleman would thank you for your hospitality, then confess. The child is indeed his own.

Antoni reached for his rifle under his desk. —Whether the gentleman fathered the child or not, Henriette is mine, where she shall remain for life, and by law that child is mine. See yourself to the main road while you're still afforded the opportunity, sir.

From the porch, Antoni and Henriette watched the tire-stirred dirt settle along the road.

—How do you suppose you shall atone for this mistake? Antoni asked, knuckles colorless against his rifle. The only mistake she made was believing this child she had willfully created with another man would kill Antoni enough to loosen his hold on her and her children.

—You sinful wretch. You've treated me criminally. What in God's name gave you the notion you were free to do as you pleased? Antoni asked. —Speak, girl.

FIVE MONTHS LATER, HENRIETTE GAVE BIRTH to a boy. Yellow, eyes black as the night sky, fat curls Henriette wrapped around her thumb while he slept in her arms. He survived croup when seven others that year did not, and perhaps it was her grandmother's whispers in her dreams that unless birds come together, a flapping sound is not heard. Henriette joined hands and prayed with the mistress of Verreaux, then prayed with the enslaved women long into the night. The women called upon Papa Legba to open the gate for them and prayed to the loas, the voodoo spirits, to spare Henriette's son.

On a night thick with fog and mosquitoes, the baby stirred in his cot. He smiled and swiped at the shadow birds his brother's fingers made on the cabin walls. Henriette held her baby boy close and breathed the sweetest part of his head. She loved all her children, but this one, he was sweet summer peaches under a magnolia at dusk. He was choice, desire, and power—all that had been stripped from her. He was joy. After the birth of her first son, Delphine told her that child was hers, and it didn't matter that he'd come into her life against her will. A woman's burden. *Delphine was wrong*, Henriette thought. *It do matter. It matter who his papa be.*

That spring while Henriette wandered the garden cutting peach dahlias for her mistress's hair, Antoni sold her baby boy in a private auction.

Then darkness came, dark as the gloomy bayou waters that opened its mouth and ate so many Black souls. Henriette offered her soul, too. Screamed at it, provoked it, pleaded with it. But the darkness wouldn't take her. She laughed, tore at her skin that held everything in for too long, and knocked the laudanum from Delphine's trembling hand. Delphine didn't see, but Henriette did. She'd searched the sullen waves for the souls of girls lured by freedom beyond *L'Aliénor*, and she'd whispered, asking for their forgiveness after she lay with Henri Rousseau. They never answered.

—It won't take me 'cause I'm already dead. I died on that ship.

CHAPTER 40

THEN

O N MY SEVENTEENTH BIRTHDAY, I WOKE TO BASTIEN SLIPPING HIS MOTHER'S ring on my ring finger. We lay, my hand extended in front of us, staring at the shine. This was my parting gift. I'd look at it in the future and remember the blinding sun in a hammock, the lake at sunrise. He would look at the empty box where his mother's ring once lay and remember me.

Bastien declined eight calls throughout the day from Mama. When she called again a little after eleven that night, I rolled out of his grasp and scooted out the bedroom door. In a black lace chemise, inappropriate with my mother's voice in my ear, I sat in Bastien's office planning a visit home. Home, where we would spend a week walking Downtown Dallas, eating brisket, and listening to music. We'd cling to those moments.

"Is your emancipation on Source or hard copy?" Mama asked. I pictured her lying on the living room sofa in the cream bathrobe she wore when she wrapped herself on Daddy's lap.

She sighed when I explained I hadn't gotten the document yet, but I would. It was still early.

"Soon," I said. "Maybe even tomorrow."

I didn't tell her the sound of my own voice in my ears filled me with uncertainty.

She heard it in my silence.

. . .

UNDER DIMMED LIGHTS, BASTIEN SAT AT the table near the window wall.

I squinted at the half-empty glass of whiskey and his firearm resting on the tabletop. "You didn't sleep."

"No."

The guilt of wanting something more, wanting to leave him, began to crest, but I couldn't allow myself to drown in it.

"Why didn't you try?"

He stood and removed his shirt and pants, ran his hand over creases, and placed them into the laundry bin.

We were in the dark room, lit only by landscaping lights embedded around trees. He slipped into bed beside me and tugged the chemise over my head so there was nothing between us.

"I need you to understand."

He never used those words. Apprehensive, I said, "Okay."

He rolled on his side to face me, moonlight capturing each time he blinked. "I can't write your emancipation papers. Not this year. Louisiana still isn't stable. I can't in good conscience send you there."

I was on a shore in Galveston, watching the waves swelling, breaking against rock, sloughing away pieces until the rough was smooth. The hush of fading waves. *Hush.*

"Okay," I said.

We lay in silence. The dark was heavy, compressing my chest until I couldn't breathe.

"This is how it will always be, won't it? I can get older, but you'll never think I'm capable of living on my own." I breathed to make sure I could. "You'll never write my papers."

Hush.

"You have to be patient."

"What if I don't want to be patient? What if I'm tired of waiting for things I deserve?"

His arm was heavy around my waist. "You will lower your voice."

"You didn't answer the question," I hissed. "You think I'm too stupid to figure out how to do things on my own."

I was too far away from him. He pulled me closer. "Baby, I know you're not stupid, but we cannot ignore that you've had a limited education."

"Who limited it? I had the education available to me—"

"And I believe you deserve to be taken care of because you don't have the skills to take care of yourself. Where will you live? What would you do for work? You haven't asked yourself these questions. You're reckless."

I untangled myself from the sheets and his limbs and pulled on the chemise from the floor. Blood roared in my ears over his voice behind me. Inside the closet, I stripped off the chemise and replaced it with a dress.

"What are you doing?" Bastien asked, watching me circle the closet, snatching dresses from the hangers and shoving them inside of my old suitcase. Where were my clothes? The stuff I brought from home?

"I'm going home. I have a month of travel passes I've never used. The Order guarantees me time home. I have the skills to understand that."

He grabbed the dress from my hand. "You are home. I need you."

Brilliant, yet he couldn't make sense of the rawness of my pain and anger. I snatched another dress from a hanger and pivoted to keep him from taking it from me. He took one from the suitcase instead, hung it.

"Safety, liberty, and freedom from tyranny for all citizens," I heard myself saying. "The Order was founded upon those words. The last line you say in all your speeches. I'm a person. If you cared *anything* for me, you'd write my papers."

Clear confusion in his eyes. He would never see outside of himself enough to make sense of this warped system we lived under. "That's illogical. That's why I can't."

"Hypocrite." I closed the suitcase and left him in the closet.

I was out on the porch. The gate, the barren maple trees, the dewy grass became more than hopeful outlines. They were real. So were the images of me in Dallas, a nobody, waking up empty and alone in my daybed with daffodil sheets against cerulean bedroom walls. Hearing doors open, knives knocking against cutting boards and wanting it to be Daddy but knowing it never would be again. But I didn't have to stay home. I would ask Officer Decuir if I could stay with him. I could be by his side without being called a maid or prostitute. When I ran out of travel passes and had to return to Bastien, I would sit in his office and do nothing until he got sick of looking at me, then I would sleep in the dorms. When he got tired of hanging on to someone he couldn't squeeze anything from, he would release me and send me home. I would marry Decuir. We'd move to the Cole Estates subdivision with only four houses on each street. I could learn to—

"Solenne," Bastien said so calmly that at first, I mistook him for Julian. The man who lay next to me minutes ago was gone. In his place was a businessman. "I made it clear to Charles Decuir he will never circumvent the algorithm to have you. He married a woman named Stacia Purdue six days ago. Your father, Charles Decuir, James Gibson—they're gone. Which man will you run to now, love? Where will you go?"

Under the lights, we saw each other. A buried woman doesn't speak. She doesn't breathe. She wonders how she lay so quiet and still when the first shovel of dirt rained upon her.

I CRIED AT THE WATER'S EDGE until Julian arrived with a blanket and his magic words that sent me into Bastien's office, sandy and still trembling from cold.

He sat at his desk, fingers steepled, head bowed like he was in prayer. "Don't look at me like that. I've never done anything to make you see me that way."

I was on his lap, both hating and loving him and wishing I felt neither. Feeling drained everything I had.

He kissed my soggy eyelashes, renaming me his sweet Sol. His kisses slipped from regret into needing. Always needing. I had nothing to give but this husk he'd created.

It didn't take him long. It never did in that chair, with the

Founders suspended above us in acrylic paints, dead blue eyes locked on their creation leaving trails of fingertip tenderness on my hips.

Signs that I wasn't just parts. I was human. A woman. A woman who understood I would never be happy with Bastien, and I would never be happy without him.

One path hurt more than the other. Burned me in a wildfire. Scattered me at his feet like gray ash. Waiting, waiting, always waiting for him.

THAT NIGHT WHILE BASTIEN SLEPT, I crept back to his office and locked myself inside. There under lamplight I saw Henriette clearer than I ever had. While the Founders watched from their place on the wall we stood in front of the windows, the fireplace, the desk where legislation was drafted. We stroked each other's cheeks where tears once spilled and whispered promises. In her letters, she wrote that she didn't understand why she hated Antoni instead of every person who didn't look like her. I understood what she never did. The world didn't owe us anything. The men who held our lives in their hands did. At any moment, they could've looked into our eyes and changed their minds. They could've given us part of what they had for themselves. They never did.

The drought left me. I rewrote the four parts of the story I once destroyed in a sink on a military base in Georgia. My story. *My Henriette.*

One day, I would love myself more than Bastien. I would look into somber waves and jump from this ship, leaving his hands empty. Alone, I would sit with my memories and Henriette's story and write part five. The conclusions to long stories would finally live on the page, not as two voices, but coalesced into one. Those who gave everything and lost, withheld everything and still lost, would hear our voice and find truth in the dark. They would understand me, her, us. The descendants of survivors.

CHAPTER 41

NOW

I SAT IN THE WOMEN'S SECTION OF BOURBON'S, CELEBRATING MY VICTORY WITH A glass of champagne. Dalena made her rounds throughout the club. Collecting interest, she called it. It was what kept men coming to the clubs. She gave me one of her real smiles. The painted one was for the men. They couldn't tell the difference.

Memphis walked in with another man. They watched the dance floor, and I watched him. He removed his beanie and swept a hand through his locs. Our eyes met. I didn't look away, and like a moment in a café five years ago, this was a beginning. It would be slower. It would be kinder. It would be.

THE REST OF THE NIGHT WAS in front of me, the lights and music behind me.

"Where do you want to go?" Memphis asked out on the crowded street.

He was a Black man, his eyes were brown, his hair was soft like cotton candy, black like mine. I wanted him to take me anywhere that would bury Bastien in the corner of my mind. I wanted to be fifteen again.

THE ROUGH, METALLIC SOUND OF STEEL wheels sliced the silence. Below us, lights diffused over meandering lines of people at stands selling drinks in paper cups, beignets, and cotton candy. A man chased a child carrying a blue stuffed animal. The roller coaster stopped.

"This is your first ride?" Memphis asked, though he didn't have to wait for me to nod to know it. The wonder on my face gave it away.

A woman in the car behind us giggled. "Oh, God," she shrieked. "Oh, Lord."

We laughed with her, our voices free. It was the buildup, to be on top of the world, to be in front of something great. My heart's rhythm was a song, and it played for me as I looked out over the palm trees and the steamboats paddling the Mississippi, their lights alive and sparkling over dancing passengers.

Memphis smiled, eyes so much like mine. "We can have dinner on one of the boats next week . . . if you want to."

It was the first time I'd ever been asked out on a date.

I reached for his hand as he reached for mine. "I want to."

Chocolate beignets churned in my stomach. I twisted against the lap bar to bury my smile in his soft locs.

I heard the wind and the wheels vibrating against metal. I heard Memphis say he didn't care that I was complicated. I reminded him of everything he missed about home.

We dropped. I didn't get a chance to scream.

IN THE FRENCH QUARTER, THE CLOP of horse hooves and the mellow sound of jazz was our music. We strolled silently, hand in hand, until we reached a squat red building converted into an all-night store. Sometime between roller-coaster rides, we decided to end the night with me retwisting Memphis's hair. We bought twisting gel, grapes, and beer and slipped back into the night that opened for us. He stopped to speak to men playing dice in front of buildings. He called out to a woman braiding a young man's hair by porch light. They called him Memphis or Ghost.

He lived in a three-story apartment building that overlooked a strip of soul food restaurants, a jazz museum, and a daiquiri shop.

Our silence led us up the concrete stairs and onto the elevator. We studied our reflections in that mirrored box.

"What are you thinking right now?" he asked.

"If I had to say, I couldn't."

"Then tell me how you feel."

Mechanical noises vibrated underfoot. The elevator door popped open.

"Free."

He punched in a code to unlock his front door instead of using Source.

"Your door isn't paired with you?"

He shouldered the door open. "There's a door somewhere in Metairie paired with me, but I don't live there. Just an address for the government."

Inside I was reminded of my old dorm room, small and absent of detail.

"I move around a lot, so I don't keep anything I can't leave behind," he said from behind me.

I smiled to reassure him. "It's so clean. Too clean actually."

He dropped the shopping bag on a tired wooden coffee table. "I don't spend a lot on furniture, but I make sure it's clean."

I opened the bag and pulled out the hair gel. "Does that mean your hair, too?"

"You've had your hands in it all night, so you already know." He emptied his left pocket. A receipt, a piece of hard candy, a stick of gum. "You sure you want to do this tonight?"

"I've been wanting to braid or twist someone for years. Believe me, I'm ready."

After washing grapes and putting them in a bowl, he collected a handful of silver hair clips and a rattail comb from his bathroom. He lowered himself to the floor and sat between my legs, the way these things are done. Images of Daddy sitting in front of me in a chair in our kitchen flashed through my mind. Clips, fingers sticky with beeswax, and Daddy dog-earing a page of *The Souls of Black Folk* and tucking it under his arm when I needed him to tilt his head.

He tested my thighs with the underside of his arms. "You feel tense."

I was. We'd danced, but doing his hair was more intimate. I focused on wetting the roots of his hair with gel and twisting them between my fingers while he told me about his last tour of duty. He was deployed to a small town in the northern part of Georgia. He and his men had orders to clear the town, and by clear, he meant burn everything. No explanation. He looked at these people who looked like him and couldn't take away their homes. The Council ordered his commanding officer to arrest and charge him with treason.

A buzz from my purse on the table interrupted us.

"You know it's Dalena. It can wait until you clean your hands."

I kept myself from answering. I would have to get used to not responding to someone as soon as they called for me. There would be time for Dalena and I to continue healing each other, but the rest of this night had to belong to me.

I finished Memphis's hair in a few hours, and we sat on his balcony drinking beer while his hair dried. He watched the vehicles below traveling the streets, and I watched him. The way he lifted his hand to the parts in his hair, feeling the tight, neat rows. The smile of satisfaction. The relaxed way he regarded his surroundings like the world was empty.

"When we brought Mekhi home, I used to sit outside with him like this and let him sleep."

"Mekhi's your son?"

"Was." He drank from his bottle. "He was born nine weeks early and stayed in the NICU for four weeks. He got used to machines beeping and nurses talking all night. He couldn't sleep at home unless there was enough movement around him. I used to tell him he was like his old man."

"He's still your son."

When he looked at me, I wished I had better words to erase the longing in his eyes. My mama said a man's character isn't hard to see. It's found in what he wants most. Memphis wanted his son.

"I fought like hell for that boy when I got out of jail. The Code teaches us a soldier's duty is to know when he's reached the end of the line. I was at the end of mine."

An insect flew around the balcony light, bumping and buzzing until it settled in place. Or died.

"So what's your next move in this game of chess?"

"Find a job. I'll probably end up like you. Keep moving. Stay free," I said.

We stood together, Governor Nicholls Street below, bright city lights unveiling secrets on other balconies, those other bodies standing like us—not two shadows but one. Time wasn't still here. It was the rushing clicks from I-10 and Source's chirp from inside the apartment.

Three men passed directly under the balcony and stopped. Clouds of smoke and laughter moved in the dark.

"I thought you wanted something more," he said.

I traced the hard disks of Memphis's knuckles, the knotty scars there, and told him the truth. I didn't know how to want more. Someone had made decisions for me my entire life.

"If that was true, you wouldn't be here now."

He finished his beer then led me inside, hitting light switches in the living room and the hallway leading to his darkened bedroom.

He stood behind me while I squinted in the dark at a floating shelf of books near the window. Ran my fingertips over the spines of *Narrative of the Life of Frederick Douglass: An American Slave, Twelve Years a Slave*, and *Incidents in the Life of a Slave Girl*.

"Can we open the curtains?" *The night should stand as witness when we come home*, Henriette had written.

Fully clothed on top of the blanket, brown limbs so inextricably tangled it was impossible to tell where either of us began or ended, I spoke. The words tumbled over each other, but I hoped he understood. This wasn't love. It was far from it, and that's why I could be free in his arms. Love would remain trapped in a curious place somewhere between fifteen and sixteen, girl and woman. Tonight, he had rewound time to the Solenne who existed before thoughts of government officials, unwanted babies, and locked doors. I left it all behind.

I stopped there in his silence, murmured a metaphor for contentment, and fell asleep. Free.

CHAPTER 42

NOW

I AWOKE IN MEMPHIS'S ARMS. THE RISING SUN LIT THE PEACE ON HIS FACE. A GOOD man with unhaunted dreams.

I untangled myself from him and slipped into the bathroom. In the small oval mirror, Henriette stared back at me. She was in my reflection, a Fulani girl with calluses on the inside. Our lips turned up into a smile that reached our dark eyes. We'd broken away from Bastien, who was denied nothing. The night I wrote four parts of Henriette's story, I promised myself this day would come. I hid that journal behind the portrait of Jefferson in our bedroom, so when I looked into his accusatory eyes, I would be reminded one day when I was stronger and wiser, I would have what he denied Sally for forty years. I didn't need Henriette's words in front of me to understand that if she could speak she would say—

"That time is now. You don't love him anymore because it was never love. We're free."

In the bedroom, Memphis flipped on his stomach and pulled a pillow over his head. I never experienced normal, the uncertainties of two young people fumbling through a beginning, but this had to be it. There would be time to do everything right—first kisses and first dates. I found a pen on his desk and wrote two lines on the receipt from the all-night store.

Today is our tomorrow. Come see me tonight.

I took a handful of grapes from a bowl on the countertop and slipped out of the apartment. In the SPV, I passed the Mississippi River textured with greens and browns, and I imagined myself there with muddy feet and misted hair. This could be home. With Dalena and Memphis, I could make this last.

I tossed a grape stem out the window, closed my eyes, and pretended the wind carried it to the water like a wishing well.

Fifteen minutes later, I stood on Dalena's porch listening to the sparrows. Those oak tree leaves I stared into should've given me peace. Instead, I thought of Lucas Magnan. I'd left Dalena alone and ignored her calls all night. The sparrows fell into intermittent silence, like a warning to grasp the fullness that hung in the air. That feeling of wandering into an empty room sparking with energy some unseen person left behind.

I pulled the firearm from my bag on my shoulder, nudged the unlocked door with my fingertips, and walked inside.

Dread in all black. Uniform, gloves, boots, fleece ski mask—only his eyes, unapologetic and robotically blue, were visible. He sat in Dalena's brother's chair, a trespass it took precious seconds to make sense of. Security monitors dead, black. Soldiers in riot helmets and pads stood behind ballistic shields like they expected to confront an army. And Dalena. She sat teary-eyed in a chair at the dining room table, rubbing her arms like she itched all over.

My knees weakened.

"I'm a man, a fool, but a man. If you were unhappy, you should've told me. I would've fixed it."

Bastien rose from the chair, and I shrank, forgetting the firearm hanging from my useless hand. Looming over me, he extracted every ounce of courage I stored for this moment. He took the firearm and dropped it in my bag.

A finger to my chin so I could look into his eyes. I didn't want to. He would know what I yearned to do with Memphis, and it would kill us both.

His mask was a blur.

"Five nights, Solenne. *Five.* You have no idea what I've been through." He pulled me into his arms and settled his face in my hair, where coconut, smoke, and castor oil—the scent of Memphis—was already fading.

It was only a matter of time. No other security had been gifted to me.

Mask now in his fist, he rested his exposed lips against my forehead. The unkempt facial hair told his story more than words could. Whispering promises we made four years ago, his arms tightened around me. "Baby, this thing we have. Do you not understand that if it could be undone and buried, it would've been me with the shovel?"

"You can release me—"

"You won't be satisfied until you drive me insane. Why do you want to break me?"

"I don't," I said. A child again. "You had time to find yourself. Why can't I have that, too?"

He lifted his head and straightened his back. The soldiers obeyed. Boots thundered forward in formation. So many of them.

The wet sounds came from Dalena. Julian tightened her handcuffs, loosening her wrist ribbon enough for it to fall to the floor. Soldiers' boots sent it in different directions. The poetry of it all—Dalena reaching for the ribbon, me reaching for her, Bastien catching my hand midair, his eyes writing messages with ice: You'll never see her again.

"Put it all behind you. We're going home."

"I have my papers." I jerked my hand away. "I'm not going."

He glanced at Dalena, then back at me. The only warning I would get.

Briefly, I imagined going for the gun in my bag, bullets shattering windows, soldiers crunching through glass to restrain me. I imagined Bastien lying dead on the old floors I considered hiding under. We both knew it wouldn't happen. He was the man forcing me into the confines of his world, but he was also the man who held me when I awoke crying because of the nightmares of Daddy wearing soldier's white. Scooping, shoveling, the thump of dirt by soldiers in black committing the first man I ever loved to nothing. *You're having a bad dream. I will never leave you,* Bastien promised. *I will always be here.* My oppressor and my savior. I couldn't untangle those either.

Out on the porch, he paused to look back into the house. His eyes roved around the place where Dalena re-created images of freedom with paint and hung them on her walls. The place where she started rebuilding me.

He lifted his eyes to the soldiers behind him. "Burn it down."

THE MV WAS PART OF A convoy I hadn't seen because they parked off a trail a mile from Dalena's house. While Dalena drank wine at Bourbon's and Memphis and I walked to the amusement park, Bastien and his men slipped into Dalena's house and waited like patient thieves. Maybe Dalena stood on the porch unlocking the door but missed the sounds inside. Maybe that's why she called me. I would never know. Like James, the friend I loved deeply and lost, I would never see her again. The men's murmurs in the MV told her fate. Strategy, they said. Hold her in a private jail until Proposition 1077 passed through the Council and negotiations with Lucas for his vote were complete. My friend, my sister, a beautiful sparrow back in a cage.

Julian had another emblem on his sleeve—his reward for his skills as a former drone pilot that found me among tens of thousands of people during the busiest time of the year in a state spanning 52,378 square miles. That emblem was an acknowledgment of his master negotiating skills that compelled Troy to enter into a secret agreement allowing Bastien access to me even after Troy voted with his cabinet to grant me asylum.

"Your grandparents moved to Detroit to escape the Klan," I said, looking at Julian's hardened profile. "You think they'd be proud of you right now?"

The men moved in sync, pulling once on the cuff of their shirts, ensuring it was perfect. "I don't think anyone could fault a man for doing his job."

• • •

ON THE JET HOME, BASTIEN WATCHED my chest rise and fall. Every breath reminded him I made it out. Every breath reminded him I made it back.

"The days felt like months, love. So, so long with no end."

My hand was in his. The silver device from his bag slid over the skin of my palm, and no, I didn't imagine the current that surged through my thumb. Source was restored.

"You're safe now."

He rested, breathed, while every muscle in my body cried out for everything that had just been, what would never be again.

CHAPTER 43

NOW

I WANTED THE SKIES TO BE GRAY, BUT THE PLACID BLUE OVER THE BUILDINGS IN Austin, the iron gates to our house, and the lake persisted.

I wandered into the kitchen, grabbed a half-empty bottle of wine from the countertop, an apple from a fruit bowl, and a knife. I would allow a day to be mad at everyone and myself, then I'd do what I'd always done. Keep from drowning in this world.

Bastien followed me into our bedroom, each of my footfalls one of his. This was our new normal, the overprotectiveness of his footsteps said. He would always be right behind me.

The bedroom door closed behind us. His firearm clicked against the nightstand. The rustle of unbuttoning and unbuckling. The bed sighed under his weight. My hope he would go to work and give me time alone to process everything vanished.

I set the stuff I picked up from the kitchen on the dresser and faced him. "No, I don't want to."

Words he hadn't heard for three years. Words he taught me to forget.

He was in front of me, belt swinging from his pant loop, hand tangled in my hair. "We've been together five years. Five days doesn't change who you are." The words brought a sudden knowing, a confirmation was in his eyes. "You lied about the treasonist. You didn't fuck him or anyone else because you can't."

"I wanted to. I was going to. But you always have to win. Why can't I ever have anything? You never let me win, you—" I pushed him. It did nothing, and that pissed me off more than the certainty in his eyes. My arms swung wildly, fists hammering a brick wall. If I hit him hard enough, he would understand how it felt to have the best night of your life tainted by memories of soldiers and fires and defeat. Was there any place on earth where he wouldn't show up? What corner of the earth did he believe he didn't have the automatic right to?

OUR BATHROOM WELCOMED ME, AND I found comfort behind the locks for however long it would last. I slid to the floor, pressed my back against the door, and drank deeply from the wine bottle. Fragrant and raw, it lazed the anger churning in my stomach. I ate the apple next, paring off slices until only the core remained.

I stripped off my clothes and scalded myself in the shower until I faded away, then worked almond oil into my skin and hair to bring myself back.

Condensation slipped away from the mirror under my finger-tips. Sad, exhausted eyes, reflecting my true colors like stained glass. Who was I before I was here? I wasn't somebody until he said I was. I didn't have a body until he touched it and showed me what each part could do.

Hush, Black girl, *hush*. Be quiet and soft.

The knife lay on the countertop. I ran a thumb against the blade. It had slipped through the apple so easily. What if I took something away from him? Would he understand then not everything was his? I swept up a handful of damp hair. Source buzzed, once. Twice.

My gaze fluttered to the ceiling where I knew I would find them. Newly installed cameras hung from the corners, their presence shouting I would never be alone anywhere. Not anymore. With my pointer finger, I flipped Source over to view the screen.

That's not a regret I'm willing to allow you to have.

I was his, without end, without fail, and there was nothing any-one could do to change that. The knife clattered into the porcelain sink, useless. I blinked at the light scattering over my reflection and searched for the place that belonged to me.

I AWOKE IN OUR BED TO his lips trailing my spine, pausing on my lower back, whispering words I didn't want to exist.

I pretended they didn't.

Body still heavy from everything he left behind, I pressed my face into the pillow and blinked in darkness. It smelled like the new us.

I squinted through the rough dark at knotted shapes outside the window wall and wondered if there was ever a time in history when this thing we were, this ugly relationship, didn't exist.

"We need each other," he whispered against my hip for the second time that night. "We always have."

My body loosened like it learned to do on his command. Parting, unbarred, limb for limb, our movements a monstrous conversation.

A quick breath against my ear splintered the silence. "You don't know how good you feel."

Only he knew. Would ever know.

"I would do anything for you. Still."

Dalena, I thought.

"Dalena," I whispered, pleading.

Bastien wasn't there to hear me.

I FRIED TWO THICK SLICES OF bread in too much butter and powdered sugar the way Daddy used to. The days when I would watch sugar dust from his fingers like magic.

Everything is the same, Bastien reassured us when I awoke under his arm each morning over the next two weeks. He was wrong. I changed. He changed. He was jumpy where he used to be confident. Suspicious where he used to draw comfort. My shadows had been stationed inside the house. I was inside of a prison within a prison, and still, he was unsettled. This was how things would be. I knew that the moment I considered boarding a train to Louisiana. I *knew* this. He would hunt me to the end of the earth, dust me off, and put me back on the shelf where I belonged.

The toast no longer looked good. I leaned against the sink, drinking lukewarm tea that tasted like dirt.

Without stopping for shoes, I slipped past my shadows in the living room, deep in conversation about bullets, of all things. In the distance, cobalt and red hulls moved so slowly in the water I couldn't tell if they were coming or going.

Waves lapped against the hull of a delivery boat docked at my pier. Back stooped, a deliveryman unloaded coolers of fresh catch. His eyes followed my bare feet down the pier.

"Be careful. Thorns are likely." He set a cooler down and dried his hands on bright orange pants.

Behind us, the boat rocked. How did it feel to own something that could take you away to solitude?

"Are you the owner?"

"She's mine." He nodded to a large plastic cooler. "This batch is for the official. Inspected them myself. You tell him that, okay?" I nodded, and he continued. "I have a couple cases of wine, too."

He climbed back on the boat, back stooped over the large wooden boxes.

I pried open a plastic cooler.

The keepers. Hairy claws twitching on ice. Bastien showed me videos of the underwater traps baited with raw chicken. The crabs crawled over each other, strategized, then maneuvered their bodies to get inside at the chicken flesh fluttering like a white flag.

The fishermen in Port Arthur and Galveston inspected them and kept the ones that measured at least six inches. They were supposed to release the females along with the smaller crabs because of the dwindling population, but they kept them to ship to Bastien. He says he can taste the difference. Females are sweeter and more delicate. They pair better with his oaked red wine. Never mind they have to catch two to equal the weight of one male.

A sweep of my foot and the cooler released the ice-stunned bodies into the water.

"Hey!" Red-faced, the deliveryman leaned over the boat's edge.

But a crab still hung halfway outside the cooler, toggling between life and death. Another nudge and she tumbled from the pier into the water.

I didn't have to turn to know my shadows had arrived. Stealthy, not even the creaking wood beneath our feet gave them away. All four, based on the deliveryman's expression. He opened his mouth then closed it, fish-faced like the creatures meandering beneath the water's surface. He thrust his hands into his pockets and gave me a smile with too many hard edges to be genuine.

THE DESCENDANTS OF PATTYROLLERS WATCHED ME from the wraparound porch. I stood at the water's edge, staring into gray that stretched farther than I could see.

One of my shadows moved closer. "Something I can do for you?"

"Yes, let me breathe. Nothing in your instructions says you need to be within three feet of me."

Source buzzed in my pocket.

BASTIEN: I'm working late. I'll be home by ten.

I could swim away before then. Sink to the bottom like the girls who abandoned the slave ships. Drift until I felt the sweet power of alone. What, then, would become of Dalena?

THE NEXT MORNING, INSTEAD OF TAKING the train like I used to, I rode with Bastien to the Capitol in the MV that was mine in name only—the MV where Julian told me Bastien loved me. Strange that, back then, I didn't see that one day he would be what I dreamed of running away from, that he was all that would keep me in one place.

"Are you feeling better?" Bastien asked.

All that had changed was the dark passenger between us. To

Bastien, all I needed was fresh air flowing through the bars of my cage to forget it.

I nodded, watching life outside the window pass in a daze.

THE DAYS STRETCHED INTO ANOTHER WEEK with Dalena in jail. Everywhere was a ticking clock. The second hand on the square desk clock with the black face. The silver galley clocks on the walls at the Capitol.

Bastien kept his head in paperwork, drafting his plan to reintroduce Proposition 1077 before the Council. Stress manifested itself in the tautness of his shoulders, the twitching trigger finger.

Dr. Bouchard stood in Bastien's doorway. "I'd like ten minutes of your time, Official."

"Regarding?" Bastien asked from where he sat behind his desk.

"Dalena Batiste."

Bastien spared him a glance. "Not with Solenne present. Schedule something for tomorrow."

"Administrator Lucas Magnan petitioned the Council for her transfer to Georgia," Bouchard continued, despite the annoyance on Bastien's face. "He said his direct messages to you have gone unanswered. Do you intend to negotiate the transfer?"

Neither Bastien nor I missed the suspicion in his tone. Without Julian present, this would turn into an hour-long argument.

"Magnan is aware of my terms," Bastien told Bouchard as I pushed the door closed.

I was in front of Bastien pleading, on his lap pleading, my lips against his, pleading. "Please don't send her back to him. He said he will hurt her."

Pleading. This was the only system designed for us. We were girls, fifteen, sixteen, seventeen. We were our ancestors, forbidden to read or write while lying under the arms of men who drafted legislation. We were educated in our mama's kitchens, passing around secrets that gave us a fighting chance against men who held our world in their hands—men twice our age with enough status to outmaneuver us at every turn. We got him to free our mamas, sisters, brothers, the old men and women with twisted backs from forty years in the fields. We kept going in a system designed for our failure because our ancestors taught us how.

He held my face in his hands. Kissed my forehead. "You must learn to separate the man from the legislation. I'm not sending her back. If the proposition is passed, the proposition sends her back."

"But you don't have to reintroduce the proposition."

"My love," he said. "Dalena Batiste aside, I couldn't consider dropping the proposition even if I believed doing so benefited the Order. You applied for asylum, and I cannot let this document stand. I have to keep you safe. I cannot give those people power to take you away from me again."

FOR YEARS, I LISTENED TO BASTIEN strategize on how to get Proposition 1077 passed through the Council and breathed hidden sighs of relief when it failed. I clung to each of his failures because they resembled hope. But this was no longer about pleasing Lucas Magnan and securing votes. I made it personal. He wouldn't fail again, and that determination is what would keep DoS buried for generations. Having no one to blame but myself, I let the guilt sink me. It was the only place I could go to be alone.

HOURS AFTER DINNER, I SLIPPED OUT of our bedroom and into the kitchen with a bottle of wine in mind.

"Source, lights," I whispered. Squares of overhead lights shone on Bastien sitting at the dining room table. A glass of whiskey sat atop *My Henriette* in front of him, a juxtaposition that lapped at my spine until I was frozen.

He looked up at me, the face of a man who had just captured an answer that had eluded him for decades. "How does it end?"

"What?"

"Your story. *My Henriette.* You didn't finish it."

"Why do you have my book?"

"Why were you writing a book?"

"Why were you going through my things?"

"Why did you have a book hidden behind a painting in our bedroom?"

I opened the wine refrigerator and pulled out a bottle with a green label.

"You want to drink another bottle? Illegally?" he asked.

"I had the equivalent of two glasses my first night back nearly a month ago. Considering all you put me through, a few glasses of wine is mild."

"Put the bottle away, Solenne."

I left it on the counter, turned to leave, and gave him the message he understood. "I'm going to bed early."

"I understand your problem now," he said from behind me. "For years, you filled your head with this treasonous story, then you left and experienced the way nonrestricted women do things. Staying out all night. Meeting people with no direction. On the surface, it looks like freedom. But they don't know what's best for you."

"Do you really not understand it's normal to want to live where you have the same rights as everyone else?" I said. "How could you be with me all these years and still think it's wrong to want more?"

"More than having the official on his knees? Do you think I don't know I was selfish? Do you think I don't know I took everything from a child? I live with it. I'll die with it. But I never treated you as a descendant of slavery. Because of my status you've suddenly decided you despise, you weren't hurt or passed around. For five years, I loved you."

In his eyes, I saw him. These were not things he said to win an argument. Like his steadfast belief his ancestor was a hero in establishing the Order, he believed he was the hero in our story. He had atoned for sins, his, and of all who had come before him. He had taken me, a sad Black girl, saved her, and given her more than anyone else ever had. He was enough. *He* was all I needed. Freedom by proxy.

"Every time you told me you loved me while holding a document giving you control over my life, you treated me like a descendant of slavery."

"How can I function with no absolutes? No certainty. Knowing you could walk away from me at any time."

"By understanding I deserve freedom, just like you."

Those words pulled him to a stand. "I haven't been free since the day we met. You change like the wind. You've always had more power over me than I had over you. You reveled in it. We're equals in that respect, aren't we?"

"I don't have the ability to strip you of choice."

He couldn't see a path for us that offered a fork in the road for me. For him, always one way. He looked Jefferson in the eye and saw his blueprint. Hold her as a child. Hold her as an adult. Hold her in servitude, even in death. *Hold* her.

His boots echoed against the wood floor of the dining room, then the kitchen tile. "I read your shadow's report. You're unsettled. It's the constant monitoring that upsets you. I can't remove your shadows for security purposes, but I removed the cameras in the bathroom and bedroom. No more truth assessments."

His weak attempt at negotiation, his concession, a step above the shiny boxes he usually had delivered.

"Maybe that would work for the Solenne you had a month ago. It won't work now."

He was in front of me now, so close that his boots touched my bare toes. "You're rewriting our story in your head because you've spent five days listening to people who know nothing about us. *Nothing* has changed other than you understanding that this is where you belong."

There was something curious in his eyes I hadn't seen since the night of my seventeenth birthday when I walked into his office after crying on the shore. Intuitively, I knew I didn't want to hear the next words out of his mouth. I stepped away from him.

"You're pregnant, Solenne."

My breath ceased. His timepiece clicked, clicked, clicked.

"You're lying."

Activated by his voice, Source opened on the wine refrigerator. GESTATIONAL AGE: FIVE WEEKS. FETAL HEART RATE: 112 BPM. HCG LEVEL: 377.

First, there was nothing, an ocean of nothing. Vast, directionless. Then I was inside a lone rowboat, reeling in a howling sea.

Bastien ran his hands from my arms to my sagging shoulders. The relief in his eyes was clear, dark like the night sky we would die together under.

....

CHAPTER 44

NOW

SINCE I'D BEEN HOME, MY DREAMS OF HENRIETTE CHANGED. WE'RE IN AN OLD house I don't recognize. I'm reaching out to still her before she drifts too far away from me. I follow her like a beacon, bright and forgiving of all I ignored or misunderstood. Her skirts wind behind her, but they slip through my fingers before she leaves me. *Remember*, she says from a room I can't enter. *Nothing is just in their world.* Then she tells me her story.

THE COMMISSION MERCHANT TRAVELED AS FAR as Virginia, searching for the boy he fathered and Antoni had sold. He found only closed doors. Every month, his driver delivered a handwritten "no news" message for Henriette through the blacksmith at Verreaux.

Their boy was gone.

When Henriette saw the merchant at a distance, she saw the boy who was stolen from her. She stopped looking. The last time she saw him on Royal Street, she passed him as she would any white man: eyes down, shoulders rounded, a carefulness to her steps. Forgotten were those stolen moments when she became loose like water for him beneath the oak trees. Trees that reminded her of freedom.

She wandered blindly through a ghost world, half alive, half dead, shriveled enough to scare everyone away from her. Antoni threatened to have her whipped. Said it would not be borne that he would reduce himself to walking on eggshells on his own property.

Henriette jerked the whip from the overseer's hand, threw it at Antoni, and screamed. —Do it yourself, coward.

The overseer couldn't help telling the story to anyone drunk enough to listen while he dealt cards for Bourré on Saturday evenings.

The enslaved women believed darkness had come to Henriette because she offended her loa by offering the voodoo spirit turtle instead of freshwater drum from Antoni's table. In a forest clearing, the women danced around a fire and called on the ancestors and the loa to bring Henriette back, to show her favor, to spare her life.

With passing time, the Henriette who couldn't eat or speak was replaced by someone who allowed her daughter's tiny hands against her cheeks to stretch a smile there.

The smile lived but a short time. Antoni's footsteps were heavy up her stairs, on her porch, and in her doorway. With his hat in his hands, he sat at the wooden table he had crafted for her, his eyes so green, green like algae in her fire-lit cabin.

—Are you going to help me pull off my boots, ma chérie?

Three months later, Henriette was pregnant.

BATHROOM DOOR LOCKED BEHIND ME, I pressed the health data tab on Source repeatedly. It refused me as it had for the past three years when Bastien decided he was a better monitor of my data. I teased through my thoughts for the date of my last period, but they wouldn't stretch enough for me remember. I didn't feel like a second heart beat inside of me. It didn't matter. Data didn't lie.

I loved my children, all of them, but I despaired. Each time I thought I'd find freedom, a new life found me instead, Henriette had lamented about her last pregnancy.

Now life had found me, too. It was always only a matter of time.

I stared into my reflections in the vanity mirrors. Five versions of Solenne. One for each year I belonged to Bastien. One of the versions pulled the makeup bag from the middle drawer of the vanity. She pushed past flat containers of foundation and cylinders of lipstick until her fingers curled around Penelope's gift as they had when Penelope slipped them to her in a bathroom four years earlier.

Source opened on the center mirror, and I waited for Bastien's message. It wasn't a threat, a warning, or a rebuke. It was an excerpt from the page he stole from that blue journal years ago.

. . . two flawed people reaching for each other in the middle of the night, finding each other where there was once silence. What could be more pure than that? This is a love story. Not every story ebbs and flows the same. Some sides of the story are beautiful, some sides are ugly. I love every side of you.

My rounded, girlish letters faded in the translucent folds of the paper. Each letter formed words as distant but familiar as my daddy's voice. Like Henriette's words brought back to life on sheets of dot-matrix paper, this was proof from another life, another time, but that was no longer me. I had left that girl behind to become a woman. Women know the difference between what is real and what is not. What is love and what mimics it. They learn from the women who came before them, the women who knew how to fly.

But women also know sacrifice.

My ancestor, Henriette's grandmother, whispered somewhere inside me, *Unless birds come together, a flapping sound is not heard.* I heard the sparrows. I knew what I had to do.

My fingers unfurled. Pushed the tablets down deep. Left them in their resting place.

A choked sob. A sigh. A requiem for what was once my resolution, my cure-all, my answer, my way out. Somewhere, there was a space and time one version of me would come back for them.

WE LAY SIDE BY SIDE IN bed. Only our breath touched.

"I don't want this baby. I don't want children at all. I never did," I admitted in the dark, freeing myself from one burden. I wasn't brave enough to be a mother.

"That will change."

"It won't change," I whispered. "How long have you known?"

"Six days."

"Why didn't you tell me?"

"I needed to mitigate any risk to my child for as long as possible. Incidents of induced miscarriage are too high in DoS."

"That's not me."

"Baby, I've known you since you were fifteen."

Once, Bastien was alone. I found him there. He wanted someone who could never leave him, so he created that certainty, shaped her, and convinced her nothing meant more than to be loved by a man who would never be killed in action. Tightened the chains. Called it love. For four years, he said he loved me, but he never said he trusted me. He read *My Henriette* and saw me in the words that told of her longing to be free. He *knew* me.

I knew him, too, perhaps better than anyone. We had grown together. It was me who learned where his soft spots lay, what caused him to stand at the water's edge in deep thought for hours, what made him fear.

"I know how *My Henriette* ends," I said when the silence pressed.

"I'm listening."

"Antoni sold the son she had with the commission merchant."

"That was part four. What happened next? The part you haven't written?" he asked impatiently.

"After she found out she was pregnant again, she ran. With two children and the fatigue of an early pregnancy, she didn't get far. In the wagon on the way back to the plantation, Antoni looked at her and said, 'You are misery, a sour note, a plague. I don't know what's stopping me from killing you.'"

"She was in her fourth pregnancy."

"Yes, and if he killed her, he had to bury her. If he buried her, she would finally be free. He accused her of using voodoo to bewitch him for so long. His stomach had been bothering him since she left the first time."

"Likely an undiagnosed ulcer."

"Maybe. He took the children away from her and locked her in the attic. He told her if she called out to the mistress, he would sell the children."

"Baseless threat."

"I can't blame her for believing. From the attic, she heard her children searching for her. The attic was so hot, she couldn't move in the daytime. She kept sane at night by writing letters to her lost son and brother that she knew they'd never read."

I listened to his even breath, imagining the scrawl of Henriette's quill under yellow candlelight.

"And?"

"Trapped in that attic, she understood she'd always be Antoni's property. He could decide how she lived. He could decide the moment she died. She finally made up her mind and grabbed her life away from him. She found a container of arsenic Antoni used for the rats stashed behind a crate."

Bastien lifted himself on one elbow. "She died by suicide."

"Or she poisoned Antoni and escaped. Or Antoni released her from the attic and life went back to normal, albeit with the daily worry the girl he enslaved would drink pennyroyal tea to get rid of the baby she carried, or that she'd slip away in the middle of the night and make it to freedom. Maybe she did. Either way, life was harder for Antoni from that day forward. He no longer held a child. She was a woman."

"You said you know how it ends."

We were eye to eye in the dark. "I didn't say I'd tell you."

CHAPTER 45

NOW

I N AN ALTERNATE TIMELINE, I'M SALLY HEMINGS IN FRANCE, SIXTEEN YEARS OLD and pregnant, explaining to a pleading Thomas Jefferson that I won't return to the United States with him where I was listed as property on the tax rolls. Other times, I'm Dalena Batiste, who decided to keep running. Often, I'm Henriette, brown skin crying out for the African sun.

That night, I was Solenne who introduced enough uncertainty to make Bastien fear her next move. I was Solenne who demanded Bastien withdraw Proposition 1077 and free Dalena. She could wander and search for a new place called Love. I was Solenne who demanded that Bastien grant her mama emancipation, end his relationship with her as her conservator, and transfer the deed to her business to her. She would become the first woman in our family post–Civil War II to hold a document of emancipation in her hands. She wouldn't be the last. Her granddaughter would be born free, ending this chain of bondage.

It would be written.

In his office down the hall from our bedroom was where secrets were created.

Julian shook his head at being called to our house in the middle of the night to have his own dreams dashed. He'd given years of his life to see Bastien as president, and now he stood as witness to its unraveling. "If you release Dalena . . . Official, *think*. If you refuse Lucas Magnan the legal right to her, you lose your working relationship with him. Five years down the drain. You lose Georgia. I predict an approval rating of thirty-eight percent with no chance of recovery in time to be confirmed to Council."

Bastien held my gaze. "Carry out the order."

"Raise your right hand," Julian said reluctantly. He lifted Bastien's hand on Source to record his fingerprints.

"DNA collection." Julian swept an oral swab against the inside of Bastien's cheek, then sealed it in a bag.

Julian held the device in front of Bastien's face to scan his retinas. "Stare straight ahead, Official."

Proposition 1077 was formally withdrawn, and the rest of my demands were set in place. Days from now, Lucas would petition the Council again to release Dalena to him. They'd discover she was gone, but they'd have no information to give him. They'd discover Bastien, their golden boy, overstepped and wrote the orders to release her without allowing the Council to vote against it, but not a single councilman would step forward and challenge him. They would fear his explanation would alter their perception of who he was and who he would become. The sun would rise each day with them doing what they always did: turning a blind eye to anything that created cognitive dissonance within them.

Julian collected proof of my identity next. The document in front of me blocked my claim for asylum now and anytime in the future, Julian said. The document erased the longing, the memories of a boardinghouse, nightclub, and lying so close to a Black man we saw our roots in each other's eyes. Bastien hoped.

Bastien pushed the document closer. "As we agreed."

"Memphis Eloi," I said.

"The treasonist who removed you from the grid."

"The former soldier who served the Order for years. He lost visitation with his son. The case should be reviewed and his visitation restored."

Bastien stretched his neck to one side. "We searched for Memphis Eloi for years on suspicion of grid-hopping. What makes you think we can find him now?"

I glanced at Julian. "You have the best drone pilot in the Order on your staff."

"The drone box is for marshals. Julian is an official."

"Then he should find him quickly."

Julian's shoulders drooped a fraction, but I caught it. He looked at Bastien, exasperated. "Are you adding this to the order?"

Bastien set a pen on the table in front of me. "Confirmed."

I STOOD IN THE EMPTY OFFICE, Bastien's hands on my hips, his forehead pressed against my lower stomach. His child, his link to the future, where I would always be. Though she was only a journey of cells no bigger than a poppy seed, that night, he called her Genevieve, his mother's name. Always absolutes for Bastien. Always one way.

"I'll give her what I couldn't give you. I swear it," he said.

I thought of those who came before me, the enslaved Black women history tried to bury, the women who left burning questions, the women who watched the man she'd lain next to for decades lowered into the waiting ground, taking with him her chance at freedom. The women, broken and ruined, knowing nothing but this man who departed with every good year she had. Fifteen, sixteen, seventeen . . .

One day, history would question me. They'd wonder if I stayed because I was afraid, brainwashed, found love in the darkest of places, or whether I looked into Genevieve's eyes, saw the years of hiding under wood floors, and knew I had to stay. They'd ask why I couldn't convince him to free me when he freed those around me.

My story wouldn't be washed into silence. I can write, so I do. Like Henriette, I would tell my story. There is freedom in releasing the words captured along the journey of a long fight.

Through my words, they would see me on a linen couch in a government office, listening to Bastien Martin's stories of survival, and how men beside him perished while he remained untouched. I thought this was proof some higher power destined him for greatness. Now I believe differently. A path had been opened for him so he could see the way, but it wasn't the divine. His brothers saw to it.

He was molded by hundreds of years of privilege and patriarchy, and what created him still lives.

Through my words, they would see me young, knowing nothing but his promises that like time, he had always been and always would be. They'd see the things I couldn't see while I was drowning—how he flowed into me, segmented my life into neat quarters he could consume. They'd understand I knew only the shape of him, the crack I widened, and his world I fell into.

Darkness always leaves a side door open. That's what I would tell my daughter. Be loud. If you make yourself too small and soft, you would slip your own chains around your wrists without noticing.

BASTIEN GUIDED ME BACK INTO OUR bedroom and into our bed, where his body curved around mine like the shape of his whispers that we'd be happy again.

His lips brushed my forehead. "Our baby, Genevieve, will make everything right. Sleep, love."

In the dark, I saw him outlined in truth. I no longer held a child's view of love. In that, I saw freedom.

And so I slipped into a quiet dream of a little girl with foreign hair and eyes. She clutched my hand while we followed the path of our ancestors, not straight, but a loop of lessons that guided us to freedom like the map songs of the runaways. The earth erased our footprints until all that was left was my final broken promise to Bastien to always stay. With her hand in mine, she wasn't Genevieve, she was Evie. When she looked up at me, I was brave. I was Mama. I became. The years passed as they always did, and Evie awoke with the memory of wandering through orange wildflowers on a hillside, a man close behind, and him tucking her into a bed with sea-glass blue sheets. "It was so warm there," she said. "How did we forget him? Why do I have his sorrowful eyes?"

I placed the final version of *My Henriette* in her hands. "To remind me to never hold on to anything too tightly."

Then I dreamed of the women as they were, as one, at the end of that long story in the fall of 1808.

The old midwife Delphine brewing pennyroyal tea and sending it to the attic on lunch trays for the Fulani girl who had to die to become Henriette.

The mistress of Verreaux, finding attic keys by candlelight and extending her hand into the cramped shadows.

The enslaved women taking Henriette and her children by the hand and guiding them to that timeworn barge swaying in the murky bayou.

Henriette, the Fulani girl with eyes like mine, gazing at two children hanging from her skirts. She couldn't look at them without thinking of the one she lost to auction and the one she left behind in bloody dressings she kept layered between her legs for eight days. She contemplated the breaths she'd never hear, the toothless smiles she'd never see, and in their eyes, the ghosts of their papas, one she loved, one she despised. The chains of both cut the same.

While her daughter Adelie stayed by her side, her son led the way and climbed aboard the boat. His papa named him Augustin, but when Henriette kissed the sweet boy while he slept each night, she called him Hammadi, her brother's name. Now she could call him Hammadi with the sun as witness. The part of her she left in Africa hummed, *You're free.*

She stepped forward for her children, for those who would come after her, for her descendants, for Evie.

The mistress of Verreaux's priest from St. Louis Cathedral welcomed them aboard with food and blankets, promising to see them safely to the ship *Philadelphia*, pointed to the free state by the same name.

"What shall I call you?" he asked.

For seven years, men called her Henriette, but it wasn't her name. She grasped his hand. "My name is Kumba."

I FOUND THE ROOT OF *THE BLUEPRINT* ETCHED IN THE BLACK GRANITE OF THE WALL of Honor at Whitney Plantation in Edgard, Louisiana.

"My ma had fifteen children and none of them had the same pa. . . . My ma had one boy by her moss that was my missis brother's child. You see, every time she was sold she had to take another man. Her had fifteen children after she was sold de last time."

It was difficult to read these stories of forgotten handmaids and their forced reproduction. Though the United States outlawed the international slave trade in 1808, slaveholders found a way to increase the slave population by exploiting the domestic slave trade. They forced Black women into men's beds, punishing those who didn't have multiple children by their late teens and rewarding those who did.

"That's how it was back then," some say about history. This distance became the foundation for the world I created that looks uncomfortably close to ours. I removed the opportunity to scrutinize the past using anything other than present beliefs and morality.

In search of a main character, I reread slave narratives, focusing on women. The stories of concubines haunted me. They were girls in arrangements with politicians, doctors, lawyers, and planters. Rarely could these girls read or write.

They were unnamed, a constitution of adjectives—beautiful, virtuous, pious—in the narratives of other enslaved people.

They were Harriet A. Jacobs, who bemoaned the fate of enslaved girls. "When she is fourteen or fifteen, her owner, or his sons, or the overseer, or perhaps all of them, begin to bribe her with presents. If these fail to accomplish their purpose, she is whipped or starved into submission."

They were sixteen-year-old Sally Hemings who stood before Thomas Jefferson and negotiated freedom for her children decades before the Emancipation Proclamation freed American enslaved people. They were sixty-one-year-old Sally who left Jefferson's plantation after his death with his reading glasses, shoe buckles, and inkwell. Being a child groomed to believe she loved a man who wrote but never meant " . . . all men are created equal" had to be a stone Sally dragged around for forty years. It dug into her, shaped who she was, then became her tombstone while she lay in the cold, dark ground.

It was out of such darkness that the voices first spoke to me. One voice held the fire of the ancestors, the other was tempered with the recklessness of a child. The voices coalesced until I imagined a young woman standing on a train platform, breathless and desperate for emotional and physical freedom. She moved forward.

The Handmaid's Tale by Margaret Atwood led the way into my world where unearthed answers seeded new questions about human nature. *Wench* by Dolen Perkins-Valdez gave me the confidence to break apart the strong Black woman archetype, the mythical superhuman who withstands trauma with emotional resilience, and create a disparate group of Black women who make impossible choices. *The Book of Night Women* by Marlon James was pivotal when I drifted toward dishonest writing, trying to avoid reader bias. In the sharp edges of his prose, I found my message. "You've placed a Black girl in the dark. Give her space to scream."

| ACKNOWLEDGMENTS |

THIS BOOK WOULDN'T HAVE BEEN POSSIBLE WITHOUT PASSING THROUGH THE hands of incredible women:

My agent, Catherine Cho, whose advocacy and love for this book in its rawest form planted seeds of success. I heard the beautiful honesty voiced in your memoir and knew Solenne and I would be understood. Melissa Pimentel, whose early collaboration created a better version of this story. My editor Sarah Ried, who intuited my characters' flaws and encouraged a fearless voice. My editor Sara Nelson, whose vision inspired growth and molded a manuscript into a novel. Thank you for guiding me and showing me the way. Edie Astley, Lydia Weaver, and the HarperCollins team, whose contributions helped get this book to readers. For each one of you, I am grateful. Always.

Chryse Wymer, thank you for keeping your candle lit through my fatigue of rewriting. I will always remember. David Boone, thank you for your calm, your wisdom, and your advice: "Let it go. You have something here. You can go all the way."

Layla, Xavier, and Norah, thank you for bringing me joy. I kept going because you were watching. Tim, my 1990s love song, my cowriter of this beautiful life we've created, thank you for walking with me.

For the women trapped in a curious place between fifteen and sixteen, I see you. May we find healing in gifting our daughters everything that was stolen from us.

Asé